Published by BRASS FROG BOOKWORKS
Grand Junction, CO
www.BrassFrogBookworks.com

Inquiries should be addressed to:

Gary Carr
717 Ivanhoe Way
Grand Junction, CO 81506

Library of Congress Control Number: 2013930321

ISBN 978-0-9847096-7-0

Printed in the United States of America

First Printing: 2013

Cover & Design: J L Leon
www.ClickCreativeMedia.com

Author Photo
by Hutmacher

Dedication

To Shirley, whom I treasure above all else.

Acknowledgement

My gratitude and appreciation to Sally
and the wonderful people of Molokai for sharing
their "Aloha Spirit."

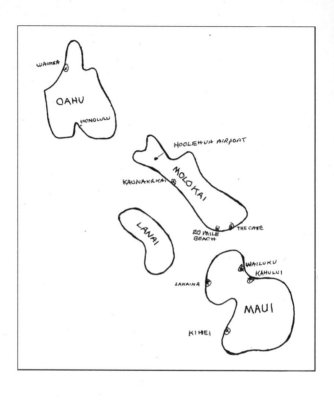

Prologue

The ocean between Molokai and Maui was quiet and bathed in shimmering shades of pink and gold. It was another picture perfect sunrise on Molokai. The sun was slowly peeking over the cloud cover on Maui. A small rainbow arched overhead. Twenty-Mile Beach was empty except for one young fisherman strolling along the water's edge. The footprints he left in the damp sand disappeared behind him as gentle waves pulled them out to sea. Just ahead of the man, the landscape rose abruptly above the water. At the base of the rise, the beach curved slightly inward, cradling a tangle of mangrove trees.

As the fisherman drew closer to the mangroves, he spotted something caught in their gnarled roots. Curious, he went to see what the tide had brought in. He dropped his throw net and bag of reef fish, peering down to the water's edge. He suddenly drew in his breath and recoiled.

The body of a man, soon to be identified as Jimmy Pualani, rested face down in the wet sand. His arms were splayed, and an army of small crabs were already feasting on exposed flesh. Waves lapped around the corpse's feet, one of his "slippahs" rising and falling with the movement. The young man summoned his wits, and swallowing the fear that had risen in his throat, looked again. He saw a large butcher knife planted nearly to the hilt between the body's shoulder blades. He quickly backed away from the scene and, forgetting his catch, ran as fast as he could for help.

Sirens pierced the placid morning air, as a police cruiser and an ambulance hurried to the scene. Two island policemen, Draper and Davis, were the first to arrive. They meticulously cordoned off the area with police tape. Draper called Maui County Police Headquarters and gave his initial report to homicide detective, Kekoa Kamu. Detective Kamu tasked the two officers with photographing the scene and collecting forensic evidence. They found a fishnet float, two beer cans, and a small pink ribbon. Kamu clamped his cell phone to his ear and called the Medical Examiner, Dr. Silas Wong.

Wong, the head of the emergency center at

Molokai General Hospital, was just leaving for work when he got the call. He arrived at the crime scene shortly after Davis began taking photos. Davis acknowledged Wong's arrival with a nod of his head. He stepped aside as the doctor slid on Latex gloves, side-stepped his way down the embankment, and began a careful examination of the body, paying close attention to the hands. He removed the knife from the corpse's back and carefully handed it to Draper, who had joined him, before rolling the body onto its back. He pushed the tattered shirt aside which disturbed the crabs, causing them to scuttle away. He felt along the corpse's side with his fingers then slid the long metallic probe into the dead man's liver to record its temperature. He scribbled a few notes, then stood up and peeled off the gloves and shoved them in his pocket. Meanwhile, Draper placed the knife into an evidence bag, labeled it, and put it with the other evidence that had been gathered.

The doctor collected his bag then wrote a tentative time of death on a paper attached to a clipboard he was carrying. "I think we can clearly state this is a homicide, but we won't have the official ruling until the autopsy is complete."

When the doctor indicated he had finished his examination, the officers bagged the dead man's hands and carefully wrapped the body in a tarp before putting it in a body bag. They wanted to preserve any potential evidence, knowing it would be scarce with the body having been in the water. Dr. Wong left, as officers finished their investigation of the site. The EMTs from the nearby Puko'o fire station hauled the body up to the waiting ambulance, shoved the gurney inside, and sped away. The beach was quiet once more.

Chapter 1

I was wrapping up notes on several upcoming cases in my small office in Kaunakakai, the largest town on the island of Molokai, Hawaii. My windows face Ala Alama Avenue, a little ways from Kaunakakai Harbor, which boasts the longest pier of the Hawaiian Islands. Ala Alama is the "main street" of Kaunakakai. Traffic lights are non-existent here, or anywhere else on the island, for that matter. The entire avenue has the charm of a movie set from the 1950s. The whole island feels like it is caught in a sort of time warp and the Hawaiian traditions have remained strong. For me, it is part of the charm I have grown to love.

There is a dichotomy to Molokai—half desert, half rain forest; half modern, half ancient; half

1

sacred, half secular. The air is permeated with the sounds of the ocean, and even on the dry side of the island you can taste the saltiness. The enchantment of this distinctive island makes you never want to leave. That particular summer afternoon, I stopped working long enough to drink it all in and count my blessings.

This office is stark compared to my plush law offices in San Diego, where I'm from. The only opulent note I allow is the gold-lettered sign stenciled on the glass front door. It reads: HAROLD WALTERS, ATTORNEY AT LAW

On Molokai, I go by Harry. I'd hung my shingle here several years ago, mostly as a tax write-off. I handle a myriad of minor legal matters, mostly contracts and deed transfers for the two local real estate offices, a few divorces, preparation of wills, and the occasional D.U.I. case. Any profit I happen to make covers my travel back and forth from California. Divorced with no children, my time on Molokai is mostly for rest and relaxation. The local saying is true, "There is nothing to do on Molokai, and no better place to do it."

My reverie was broken when the phone jangled. The caller was a woman named Taniko Tagahashi. I could hear the distress in her voice as she asked if I could help her daughter, Tala Pualani. The girl was being questioned by the police in the death of her father, Jimmy Pualani.

Molokai doesn't have a daily newspaper. All the

broadcast media is by cable from Maui or Oahu, or by satellite. That doesn't deter the local populace from keeping up on events, however. Cell phones and "talk story" suffice quite well. Very little stays secret for long. I was sure news of Jimmy Pualani's murder had already circulated to all corners of the island, and now, it reached me.

Ms. Tagahashi and I arranged to meet at seven o'clock that evening after I finished a real estate closing I had for a client at Wavecrest Resort. She was staying with her sister and brother-in-law, Pearl and Isaac Roland. They lived at Ualapue, about a mile from Wavecrest. Since the closing was a mere formality of exchanging keys for money, I should have no problem getting there on time.

I ended our conversation by advising her daughter not to say anything to anyone unless I was present. Ms.Tagahashi agreed to get that message to Tala right away. I also told her I'd need more information from both her and the authorities before I'd officially accept the case. She understood.

After hanging up, I called Patty Alemo, who works for me part-time as a law clerk and secretary. Patty is a beautiful young woman, a local who has dreams of becoming a teacher. She takes online college classes in the afternoon and lives with her sister, off Kokio Street. The salary I pay her is generous, and in return I get an excellent worker who can unearth even the most obscure bit of information.

"Hello?"

"Hey, Patty. Sorry to bother you this late in the day." I put just the right amount of regret in my voice. She hated to be interrupted during her classes. "We may have a case, and I need you to find out all you can on this Jimmy Pualani murder. I'm meeting his wife this evening."

"Oh, yeah! I heard about that. His daughter's being questioned, isn't she? Totally lolo!"

I imagined Patty circling her ear with the international symbol for crazy and smiled. "Yep. Get back with me before six forty-five, okay? Thanks, Patty."

"Oh, you'll be paying for this, *big* time, *haole*!" In the best of translations, *haole* means an outsider. You don't want to know what the worst meaning is.

"That's *Mr*. Haole, to you." The phone went dead.

It took about twenty-five minutes to drive to Wavecrest from my office. The rugged slopes of the Kamalo Mountains are a backdrop for some of the most beautiful ocean front property on the planet. It was a no brainer to see why my client bought the Wavecrest condo. From the lanai, one could watch humpback whales in season and spectacular sunrises over Maui almost every morning.

During the ride, I began to contemplate my meeting with Ms. Tagahashi. I would learn as much as I could about the case from her, and then would need to find out what the District Attorney's Office had on Tala. I ran several scenarios around in my head on how to approach Keone Akumu, Maui County District Attorney. Unless there are mitigating circumstances, I figured this will probably turn out to be another case of an impassioned family member killing a relative because they were abused, betrayed, swindled, or in fear of their life.

Nine times out of ten, when a child kills a parent it is in self-defense or they are trying to protect someone they love, usually the other parent or a sibling. If that turns out to be the case here, then the best I can hope for is a sympathetic jury. The problem with that is even sympathetic juries hand down guilty verdicts when it comes to murder. That is why I try to get the charges and sentence lessened when possible. This is an election year, however, and the DA is facing a tough challenger. He would be looking at every case as a potential publicity tool, and push it to the limit to keep his seat–especially if he has a strong case.

Patty called my cell at six forty-five. She hadn't found anything substantial. At precisely seven o'clock, I knocked on Ms. Tagahashi's door. The woman who opened the door introduced herself as Taniko Tagahashi. I was welcomed into the house with the reserved politeness that Hawaiians have for outsiders. I shook her hand and followed her into the living room. She wore a traditional island muu-muu, but ruffled shoulders and a fitted waist made it stylish and added a girlish touch. She was trim and shapely, even in middle age. Short, dark hair framed an elegant face, but her almond eyes were expressionless. I wondered what secrets she held behind them.

Hawaiians are very tolerant and gentle people, but if you pay attention, you'll see they are not overly fond of outsiders. They don't really care if you like them or not. Truth be known, they would just as soon have you go away and leave them alone. It probably had been very hard to call me, so my help must be deeply needed.

The woman seemed nervous as she motioned me toward the kitchen table. "Have a seat Mr. Walters." She sat down near me, ankles together and folded hands on her lap. "I need your help. Tala shouldn't be in jail. She hasn't done anything." A slight tremble entered her voice. "There is no way she could kill anyone, even if it *is* her father."

"I'll help if I can, Ms. Tagahashi. But, before I commit to representing your daughter, there are a lot of questions I need to ask you."

"What do you want to know?"

"First, why do you go by Tagahashi? Is Jimmy Pualani your ex-husband?"

"No. We are still married. I stopped using my real name when Tala and I ran away to the mainland. Tagahashi is my maiden name."

6

"I understand." I wondered why she and the girl had to run away, but would get to that eventually. "Can you tell me what happened when Tala was arrested?"

"We were having breakfast when that detective from Maui knocked on the door. He said he needed to talk with us about Jimmy's murder. After he told us about Jimmy's body being found, he asked if he could talk with Tala. The first thing he did was ask to see her hands. Then he asked her if she had killed Jimmy. I couldn't believe what I was hearing. I ran over to Tala and pulled her behind me. Then I told the detective to get out of our house. He said he would be back with warrants to collect DNA samples from everyone, and that we needed to stay on the island."

"Why did he want to see Tala's hands?'

"I'm not sure. The detective saw the bandage on her left thumb and took out a note pad. He wrote something in it."

"Why did she have a bandage on her thumb?"

"She cut it while preparing the Huli Huli chicken for our family reunion."

"Is that all the detective asked you about?"

She looked down at her hands, her brows coming together in thought. "Oh! And he asked Tala if she had threatened to kill Jimmy."

"Did she answer him?"

The woman looked at me with agony in her eyes. "We have had our share of pain from that horrible

7

man for too many years. Tala said no, she hadn't threatened him, but then she yelled, 'I'll kill anyone who tries to hurt my mother!' What a foolish girl! She was just reacting, I suppose."

"Ms. Tagahashi, do you know why anyone would want to kill Jimmy?"

She shook her head. "Any number of people. But, Mr. Walters, I assure you Tala didn't kill him, and neither did I."

She peered at me for a moment. "Are you a *good* lawyer, Mr. Walters?" Her eyes searched my face. "I want to make sure I hire someone who can get Tala out of jail."

"I like to think I am. I've handled numerous murder cases back in California and have never let an innocent person get convicted. If Tala is guilty though, the best you can hope for is a plea bargain that gets a reduced sentence. You also need to know this could get very expensive." I then laid out the very real possibility of Tala going to trial, and the arduous ordeal she may have to endure.

When I finished my discourse, she replied, "I have plenty of money, Mr. Walters. What I *don't* have is my daughter sitting next to me, unshackled and safe."

She again vehemently denied Tala's culpability. I believed *she* believed this to be true. I don't know exactly when I decided I was going to take the case, but ultimately knew I would. Perhaps the questioning of my abilities challenged me, or maybe it was the palpable fear revealed oh-so-briefly in those mother's eyes, that convinced me her daughter was innocent. But, the moment I decided, come hell or high-water, I was going to see her daughter free.

"I'm a little concerned about Tala's outburst to the detective. Why would she say that?"

"I don't know," she sighed. "Tala can get quite dramatic at times. Teenagers!" She gave me a rueful smile. "Mr. Walters, do you know how island people are about family? We are emotional, but most threats are just that—threats. Jimmy was an animal, but there is no way Tala could have killed him."

Glancing out the window, I caught sight of the waves breaking on the shore and thought how very out of place murder and legal procedure seemed in this tropical paradise. Turning back to the distraught woman, I asked, "Ms. Tagahashi, may I ask why you had to run away from your husband?"

Her voice grew soft and she leaned her elbow on the table, cupping her chin in her hand. "Oh, Mr. Walters if you only knew."

For the next half hour I heard stories of drunkenness, infidelity, neglect, and abuse that no one should have to suffer.

"When Jimmy and I first married, he was a good man. Then about a year later, he lost his job, and I had to go to work to support us. He didn't like the fact that he suddenly had to ask me for money and started blaming me for his not being able to find work. We had more and more arguments, and he started drinking heavily. He would leave for days at a time. Then he would come home drunk and expect me to do 'my wifely duty.' When I refused, he would slap me around, call me names, and say everything was my fault.

"The first time I left him I stayed with my parents for six months and wouldn't let him come near me. Then one day, when I came home from work, he was sitting in my parent's living room, waiting for me. He conned my parents into seeing me by telling them how sorry he was and how he had changed. He told me the same thing and kept saying how much he loved me and how he wanted me back.

"Convinced by the fact that he had a new job and swearing to me he had quit drinking, I moved back. A few months later, I found out he was selling drugs in addition to working at the landfill. When I confronted him about the drugs, he became violent and threatened to kill me if I told anyone. To make his point, he beat me badly enough to put me in the hospital. The police tried to get me to press charges, but I was too afraid he really *would* kill me, so they didn't arrest him.

"From there, things only got worse. When Tala was born, I feared for her safety as well. I just kept my mouth shut and let him sell his drugs and wondered what would happen to us. By then, he was chasing other women, too. I didn't even care as long as it kept him away from us. I concentrated on raising my daughter."

She told me of several other instances where Jimmy had abused her. After one particularly bad beating she ran away with Tala to Oahu. They were able to stay hidden for a couple of years, but eventually Jimmy found them and forced them back to Molokai.

When a tsunami warning sent Jimmy out looking for food and water to tide them over, mother and child escaped to a domestic abuse shelter and reported Jimmy to the police. When the police failed to find him, the shelter decided to send them off the island to the mainland. The counselor knew farmers in central California who were looking for workers and saw an opportunity. The shelter provided the two with enough money for plane tickets and food for the trip. When they arrived, Taniko used the contact numbers she was given, and soon found vineyard work in the small community of McFarland in California's San Joaquin Valley.

They remained safe until Tala entered high school. Unfortunately, her prowess as a soccer player led to them being found again. Tala gained local celebrity status, prompting the publishing of a picture in the paper. This may have been how Jimmy found them, but find them he did. Taniko heard from a neighbor who worked as a cashier at a local gas station that a man fitting Jimmy's description stopped at the station asking a lot of questions. He showed her Tala's soccer picture and said he was looking for her. The neighbor knew some of their story and steered the man in another direction. She said he seemed very determined to find her.

This scared Taniko and sent her into a panic. She picked Tala up at school, and when they got home, they packed the car with a few belongings and drove south.

Taniko's sister and two nieces lived in San Pedro and welcomed the two with open arms. Soon, Taniko had found another job, and Tala was registered in another school. This time, she didn't sign up for soccer.

"We had many discussions on what to do if Jimmy showed up again and put a plan in place," said the woman. "We weren't going to run anymore!" She balled up her fists. "Tala and I decided we'd call the police immediately and demand protection."

For several more years, the urge to look over their shoulders persisted. Eventually, the mother and daughter felt they were safe. The nieces went off to college, and Taniko stayed with her sister who had been diagnosed with cancer. Both she and Tala helped take care of her. When her sister finally died, Taniko discovered she was a beneficiary of her sister's estate and inherited about a million dollars.

Being financially set for life, and believing that

Jimmy had probably moved on, Taniko felt they could attend her family's reunion on Molokai that summer.

"How'd he wind up at the reunion?"

"I can only guess that someone let it slip we were coming. I wish I knew who it was."

The woman suddenly sank with exhaustion. "Do you think it's wrong of me to be happy Jimmy is dead?"

I shook my head. "Now you can start living without fear." I neglected to tell her that what she had disclosed was a strong motive for murder. It was clear to me that I'd have to find the real killer in order to take Tala out from under the umbrella of suspicion. Tala needed a chance at happiness, too.

When our meeting was over, we walked to the front door. I took her hand and said, "Don't worry, Ms. Tagahashi. Everything will work out."

"Call me Taniko, Mr. Walters."

"And I'm Harry."

The first order of business for tomorrow was to head to Maui and the Juvenile Detention Center to talk with Tala. She'd know by then that her mother had retained me to represent her. I would caution her not to talk with anyone and see if I could get her some phone time with her mother. Then, I'd find out if and how soon the DA intended to charge her. With that information, I could determine when her advisement would be scheduled and see if she could be released on bail.

I pulled into my driveway about eight thirty. After going inside, kicking off my shoes, and tossing my keys onto the credenza, I hooked up my private "security system." It consisted of a length of fish line tied across the door and attached to the large bell hanging on the doorpost outside. This was part of my mainland mania. I had been burgled in San Diego, and this was my feeble attempt at thwarting any potential break-ins here. I was sure it could be breeched with a mere breath, but it brought me some peace of mind.

My ritual was interrupted by the tune, *Tiny Bubbles*, coming from my cell phone. It was the ringtone signifying Patty was calling. She had been in touch with both the police and DA's Office. She informed me Tala had not yet been formally charged but was being held in police custody as a "person of interest." Good. That gave me time to see what I was dealing with.

Patty proceeded to recount the details of Jimmy's murder: "Yesterday, about dawn, a fisherman strolling along Twenty-Mile Beach happened to notice a large lump in the mangrove roots and went to see about it. It was the body of Jimmy Pualani, lying face down in the sand with a large butcher knife

14

planted in his back. Officers Draper and Davis were the first to arrive at the scene. They called Dr. Wong, the ME, and collected forensic evidence. The ME examined the body at the scene and has determined the preliminary cause of death to be homicide."

Patty paused for a moment and interjected, "Duh!" I smiled.

"He won't have the official ruling until he finishes the autopsy. He thought he'd have a report sometime late tomorrow, depending on his schedule at the hospital."

I felt I needed to interrupt her long dissertation if only to let her take a breath. "Patty, can you call the ME's office first thing tomorrow? I'd like a copy of his report ASAP."

"Sure thing," she said. "The DA is waiting to make a formal arrest on murder charges until results of blood tests from samples taken off the knife are known and the official cause of death is determined by Dr. Wong."

"Wow, your ability to get the goods is amazing!"

"Thanks. I got all this from Kekoa Kamu. The detective and I had a sort of 'thing' once, and I still have some sway with him. Good thing, as the grouch secretary at the DA's Office really didn't want to talk with me. She just gave me a bare outline of what was going on, but Kamu said Tala was their prime suspect.

I grimaced as Patty pressed on.

"Earlier in the day, at a family reunion, Tala was seen holding a knife like the one stuck in Jimmy's back. When she was questioned, she blurted out she'd kill anyone who tried to hurt her mother. Apparently, they've been running from Jimmy for years." Patty lowered her voice. "He abused the mother, I heard."

That's putting it mildly, I thought, remembering my conversation with Taniko.

"That was enough for her to be brought in for questioning."

"This seems like pretty flimsy evidence to hold the girl on," I said. "Why connect her to the murder, in the first place?"

"For one thing, Jimmy showed up at the reunion yesterday and threatened the mother. He was stinking drunk. He was tossed out of the party by some of the family, and that would have been the end of it if he hadn't been found this morning with a butcher knife in his back.

"That's all I have right now. I'll be in first thing in the morning and will call the ME. You have me all morning, but I've got classes in the afternoon."

"See you soon, Patty." Even as a part-timer, Patty's knowledge of Molokai, and her occasional "things" with some of the more notable men around the islands, would buy me far more than a full time employee in San Diego.

After my conversation with Patty, I called the chief jailer, Billy Noland, on Maui and scheduled a conference with Tala for nine the next morning. Billy said Tala was being held in a solitary cell in juvenile detention but was holding up pretty well. The jailer was an easy going guy and, because he had a soft spot for wayward teenagers, he arranged for Tala to call me a few minutes later.

I was surprised when I first spoke to Tala. Considering the circumstances, and the fact that her mother said she was scared to death, I expected a frightened young lady in tears. Instead, the voice I heard was strong and determined. When she learned I was her lawyer, Tala demanded I get her out of jail "this very minute!"

"I wish I could, but that will have to wait for your bond hearing, hopefully tomorrow."

"Mr....what was your name, again?"

"Walters."

"Mr. Walters, I didn't do this!" She practically screamed into the phone. *There* was the scared child I expected.

"Look Tala," I said, in my "calming" voice. "This is a very complicated situation, but I assure you, I'll be there in the morning to talk with you and do everything I can to get you out. Get some sleep, and I'll see you in the morning."

GARY CARR

CHAPTER 2

The flight to Maui was quite bumpy due to an early morning storm. The little eight-passenger, island-hopping Cessna bravely fought the crosswinds and arrived in Kahalui shaken and stirred. I had reserved a rental car the night before and was quickly on my way over to the correctional facility in Wailuku. After clearing security, I made my way back to the jailer's office to see which room had been set aside for my conference with Tala. Billy had arranged one of the more comfortable meeting rooms for us to use.

As I waited for Tala, I called Patty, who informed me the ME still had no report ready. "Shoots!" I exclaimed, using the common Hawaiian term.

The door opened, and a matron brought Tala in, handcuffed and looking vulnerable. I felt a surprising surge of protectiveness. Why, she could be my niece or little sister!

Tala was tall and slender, making even her orange jail suit seem elegant. Her sleek ebony hair reached her waist, and her pixie face prettily reflected her Polynesian heritage. Worry and anger marred her eyes, easily her best feature. She looked at me with wariness, and I sensed the same mistrust of men that I'd gotten from her mother.

After the matron removed Tala's restraints and seated her across the table from me, she stepped outside, just out of earshot but where she could still keep an eye on the girl. I introduced myself and explained all of the procedural matters. I went down the list of all the ordinary background questions to verify the facts I had on hand.

When I reached a pause in my questions, Tala skewered me with a defiant stare. "Aren't you going to ask me if I did it?"

I looked up from my paperwork and put my pen down. "Did you?"

"I told you on the phone I didn't do it. But," and here I saw a fierceness that rivaled any beast, "he would have had me to contend with if he'd ever hurt my mother, again!"

"You've got to quit saying that," I admonished, "This is not the time to act tough. You need to act like an innocent, helpless little girl."

She gave me a scornful look. "You're a little late with that. I lost my innocence the last time I saw my father beat my mother up. No way will any man hurt her or me, ever again! I'll see to that!"

"You've got to understand something, Tala. If you get convicted of murder, your life as you know it is over. Running and hiding will seem easy compared to what you'll go through spending the rest of your life in prison. So pay attention and let's see if we can do something to get you out of this mess."

She stared at me for some time without saying anything. Finally, she gave a little shrug. "I don't want to leave my mother alone. Tell me what to do and I'll do it." There was resignation in her voice.

"Tell me everything you did the day before your father's body was found–the day of the reunion."

She closed her eyes as if it would help her remember. When she spoke, she seemed far away. "Mom and I have been staying with Aunty Pearl and Uncle Isaac. We'd spent most of the morning down at the beach preparing food for the reunion. At about eleven o'clock, we piled into the jeep and drove out to Twenty-Mile where we joined in and helped set up tables and canopies.

She smiled crookedly. "It was the first time Mom and I had been to a reunion, at least together. Mom had been to many growing up, and really regretted my not having that experience. We were happy and felt safe for the first time in a long while.

"My cousin, Tina, was there." She looked at me. "She's Aunty Pearl and Uncle Isaac's daughter.

Everyone says we look more like sisters than cousins! I was finally starting to get to know my family, until *this* happened!"

Tala wrestled with her tears. I waited while she swallowed hard and then started again. "Aunty Pearl assigned me and Tina the job of dissecting the chickens and soaking them in Huli Huli sauce. After they marinated for a while, we'd place them on the barbecue grills." She smiled at me. "I can still smell the delicious aroma. After everyone had eaten and played awhile, the adults settled down to naps or talking story. Many of the kids played on the beach or in the water."

She told me it was around four o'clock when Jimmy, and his friend, Lono Barton, showed up, much to everyone's surprise. Jimmy demanded to talk to Tala's mother, who was quietly sitting in a chaise lounge watching the children play. Jimmy was clearly drunk.

Her mother ran to her sister as soon as she realized Jimmy was there, and they were quickly surrounded by relatives. Several of the men, including Uncle Isaac, tried to corral Jimmy and send him away, but he insisted he had a right to talk with his wife. After convincing them he only wanted to talk, they finally agreed to let him see Taniko, if it was agreeable with her. She said it was as long as they talked in the open where people could watch Jimmy.

Just the Right Amount of Wrong

They only talked for several minutes before the conversation escalated into yelling at each other. The men stepped in and demanded Jimmy leave. He finally did go, but shouted at Taniko that he would be back and he'd get what was coming to him.

Tala had heard the commotion, and ran towards her mother. As she got closer, several of the men stopped her. Her uncle said it wasn't safe. One muscle-bound cousin put her behind his back, so Jimmy couldn't see her.

When Jimmy and Lono Barton got back in their vehicle and headed toward town, Tala scrambled to her mother. Taniko assured her daughter she was all right, and said her father was just trying to act tough in front of the other men. She wouldn't say any more about their verbal exchange, but she warned Tala to stay close the rest of the day.

Everyone eventually relaxed, and the reunion returned to its happy tone. Tala and her mom went home with Aunt Pearl just after dark. There, they did some cleaning up, took showers, and went to bed.

Tala was awakened by her Aunt Pearl about eight o'clock, the next morning. She told Tala to dress quickly and come into the kitchen because there was a detective talking with her mom. He also wanted to talk with her mother. When Tala walked into the sun-drenched kitchen, she immediately saw that her mom looked scared. She was introduced to Detective Kamu, who informed them of Jimmy's death. He didn't offer any details, but he asked numerous questions.

Tala said, "I told him just what I told you, but he kept going over and over the same stuff, like he didn't understand the answers. He asked me if there was any reason I might want to hurt my father. What a joke! I told him I had *lots* of reasons because my father was a monster and that I would kill him before I let him hurt my mother again." She looked at me and shook her head. "I guess that was a dumb remark since I had just learned he was dead, but the cop acted as if it was an admission that I had done it!"

Detective Kamu warned them not to leave the island, and said he'd probably be back later with a warrant to collect DNA samples from them and everyone else who was at the reunion. He made good on his words later that afternoon. He left after taking samples from everyone in the household.

"We sat around talking about my father being dead, and then the phone started ringing non-stop. We learned from several relatives that his body had been found close to our reunion site, and that he'd been stabbed to death sometime in the night.

"Around dinner time, Detective Kamu was back. He said they were processing blood evidence, and though it would take awhile for all the DNA profiles, because of the preliminary blood test results, I would need to come with him and provide a blood sample. He actually had a warrant for my blood! Mom started weeping when he said I was being held as a person of interest. I kept telling him over and over that I didn't kill anyone, but he wouldn't listen.

"Mom told me she would find a good lawyer and not to worry. Detective Kamu drove me to the airport where there was a police plane waiting, and I was flown here and placed in a jail room."

We went over the other questions Detective Kamu had asked, as well as what she had said in response. I knew there had to be something important about the blood tests that had yet to surface. I asked if she had been anywhere near her father at the beach or anywhere else, and she assured me she hadn't. Her uncle had seen to that. She said the only time she wasn't with her family was about ten minutes, when she went for a short walk right after they got home. She'd walked down to the water at the edge of Aunt Pearl's property, but headed back only a few minutes later.

I took a few additional notes, asked Tala if there were any personal items or specific toiletries she needed, and told her I would be back soon. I explained I would be talking with Detective Kamu, the District Attorney, as well as the Medical Examiner. I reminded her to be nice and act innocent before I motioned the matron to come in.

The stern looking matron came in and placed Tala in restraints once again. As she was being led away, Tala turned and smiled for the first time.

"Thank you, Mr. Walters. Please tell my mom I'm okay."

I was feeling pretty good until Patty dropped off the preliminary results from the blood tests later that afternoon.

CHAPTER 3

I awoke suddenly in that still part of the night when everything is quiet and the only thing you hear is the voice in your own head. I was arguing with myself about bringing my investigative staff over from California, but decided it wasn't a good idea. They would run into a lot of resistance from the locals, and that would eat up valuable time. That meant me doing a lot of the work on my own.

Investigating on my own could muddle my actions as an attorney, but if I was to get this cleared up quickly, I'd have to take the chance. As I weighed the pros and cons, and the fact that it could get dangerous, I remembered a private investigator on Oahu I had used a few years ago. Maybe I could get him over here to give me a hand. I would give him a call as soon as I found his number.

I knew Tala could be charged with murder at any time, and for some reason I was nervous about

27

that. A strange reaction, as I'm usually quite confident when I start a case. I guess it was because I felt like I was flying by the seat of my pants.

Perhaps it was the girl. My thoughts drifted to Tala, who'd suffered tremendously in her young life. No child should endure what she had with her father, and very few would fault her if she had killed him. After meeting her, there is no doubt in my mind that she is innocent. In order to prove that, however, I'm going to have to find the real killer. Now *that* made me really nervous!

Nature called. I tried to shut off the nagging voice in my head on the way to the bathroom. Walking back to my bedroom, I realized I wasn't sleepy anymore. I detoured to the kitchen and made a pot of coffee. Sitting down at the table, I took a notepad and pen and disassembled the facts of the case from the beginning to the present.

Five days ago, Tala and her mom arrived in Hawaii. They had traveled to Molokai to spend time with their relatives. The third day of their visit included the big outdoor barbecue at Twenty-Mile Beach. A large crowd attended. Kids were squealing and playing in the water, adults were cooking and drinking, talking story, and just happy to be there with everyone else. When Tala's father showed up uninvited, the mood turned sour–particularly for a lot of the family who did not like him. His sudden presence was especially unpleasant for Taniko. An argument ensues, and Jimmy leaves mad. The next morning, he's found stabbed to death with a knife used at the reunion. There were no fingerprints on the knife, but blood test results showed that Tala's blood type, along with that of her mother and her cousin, Tina, was on the knife. And then there was Tala's outburst. Bit by bit, this all this added up to enough circumstantial evidence for the District Attorney's Office to hold Tala as a person of interest in the murder of Jimmy Pualani.

I couldn't even think ahead and anticipate DNA profiles. Right now the blood test results are what will send this over the top to murder charges. With Tala's blood type on the knife, I'd have to scrutinize the interviews and forensic reports until I came up with something that works in Tala's favor. If only Tala had kept her mouth shut with Detective Kamu. I might have been able to get a lesser charge based on circumstantial evidence. I would just have to wait and see where the evidence takes me. The weight given to Tala's statement by the DA still seemed ridiculous to me.

An hour later I found my way back to bed. I was awakened at daylight by dogs barking and roosters crowing. The large numbered LED clock on the bed stand read five fifty-eight. Glancing out of the bedroom window, I witnessed a glorious sunrise over Maui. When the alarm went off, two minutes later, the Francolin game birds began their cackling. Right on time! Ah, the wonderful fabric of life on Molokai. I quit fighting the urge to go back to sleep, and hauled my butt out of bed. Ready to face the world after showering and dressing, I fixed a fresh carafe of coffee and a light breakfast. Taking my meal on the lanai, I planned out my day.

After my six-minute commute on the nearly deserted Kam V Highway from my home in Kawela, I arrived at the office at seven thirty. It had been a long time since I was up this early. As I sat at my desk waiting for Patty to come in, I watched Kaunakakai get ready for the day. Cars began filling the street. Delivery trucks were hurrying to make their rounds. People scurried back and forth. Even at the height of this activity, the town exhibited a sense of purpose that was relaxed and non-stressful.

I saw Patty pull up in front of the office just before eight. She bounced out of her late model high-rise pickup and burst through the door with a hearty "Aloha." She was more athletic than dainty, but moved with the fluid grace of island women. She tossed her purse on the chair by the door and brandished cinnamon hot bread under my nose.

"I already ate."

"Bran muffins and coffee?" She propped a hip on my desk and made quite a show of devouring the gooey treat.

"Something like that." Oh, to be young again, and eat whatever you wanted and never gain a pound.

"Talk to me."

Between sips of her coffee, Patty recounted a litany of details she'd managed to elicit from the DA's Office, yesterday. When she was done, with her information and her hot bread, we set to work preparing our case, should Tala actually be charged. We suspected she would be.

It wasn't long before we got the call from a clerk in the DA's Office. It was just after ten o'clock, and the "grouch" assistant informed us that Tala would be charged with murder. The clerk also told us that Tala was being moved out of juvenile detention to a secure cell at the main prison facility until her advisement, and that the DA was going to push for trying her as an adult. I knew it wouldn't do me any good to try to persuade the DA into letting Tala stay at juvie. The assistant said they were faxing the arrest warrant over to me this morning, and that the DA had scheduled a press conference for two o'clock this afternoon to announce an arrest in the case.

GARY CARR

CHAPTER 4

I flew over to Maui to be on hand for the DA's press conference. I wanted to make sure Tala's name was not released, since no determination had been made yet to try her as an adult. I let the reporters know that I was representing the accused, and that my client was innocent of any wrongdoing. Since this was an election year, I got a barb in that the DA had made a hurried arrest just for publicity. That little bit of gamesmanship probably cost me any future favors from the DA, but it was necessary for Tala's sake.

Truth be known, I liked the DA. He had been fighting to clean up the growing drug problem in Maui County, and wasn't afraid to try cases on thin evidence if it meant getting some of the criminals off the street. This case was different, however. Tala was a teenager who, as far as I could tell, had never done anything except show a strong devotion to her mother.

I went to the prison to check in with Tala and explained what was happening. I warned her the next couple of days were not going to be easy, but reassured her I would be with her each step of the way. We went over what she had previously told me a few more times. She was adamant that she'd left nothing out. I told her Patty would get with her mom and select clothing for her to wear to court. I reminded her about acting like an innocent, scared little girl.

"I don't need to act, Mr. Walters," she said. "I really *am* scared!"

I toyed with the idea of taking the Molokai Princess back home rather than another bumpy plane flight. The ninety minute ferryboat ride in the fresh air would give me some time to think. However, one look at the choppy seas changed my mind.

When I got back to the office, Patty had all the faxed information from the DA's Office neatly arranged on my desk. I read the arrest information and then re-read it. The premise of the warrant was thin, but district attorneys usually play things close to the vest until they get past the advisement.

Before going home, I decided to walk over to Friendly Market Center to see if they had any new culinary delights. Since this is Tuesday and the barge had just come in, I wanted first shot at any choice meat or specialties. I found a nice package of tri-tip beef that I envisioned as fajitas for my dinner. I chose a few fresh vegetables, and then picked out a large chocolate candy bar for dessert. It would be bran muffins for breakfast, again, but chocolate is worth it.

My fajita dinner turned into a beef stir-fry on rice, because I changed my mind on the way home, deciding I'd rather have a good night's sleep, than Mexican food and heartburn.

After dinner, I turned on the television to catch the news. As expected, the lead story was "Arrest Made in Molokai Murder." No names were mentioned, following protocol for a juvenile who had not been formally arraigned. If the DA got approval to try her as an adult, her anonymity would disappear. I fumed at the thought that the DA was turning this into a circus in order to get votes. I shut the TV off, grabbed a beer, and went out to the lanai. Sipping my beer, I listened to the trade winds and night sounds until I started getting sleepy, then got up and went to bed.

GARY CARR

CHAPTER 5

I arrived at Maui's courthouse Wednesday morning for the advisement. The matron brought Tala in, and we discussed what she could expect to happen. I told her the purpose of this appearance was for the court to advise her of the charges against her. It was also to determine if she could be released on bail until her appearance in court. I told her it was unlikely she would get bail because she was charged with murder.

The bailiff briefly summarized that the matter before the court was the advisement of one Tala Pualani on the charge of homicide in the first degree. The judge acknowledged the summary and asked if the accused was in the courtroom. I stood and informed the court that the young lady next to me was Tala Pualani, and that I was the attorney representing her. The judge asked Tala if she

37

understood the charges and her rights, which included the right to counsel. Tala replied that she understood and that she wished me to represent her. He jotted a note down on a tablet in front of him and then asked for motions. The DA stated that he didn't have any motions, so I asked the judge to set bond. He said because of the nature of the crime being a capital offense and the possibility of flight by the accused, he would not set bond. He remanded the case to a higher court for any further hearings.

I then filed an Entry of Appearance, a Motion for Discovery, and requested a preliminary hearing as soon as possible. The judge looked at the district court calendar and asked the DA if he could be ready for the hearing by tomorrow morning. Startled by the very unusual short timeline, the DA registered a strong objection, stating he needed more time. I responded that I saw this move as another publicity stunt by the DA.

The judge got angry and said he needed to accommodate his very busy schedule. He peevishly offered to move the timeline to one o'clock in the afternoon on Friday or he could delay the process by three weeks. That meant nearly a month in jail for Tala. I reluctantly agreed to the short time frame, as did the DA. The judge left the court, and Tala was taken back to her cell.

Chiding District Attorney Akumu, I told him, "Make sure I have everything."

Akumu stiffened. "I'll have my office **fax you all** we have as soon as I return to the office. **You do have** a fax, don't you?"

"I have two," I said, with a churlish smile. I strode out of the courtroom.

After a quick, chartered flight back to **Molokai, I** hurried to the office. While I'd been flying, **the DA** had faxed the documents to my office. **Patty and I** began our fine-toothed comb examination **of the pile.** About six thirty, I told Patty to go home. **There were** stacks of paper scattered everywhere. I spent **the next** three hours making a list of witnesses **and** constructing a perk chart on anyone **connected to** Tala, both as a relative or possible witness. **By the** time I left, I felt better about my chances **of getting** this matter thrown out before it ever came **to trial. I** wasn't buying the DA's flimsy evidence **against Tala,** and the lack of a substantial motive.

GARY CARR

CHAPTER 6

Friday morning, I met with Taniko. We flew over to Maui together, and spent some time with Tala prior to the hearing. Precisely at one o'clock, the bailiff announced the arrival of the judge. All rose and followed the pomp of judicial proceedings. The judge asked the DA to list the charges against Tala, which ranged from assault with a deadly weapon to murder in first degree. Turning to face the audience of reporters in the courtroom, Akumu began to lay out the details of Jimmy Pualani's death and the forensic evidence that had been gathered. He then called on Detective Kamu. Kamu testified that Tala had told him she would kill anyone who tried to hurt her mother.

Tala, in a fiery outburst, yelled, "I didn't kill anybody! I told you that."

The judge glared at me over his glasses and admonished me to control my client.

41

The next witness was an elderly lady, generally known as Aunty Kiolani. She said she'd seen Tala have "words" with Jimmy. She couldn't remember exactly what was said, only that Tala seemed very upset. She said Tala was preparing food for a family reunion, and when her father approached, she started waving the butcher knife in his face and yelling at him.

This was news to me. I looked at Tala, who shrugged and raised her eyebrows to indicate she had no clue what the witness was talking about.

I tried to discredit the witness, but she was the epitome of truth and sincerity. Nothing I said would make anyone think differently. I didn't think she was lying, but why was she so sure Tala had done this? From the discovery, I'd read the DA had picked up information from several of the children verifying that Aunty Kiolani was standing close to Tala and her father, when they were arguing.

Having an argument doesn't equate to stabbing someone, I pointed out to her. I tried to cast doubt about her identifying Tala. Her eyesight wasn't very good, and maybe she saw someone who simply looked like Tala. I returned to the defense table unsure if I'd accomplished my goal.

Next, an insurance company rep was called to the stand. He verified that Tala's mother had recently inherited over a million dollars from a sister who'd passed away. The DA then called Police Officer

Draper to the stand. He testified that a young fisherman had found the body washed up in the mangrove roots. He stated that all of the personal effects such as wallet, watch, etc., were still on the body. He found no other evidence to speak of except a pink satin ribbon that was caught on a branch, a couple of empty beer cans, and an old fishnet float near the body.

Following the officer, the forensic pathologist, Dr. Wong, in his role as Medical Examiner, testified that Tala's father had died as the result of homicide, namely, being stabbed in the back with a large butcher knife. It had penetrated a lung and embedded in the heart. His testimony about the force needed to inflict such a wound was shaky, but he offset that by stating the sharpness and shape of the blade were such that even a young person or woman could have easily wielded it.

In my cross examination, I tried to use that to my advantage, pointing out there were numerous young people around Tala's father at the reunion. I noticed a slight nod of agreement from the judge, and felt I had planted at least one small seed in Tala's favor.

I asked Dr. Wong if he could read the report as it had been written and submitted to me and the DA.

He read: "Subject is a male of Polynesian descent, approximately forty-eight years-of-age; six foot, one inch in height; two hundred seventy pounds in weight; black hair and dark brown eyes. Victim has

Samoan tribal tattoos surrounding both biceps, and a small honu tattoo below the left earlobe on the neck. Subject was found at Twenty-Mile Beach on Molokai with a ten-inch butcher knife protruding from his back approximately two inches left of the spine just below the rib cage. Cause of death is exsanguination from punctures to the left lung and right ventricle of the heart. Death is non-accidental homicide caused by person or persons unknown.

"Blood samples were taken from the knife blade and handle, and were type AB. No discernible fingerprints or other foreign matter were on the knife. Blood tests from the victim also confirmed traces of alcohol and methamphetamine in the body. Foreign matter on the body was consistent with material on the beach and not considered relevant. The victim was dressed in a tank top T-shirt and board shorts. One slipper was on his left foot. The other slipper was near the body in the mangroves. He was wearing a gold-plated watch on his left wrist, and there was a wallet in his pocket that contained $42.00, a Hawaiian driver's license, several scraps of paper with phone numbers and e-mail addresses, and a newspaper clipping of his daughter, Tala, playing soccer.

"Additional blood tests taken from persons at the reunion show three were determined to have the same blood type as that found on the knife. The three are: Tala Pualani, Taniko Tagahashi, and Tina Roland."

When he finished, I began my questioning.

Q: I see from your report and your previous testimony that blood samples were taken from people at the reunion. Were samples taken from everyone?

A: No. DNA swabs were taken from almost everyone, but not blood samples.

Q: Who did you take samples from?

A: Just the seven people listed in my report.

Q: Why only these seven?

A: We thought we would focus on those who had been seen preparing food and had immediate access to the knife.

Q: We?

A: Yes, myself and Detective Kamu.

Q: Why weren't others checked?

A. Detective Kamu said it had to be someone messing with the food, and it would be a waste of money to run a bunch of tests for nothing. He checked the people we tested and discovered small cuts on Ms. Tagahashi's and Tina Roland's hands. There was a larger, bandaged cut on Tala Pualani's left hand.

Q: Did you have DNA tests run on the blood?

A: No.

Q: Why not? Didn't you say that DNA swabs were taken from almost everyone in attendance?

A: Detective Kamu told me blood tests would be enough.

45

Q: **Do** you have a list of everyone who was at the reunion?

A: Yes.

Q: How many were there?

A: Thirty-two.

Q: So out of the thirty-two, only seven blood types were checked?

A: That is correct.

Q: So there are twenty-five additional people who could be suspects that were never even checked?

A: Stated that way, you are correct. However, I would like to point out that eighteen are children. The three oldest relatives are in their late seventies, leaving four individuals who were not checked.

Q: Who are the four individuals?

A: Isaac Roland and the three Iono brothers, David, Samuel, and Jonah.

Q: Is there sufficient blood or tissue from the knife to run a DNA test?

A: Yes.

Q: Is there some reason DNA tests were not conducted?

A: Detective Kamu said the prosecutor only needed a blood type match for an arrest.

Upon hearing that DNA swabs had been collected, but never processed, and that four

46

individuals were not even blood tested, I said, "Your Honor, I would like to move that charges against my client be dismissed for lack of probable cause due to an insufficiency of evidence."

The DA objected, stating, "Miss Pualani was seen with the murder weapon, her matching blood type was found on the knife, she demonstrated dislike of the victim, and stated she would kill him. The state believes that this is more than sufficient evidence to bring this matter to trial."

The judge called for a brief recess to consider the motion and retired to his chambers. Less than a half hour later, he returned and denied my motion. As there was no further evidence presented, he set Tala's arraignment for Monday after next, barely meeting the ten day timeline.

My questioning of Dr. Wong on the blood tests, and the fact that no DNA tests were done only gave fodder to the DA. He probably told Wong to start the tests immediately. The problem with that is if they come back with solid evidence against Tala, I'm going to have a tough time convincing a jury she didn't do it.

None of this helped me cast doubt that Tala had murdered her father. Here was a body on a remote beach, on a remote island, and little evidence. Certainly nothing that would prove my client innocent. The big curtain I had to lift was Tala's statement which, here in Hawaii, seemed to carry a lot of weight. If we were in San Diego, it would be a different story.

Tala's arraignment was procedural with a summarized presentation of the charges and evidence presented in the advisement hearing by the DA. Upon completion of the presentation of evidence, the judge addressed me.

"Mr. Walters, having heard the statements presented here today, do you wish to enter a plea on behalf of your client at this time?"

"Certainly, Your Honor. We would like to enter a plea of not guilty."

The judge asked Tala if she understood the proceedings and agreed with the plea. She stood and, with a crack in her voice, replied, "Yes, Your Honor."

I then asked that my client be released to her mother since she was a juvenile, and that all proceedings in this matter be dealt with in juvenile court. The DA objected, claiming Tala was a flight risk. He also said as this was a homicide case, Tala should be tried as an adult. He strengthened his objection by stating it was only two months until Tala turned eighteen, and she was fully aware of her actions.

The judge took a few minutes to consider the matter. He then ruled that bond would be denied, and

Tala could be tried as an adult. Tala gasped, and I took her hand and squeezed. She was trembling.

The earliest available trial date that accommodated both sides and the court was nearly two months hence. I would have plenty of time to prepare a case. Unfortunately for Tala, it meant a lot more jail time.

I received word later that day from the District Attorney's Office, that they had been unable to locate two of the people from the reunion that were supposed to have blood and DNA tests. Well, at least I knew the DA was performing tests. Nothing was done according to normal protocol here, so I had to be on my toes. Now I had to bring my own experts on board to counter the DA's findings. I found it interesting that one of the missing persons was Tala's uncle, Isaac Roland. I called Patty, to pick her brain about him.

"Really, Boss? Again? I'm going to flunk my Early Childhood class."

"Sorry, Patty. It's important." I asked her about Isaac, and wasn't surprised she already knew of his disappearance.

"It's believed he's hiding somewhere in Halawa Valley. It could take weeks to track him down.

"The locals won't be much help, Boss. You know

that's where a lot of 'creative agriculture' takes place."

"Creative?"

"You know…" I heard her take in a breath and hold it.

"Ah, Marijuana. Pakalolo."

"Now, Isaac has led an interesting life. He probably has lots of reasons to hide. Besides being a drug dealer, he's known Jimmy all his life, and his name has been tied to several unsolved break-ins and robberies on the island."

"He's a drug dealer? No wonder he doesn't want DNA testing done on him!"

"No kidding. The other person missing is Isaac's daughter, Tina, who also happens to be Tala's cousin. She's been gone since the day after the murder."

"That's weird. Father and daughter are missing. I wonder if they are together."

"I wouldn't know."

"What? The island grapevine hasn't told you, yet?"

I could almost hear Patty's shrug. "Give it another hour."

"Her blood type matched what was on the knife, and they want a DNA profile. There is something weird here."

"You might have something there, Boss."

I signed off, promising to call Patty with any new information, if she promised to do the same.

Just the Right Amount of Wrong

I called Detective Kamu and was told there were intensive searches going on for Isaac and Tina, headed by the local police. They were particularly interested in Tina's whereabouts, he told me. He also said the DA was making noises like he was afraid she'd been hurt, possibly from someone who'd seen what had happened the night Jimmy was killed. Kamu shared that upon interviewing family and friends, no one could think of a reason why she'd just disappear like that. Her Toyota was last seen in Kawela II Subdivision the day after the murder, but the driver could not be identified. The vehicle was found later that day in Friendly Market's parking lot, in Kaunakakai. The initial search of the vehicle hadn't turned up anything useful, and the only fingerprints found on the vehicle belonged to Tina.

I called Taniko, who said Tina had lived on the island her whole life and knew almost everyone, and that she worked as a clerk at Misaki's Market.

"Do you think Tina saw something, and that's why she's gone into hiding?"

Taniko was quiet for a moment, and then said, "It's plausible. But, I'm worried her disappearance has a more dire reason. My sister is frantic, especially since Isaac has disappeared, too."

I hated to ask this, but I did anyway. "Taniko, please don't take offense at this, but do you think Tina had anything to do with Jimmy's death?"

"I don't know, Harry. I wish I did."

51

I thanked her, and said I'd be in touch. "Please call me, if either one shows up, okay?

Tina needed to be found right away. Fortunately, she was going to have a tough time hiding from me. I knew the island as well as she did. Maybe I'd find Isaac, too.

Isaac seemed a complex person. A drug dealer, and yet he was one of the men who guarded Taniko, and warned Tala to stay away from Jimmy. A bad guy with a good streak? Interesting.

CHAPTER 7

If I was going to find these two, I needed help. Fortunately, I'd finally found the contact information for the private eye on Oahu. I placed the call to Melvin Momi and hoped he had the time to help in this murder case.

Melvin is one of those nondescript men whom no one notices. Living in Hawaii, and being of Japanese-Hawaiian descent, he can blend into the local population, something that comes in handy in his line of work. He speaks all the languages of the islands, including Tongan and Samoan. A "kama`aina" or Hawaiian born, he has lived and worked on all of the islands, and has one of the best underground networks anywhere. The big problem with Melvin, however, he is extremely protective of himself and his network. If he decides to omit information to cover his own butt, he does. Usually that is not a problem.

I wanted to ask Melvin to put together a list of Jimmy's contacts. This would give me a starting point for possible suspects. When his voicemail asked me to leave a message, I sighed and asked him to call me as soon as possible.

Melvin returned my call a few hours later with a hearty, "Hi-ya Boss."

"Aloha, my friend!" Finished with social niceties, I got down to business. "You heard about the murder of Jimmy Pualani?" I asked.

"Yeah, I read that drug dealer got stuck like a pig. I was a little surprised to see his daughter nailed for it, but figured it was just bad blood in the family."

"She's innocent," I assured him. "But someone had bad blood with him. I need your help."

"I'm at your service."

"How soon can you get here? The sooner the better, as this is really important."

"How does this afternoon sound?"

We set up a time for him to fly over to Molokai on Island Air. I would meet him at the airport with a packet of information, which included the details of the case so far, and a small collection of photos, depicting some of the key people involved. I was sure Melvin would bring his camera equipment, but asked him anyway. He had all the latest digital surveillance gadgets: still and video cameras with telephoto and macro lenses for long distance and close-up shots, as well as listening devices and bugs. I hoped the little rental car I was meeting him in had sufficient room to hold everything.

It was several hours until the two-fifteen flight came in, so while I waited I decided to do a little grocery shopping in downtown Kaunakakai. While there, I might just ask the locals if they had any insight into the murder. I may be able to glean some interesting tidbits of gossip.

Strolling down the street, I marveled that little had changed since King Kamehameha V established the town as his summer home in the 1800s. Kaunakakai has a population of about 3500, half the island's population, and covers approximately sixteen square miles. The king's coconut grove is still a minor tourist attraction. Somewhat worn store fronts still allure shoppers and day trippers fade in and fade out from the harbor. The nice thing about Molokai is that very little changes. I arrive every month or two and each time, it is like I never left.

The people are special, too. One time, as I sat waiting at the airport, I watched a teen-age girl look after her grandparents. She really cared that they were comfortable and seemed to appreciate that she could be of help. I've seen this sense of family in other places, like Italy, but none better than in Hawaii. The island people are proud of their family and friends, and it bonds them to their roots and culture. In some ways, watching the cultural differences between the Hawaiians and outsiders is an echo of the time I spent on the Navajo Reservation in Arizona as a youngster. Fiercely proud native people in both instances, clinging to traditions not only because of the oneness they have, but in many cases, because of the inability to grasp or accept the changing world around them. Whatever it was about these people and this place, it drew me here and held me fast.

After picking up some Portuguese sausage and a few vegetables at Friendly's, I headed over to Misaki's to purchase a couple bottles of wine. The little corner liquor display in Misaki's Market has always been one of my favorite haunts. You never know what you will find. They acquire the odds and ends of liquor destined for Japan, or coming to the States from Asia, and their prices are one of the few things on the island that are generally lower than on the mainland. Today was an especially good day. I picked up three bottles of Italian Prosecco for $3.99 a bottle and a sack of licorice candy for Melvin.

I recalled him switching to licorice when he gave up chewing tobacco. It always fascinated me to watch him take a gob of candy and tuck it under his lip. He occasionally forgot it was licorice, and gave a big cowboy spit. Then he would shoot me this bull-at-a-bastard-calf stare, like it was *my* fault or something.

Just the Right Amount of Wrong

I ran into a couple of acquaintances at the post office, and they wanted to talk about the murder. They learned more from me than I did from them. Next I strolled over to the Fish and Dive Shop and stumbled into a conversation between two men jawing about the murder. When they finally noticed me standing nearby, they quickly changed the subject. I asked what they had been talking about, and they said they were just kicking around some of the things they'd heard about the murder. They asked me why Tala was arrested and whether I thought she was guilty. I gave a cursory answer and said as far as I was concerned she was more a "person of interest" than an actual suspect, but it was early days as far as the investigation was concerned.

The two men were talkative, and that was all right with me. They enlightened me about the shady nature of Tala's Uncle Isaac, and him being missing. They figured he was "backside," hiding out. He had been involved in pakalolo and other drugs since he was a teenager.

"He and his brother-in-law, Jimmy, had lately been dealing the heavy stuff," one man said.

The other one lowered his voice, and informed me there was an older Filipino guy we should be looking for, too. "We don't know his name, but he's been hanging out with Jimmy for a while." He gestured with two fingers that they were closer than brothers.

Hmmm. Melvin can look him up, too. I made a mental note.

Happily, my little shopping trip gleaned unexpected riches. I drove the groceries back home, and after putting them away, wrote everything down that I'd learned. This was always a good way to see if I had unanswered questions roaming around in my brain. Soon, it was time to pick up Melvin.

CHAPTER 8

Murder is mainly personal, the majority of them taking place between people who are close to one another. A large percentage are family members, followed by close acquaintances and business associates. While watching for Melvin's plane to coast to a stop, I pondered the family around Jimmy. It was a mixed bag, for sure. Taniko, Tala, and Tina were family, as was Isaac–sort of. Throw in a beach full of relatives who didn't like Jimmy, abuse, drugs, and who knows what else, it's a wonder murder hadn't happened sooner.

Something for Melvin to look into was the Filipino friend of Jimmy's. There had been no mention of him anywhere in the police reports. That was odd considering he was supposed to be a close friend of Jimmy's.

In spite of his upbeat phone voice, Melvin was reserved, when I picked him up at the airport. I remembered he used disguises, a lot, and today he was sporting a long black wig and a pair of dark sunglasses. It had taken me a moment to recognize him, and at my questioning glance, he said, "It makes me seem younger, and less like a narc."

This information was conveyed to me in pidgin, knocking out any doubt that he was native born. I deciphered his meaning, and then placed my information packet in his outstretched hand. Before I left home, I'd thrown in my latest batch of notes and the questions I still had, before dashing the fifteen minutes to the airport.

Melvin thanked me, this time in English, and handed me his latest business card. It said "Fish Surveyor," with the Hawaiian Department of Tourism. Shaking my head, I followed him to the car rental counter. I said I had a rental, but he said he preferred his own. He'd also wanted to stay at Wavecrest Resort on the East End if they had a condo available. It would be closer to the scene. If not, he'd stay at Hotel Molokai.

I held out the business card. "Fish surveyor?"

Melvin shrugged. "I can ask a lot of questions without arousing suspicions. Just a local yokel asking tourists where they are from, what they are doing, where they are staying. I can garner a lot of information that may come in handy down the road."

We climbed into our respective rental cars, and I called through the open window, "Contact me when you are settled."

He saluted me, as he sped off.

My cell rang later that day. Melvin was ensconced at a condo he had rented at Wavecrest Resort. He had made the arrangements through Friendly Isle Realty and was renting it for the week. He thought that would be enough time for him to snoop around and get most of the answers I wanted.

I introduced Patty and Melvin and later told her he would be working with us on the case. She had never met Melvin before so I asked what she thought. She gave me the strangest answer.

"I wish I could like Melvin, but I'm a little *afraid* of him. He has dead eyes. People with that look wouldn't hesitate to kill someone. I can *feel* it."

"Before you get started, Melvin, perhaps you can give me some of your insight on why Tala was arrested on what I think is very slim evidence."

We were sitting in my office, enjoying the late afternoon sun streaming through the windows. Melvin slumped slightly in his chair, absentmindedly pulling on an earlobe. He'd shown up without the beard and sunglasses, so I was able to see his eyes weren't as dead as Patty thought. They were wily, intelligent eyes that showed a surprising glint of humor.

61

"You need to remember, this is Molokai. It's a lot different from Oahu and Maui. Most everything anyone does here is right out in the open. The family reunion was no secret. Neither was the flap Jimmy had with his wife. People were talking about it on the plane trip over here. There was even a lot of gossip about someone seeing Tala threaten Jimmy with a knife. For the most part there wasn't any reason for the DA to dig any further. So, it looks like we're going to have to find a reason."

"We need something to counteract the DA's so-called evidence."

"Well, I'm already digging around for you, and while I'm doing that, I was hoping I could work on my own investigation. I'm trying to track down some of the drug underground, here."

"No problem, most likely drugs will have a lot to do with Jimmy's murder. We need more information on how Jimmy's friend found Tala and her mom, whether he knows the Filipino, and if there are any ties beyond drug dealings."

"Right, Boss."

I asked Melvin to report to me a couple of times each day, or sooner, if he found anything really pertinent.

His pidgin response was, "Coming good, Boss." I smiled to myself.

One of the ironies of the Hawaiian Islands is that it is the kind of place where you really wouldn't think violent crimes happen–on Molokai especially. Molokai is considered "old" Hawaii and has a different feel than its neighboring islands. It has a rich history, a diverse landscape, and was even home to a leper colony where a remnant from the original patients continued to live after the segregation policy for those suffering with Hansen's Disease (leprosy) was lifted. Molokai still models a reserved lifestyle based primarily on agriculture and fishing with a strong sense of Hawaiian traditions. Days begin with sunrises and rainbows. Citizens move at a slower pace, and delight in stopping almost anywhere to "talk story." You're not on Molokai very long before your movements mimic the flow of the ocean and become in tune to the nature around you. Murder definitely throws a kink into the flow.

I did some online research on DNA profiling, and after wrapping up my work with a few more phone calls, I headed to the kitchen to prepare dinner. I put a salad together, and then fried up some Portuguese sausage. I placed the sizzling meat between two slices of bread, sprinkled it with fontina cheese and Mexican salsa. Feast in hand, along with a chilled bottle of the Prosecco, I settled on the lanai to watch the sun go down and see the spectacular contrast of the Wiliwili tree against the subtle shades of orange, red, and pink of the sunset.

Melvin called just after I got out of the shower the next morning. As I was trying to shake the last of the wine cobwebs from my head, he said he had picked up a lead on the Filipino from one of the patrons at Wavecrest. His name was Moses Silva, and he and an old girlfriend from Maui had been holed up at her place on the west end of the island for the past few days. She supposedly came over on the ferry the day before the murder, and they haven't been on this end of the island since then.

Melvin then updated me on his conversation with some folks at Paddler's. For the price of a couple of drinks, he'd learned a little more about Jimmy's friend. His name was Lono Barton, and he could possibly connect him with Isaac. Melvin said he was leaving right away to locate Barton, and would get back with me on what he found.

Good news, I thought.

Before he left, one of Melvin's "watchers," as he called them, located Barton at a restaurant in Kualapu'u, and snapped a picture. He forwarded it to Melvin's phone. Melvin hurried to the restaurant and parked his car, nose out. He was heading to the entrance when he spotted Barton just as he climbed into his truck. He tapped him on the shoulder, and asked if they could talk. A few beers later, Melvin had gathered most of what he thought was relevant to Jimmy's murder.

Barton and Jimmy had been drinking buddies, and he helped Jimmy sell "weed" to tourists now and then. He said Jimmy really wasn't a friend, just someone he hung with once in a while. He said the day before the murder, he and Jimmy had a few beers down at the wharf.

"Jimmy started talking about his wife, and said she had inherited a lot of money. He wanted me to drive him to the reunion to remind her that they were still married. He was going to make a deal for some of the money, and if he got it, he would agree to a peaceful divorce. He promised me he wouldn't cause any trouble–he just wanted to talk. When we got there, he kept his promise, partly because all of the relatives were there to make sure he did. His brother-in-law, Isaac, was there and he stuck to Jimmy like a bur on a bear's butt. They had a falling out several months ago, and so there is bad blood between them. Word was Jimmy stiffed him on a drug deal. He'd wanted Isaac to deal heavier stuff for a bigger profit. Isaac didn't want to go there.

"Well, Jimmy tried talking to his wife, but she told him to 'go to hell.' She threatened to have him arrested if he came anywhere near her and her daughter, again. Jimmy got real mad and ranted all the way back into town. He said he'd 'show her!' I dropped him off at Paddler's, and that was the last time I saw him."

"What about Isaac? Do you think he had anything to do with Jimmy's murder?" Melvin asked, placing a twenty on the bar. The bartender swiped it up, and placed two more beers in front of the men.

Barton said, "Isaac and Jimmy used to be good friends, having grown up together on Molokai. They attended the same schools, worked construction when they could, but then sort of drifted apart after they got married and started spending more time with their families. After Tala and her mom left, Jimmy started drinking even more and exhausted a lot of his time getting high. Isaac spent less and less time around him."

"Is he still in the drug business?"

"Isaac grows a little 'medicinal marijuana' in Halawa Valley, but hasn't been into 'pushing,' like Jimmy."

Barton said he didn't know where Isaac was, but most likely, he was hiding in Halawa, because he was afraid of police. More important, his "crop" was just about ripe.

The next day, the island's "creative"

agriculturists started brush fires near the landfill to distract the fire and police departments. While the authorities were busy with the fires, the growers were dissembling at the other end of the island, packing the pakalolo out of Halawa Valley. Their contraband would wind up at a safer location on the island.

Melvin was familiar with the old ruse, and so was Detective Kamu. Both spotted Isaac at the same time, when he made a stop at Manae Goodz and Grindz, a small local store and food counter on the East End. Isaac was immediately arrested and taken into custody.

Melvin called and filled me in on the info he had gotten from Lono Barton and on Isaac's arrest by Detective Kamu. Now that he was in custody, I would have Melvin interview him to find out why he disappeared and if it was related to the murder. Having Melvin do the work kept me off the possible witness list, and not subject to examination on the stand.

I told Melvin to see if he could talk with the Filipino, Moses Silva, and let me know if he came up with something.

Melvin headed out to Maunaloa and, within a few minutes, contacted Moses Silva. He was a weathered little man in his early fifties, with a constant, genuine smile. He didn't seem concerned about answering questions. He told Melvin Jimmy had always been a bad sort, always getting into a lot of trouble, and sometimes causing trouble, just to let everyone know how tough he was. Silva explained he hung around with Jimmy to pick up weed that he could sell in the Filipino community. He only dealt in small quantities, he hastily assured Melvin.

"There is less chance of getting a stiff sentence if I get caught," he said with a slight shrug.

Melvin was in no hurry to shut Silva up. He nodded at the man, who blithely went on.

"Jimmy sort of went crazy when he found out his wife had inherited a lot of money. He was always talking about finding her and getting his share of the money. When he heard she was actually on island, he really went nuts. He wanted me to drive him out to Twenty-Mile, where the reunion was. Jimmy said he didn't want any trouble. He just wanted to tell Taniko if she gave him a couple hundred thousand, he would agree to a divorce and leave her and the girl alone. I said I couldn't oblige as my girlfriend was coming in on the ferry. I offered to drop him off at the wharf, but just then he spotted Lono and asked him for a lift. He hopped into Lono's car, and that was the last time I saw him."

CHAPTER 9

Tina had heard from other members of the family that the cops were going to make them do DNA tests and she didn't want anything to do with that. Tina had a secret that only she and one other knew, and it made her shudder in fear. She hadn't done anything wrong, but neither had Cousin Tala—and look where she wound up!

She hastily packed a few clothes, headed into town, and left her car in front of Friendly's. She called a girlfriend who picked her up and took her to Young Brothers Shipping where her boyfriend, Danny Ipo, worked. He had promised he would help her get off the island.

Danny was head-over-heels in love with Tina,

and would do anything to keep her safe. He knew she was in danger—heck, he may be, too—because of her father. And because of Jimmy's murder. Until the situation cooled down, Tina didn't need to be anywhere near her family.

He asked Tina to meet him before seven a.m. The shipyard employees typically began dribbling in at seven thirty, so he and Tina would be alone for only a short time. He called her cell to let her know the coast was clear, and then her friend dropped her off at the locked front gate. Danny emerged from behind a small building where he had been waiting. He fumbled with the lock and swung the gate open just enough to let her in. The hinges squealed and he cast a furtive glance over his shoulder before shutting it with a clatter and locking it behind them. Tina's eyes darted around as he motioned for her to follow. The two of them strode down the wharf to where a mountain of stacked shipping containers stood two high. There was little activity, but that would change in a short while. They had to hurry.

At the end of the pier was an area where smaller containers would be loaded onto barges bound for the other islands. They had almost reached the end of the dock when Danny stopped and jerked his thumb toward the container behind him. "This is it," he announced, swinging the door open. It yawned irritably.

Tina just stood there and blinked for a moment

as she stared at the gloomy interior. A stack of soiled moving blankets was piled in a corner. A five-gallon bucket lined with a trash bag sat against the back wall. It was meant to serve as an emergency toilet. A roll of toilet paper had been thoughtfully placed next to it. Danny and two of his buddies regularly used this system to smuggle illegals and other things back and forth on the islands. He saw the dubious look on Tina's face and assured her the plan would go smoothly.

It was a standard container headed for Oahu. It would be off-loaded there and picked up by one of his friends later that morning. He warned her to hang on to the safety ropes he had installed any time the box was moving, and told her to keep quiet until his buddy let her out.

Tina took a deep breath as she stepped inside and walked through the hollow interior toward the blankets in the corner. She sucked in her breath as Danny shut and bolted the door enveloping her in darkness. His muffled reassurance from outside did little to calm her nerves. She plopped down in the corner and got as comfortable as one can in a storage container. She clenched her teeth and held on for dear life through the frightening experience of the container being loaded.

That afternoon, it arrived at the docks in Oahu. By then, she was fighting claustrophobia. The heat was sweltering and her clothes were damp with sweat. The snacks from her bag were almost gone, and she had only a half a bottle of water left. She'd made up her mind that there was no way she was going to pee in that damn bucket, but her full bladder was very uncomfortable.

Thankfully, she heard voices outside the container, and thought the door would open any moment. She waited. Nothing. Instead, the container was hoisted upward. She clung tightly to the safety straps, feeling the sensation of the box being lifted, then set down with a thud. Her ears listened intently.

There were voices again. A vehicle door creaked open, then shut. Someone was asking about the contents of the containers and for a shipping invoice and identification. Another voice answered in a casual tone, "Just house stuff from folks movin' over from Molokai."

"It must be special to ship it in a container." There was a tinge of suspicion in the comment.

There was a pleasant chuckle. "Yeah. You know these crazy *haoles*," he commented, shaking his head. "They even ship stuff from the mainland that they can buy here."

By now, Tina figured the container had been loaded on a flatbed truck. There was a ripple of laughter and the vehicle door opened and closed again. She felt the gentle movement as the truck lurched forward and began its trek, Tina tried to relax. They had traveled only a short distance when the brakes squeaked, and movement stopped.

Tina really had to go to the bathroom! She was warily eyeing the bucket, when a loud slap on the side of the container made her jump. Must be the clearance sticker, she thought. Outside, she heard confirmation.

"Okay, braddah, you good to go."

The truck started moving again, and Tina sat against the wall contemplating her bathroom options. Just as she'd resigned herself to the bucket, the truck slowed again and then seemed to be maneuvering itself into place. When it stopped, she heard the driver side door open and close.

Through the wall, she heard him say, "Everything's okay now. We gonna have you outta there in a minute."

She heard pry bars pulling at the container door, and in a moment, bright sunshine poured in and flooded the inside as the door opened. The sudden brightness caused Tina to shield her eyes with her hands. A sense of relief settled over her like a warm blanket. She barreled out of the container and wildly looked around.

"Bathroom?"

The driver grinned, and she ran in the direction he pointed. She made it to the Porta Potty just in time.

When Tina emerged, wiping her hands on a tissue, the driver was leaning against a dark blue sedan that had not been there moments before.

Answering her questioning look, he said, "Had it hidden in the bushes." He opened the passenger door and bid her to enter. "Your suitcase is in the trunk. We are heading to Waiamea, where friends are waiting for you."

Tina settled in and began to relax as she watched the scenery roll by. She thought of Tala and Aunty Taniko. How hard it must have been for them having to run and hide for all those years. She felt sorry for them and hoped they could get through this ordeal so they could finally live a normal life. After managing her own escape, she had a sense of what it felt like to live in fear. She vowed, when all this was over, she would appreciate her life more.

CHAPTER 10

The DA instructed Detective Kamu to detain Isaac in the holding cell at Molokai Police Station until he could get someone there to take new blood and DNA samples. The DA told Kamu that it would give him more time to decide if he had enough evidence of Isaac's drug activities to arrest him on those charges. I sent Melvin to the station to talk with Isaac on the pretense of offering our services. What I really wanted was information that might help Tala.

Isaac was far from cooperative. After Melvin told him he was working for Tala's attorney, he softened a bit, but was still reacting like someone who had been in this situation before. Melvin knew from his rap sheet that Isaac had been arrested several times, but never for a major felony. Still, the hard face and folded arms didn't bode well for extracting information. This may take some effort, he thought.

When Melvin asked him why he ran away, he said he wasn't running anywhere. He didn't even know they were looking for him until Detective Kamu slapped the cuffs on him at Goodz and Grindz. He thought he was being busted for selling grass. He said he didn't know anything about any DNA or blood test, and demanded to know why they needed those tests on him.

Isaac insisted he didn't have anything to do with Jimmy's murder, that he had only spoken to him for a few minutes when Jimmy showed up to talk to Taniko. He and Jimmy had parted ways several months prior because Jimmy wanted to push hard drugs, and Isaac didn't. He'd gone to Halawa Valley to harvest about a dozen pakalolo plants and get rid of them before the "green police" found them. He knew the bigger growers were getting ready to move their crop, and wanted to take advantage of the brushfire diversion they'd created on the other end of the island.

"I'll admit to selling a little weed," he told Melvin, "but I ain't guilty of anything else, and for sure not murder!"

Melvin questioned him extensively about Ms. Tagahashi and Tala, confirming what was already known. Isaac said that he, too, had always been a little afraid of Jimmy and what he might do to Taniko and Tala. He said he had helped them a few times with money without Jimmy's knowledge, but was afraid to interfere too much because Jimmy was such a loose cannon.

Dr. Wong showed up just as Melvin was completing his talk with Isaac. Warrant and test kits in hand, he dutifully took his samples, and avoided any conversation. Melvin watched the process very closely to make sure all was done according to Hoyle. Hoyle, in this instance, ensured proper evidentiary processing. When Dr. Wong had all he needed, he left.

Melvin prepared to leave, but asked Isaac if he could pose one last question.

"Off the record, of course."

Isaac sat back. "Depends on the question."

"Why would anyone want to kill Jimmy the way they did? Sure, he was a badass, and it makes more sense that he'd be killed in a drug deal gone bad. But, this seems personal. Do you know of any family members or close friends who might want to kill Jimmy? And, do you think Tala could do it?"

"That's more than one question, braddah." Isaac leaned his head back and assessed Melvin through half-closed eyes. "You know as much as I do about his murder. I was as surprised as anyone else that he was killed. Was it personal?" He shook his head. "I don't know of any family who'd want him dead, even his wife and daughter. They had other ways of dealing with his abuse, like going stateside. As for friends, Jimmy had no one close to him. He was lolo."

Melvin thanked him and called the officer waiting outside the door. He handed his card to Isaac. "If you do think of any reason or person that could be involved, call me."

Isaac looked at the card. "Fish surveyor?"

Bland faced, Melvin replied, "That's right."

"Whatever, braddah."

CHAPTER 11

I met Melvin at the police station to get his report on Isaac, and then walked back to my office to get a little exercise and fresh air. This whole mess is beginning to get to me. Usually, I'm so bogged down in facts and evidence in a case that it's hard to keep track of everything. Not this time. It feels like I'm racing in deep mud and am miles from the finish line.

Patty was all smiles when I walked into the office. After asking how Melvin's talk with Isaac went, she said she had just heard from Melvin, and that he might have a lead on Tina.

"It's the afternoon. Why are you here? What about your courses?"

"Things are getting too exciting! I need to be in the middle of this, Boss. There's all kinds of talk-story around town about the murder. Nothing new," she said to my enquiring eyes. "But I did find out Jimmy had a new girlfriend, and he was supposed to go to her house the night of the murder. She says he never showed up."

"Do you think this girlfriend could have anything to do with his murder? Maybe he broke up with her, and she was mad? Or maybe she had a jealous ex?"

Patty's eyebrows came together in thought, but lifted when she said, "Nah. I don't think so. She is a single gal who had been divorced for several years. Her ex wasn't jealous. He was happy to get rid of her so he could marry his girlfriend! She had relationships with a couple of other men, but they didn't hang around. She was getting into drugs."

"She should be questioned, anyway."

"Should I call Kamu?"

"Why do his work for him? I'll call Melvin."

I was reviewing the notes on Melvin's conversation with Isaac, when the phone rang. It was Detective Kamu. He said the police had checked Isaac's and Tina's cell phone records and picked up on a couple of calls from Tina to a Young Brothers' employee by the name of Danny Ipo. Danny and Tina have been dating, and he probably knew where she was. Detective Kamu was headed over to talk with him, and would keep me posted.

As I rang off, I thanked the island gods for Patty. Her "things" were paying off again.

Instantly, my cell rang once more. It was Melvin. He said he picked up some talk in front of the bank that Tina had a boyfriend, and he was headed over to talk with him. I said he needed to work a little faster, because Detective Kamu had just called with the same information.

He took my jibe lightheartedly, and said something about a blind hog finding corn. "Maybe we'll bump into each other."

Kamu and Melvin showed up at the shipping yard at the same time, and were let into the secure yard when Kamu flashed his badge. He asked for the boss.

"Thanks for letting me tag along, Kamu. I usually have to pass a twenty to get anyone to talk to me."

"How about you make a nice donation to the policeman's fund this year, and we'll call it even?"

When the boss appeared, a bulldoggish man with a butch haircut, Kamu said he wanted to talk with Danny Ipo.

"Let me call him." He went back to his office, with Kamu and Melvin following, and said Danny's name over the loudspeaker.

A tall, nice-looking young man sauntered up to the office, but when he saw the other two men, he stopped. "Hey, Boss, whatcha need?"

"These fellows wanted to talk to you."

His eyes darted between the men, and he said, "Is there something I can do for you?"

"Just some routine questions in a disappearance,"

81

Kamu said, showing him his badge. "We're looking for Tina. I understand she's your girlfriend."

Danny paled. "Um, I haven't seen her for a few days." He glanced at the door. "Sorry I can't help you."

"Uh huh. No phone calls, either?"

"Well, she did call me and said she was going to the Big Island for a couple of days to get away from relatives. She said she would call me when she got back."

Melvin asked if he had her cell number, and Danny gave him the number. He didn't seem happy about it, though.

Kamu watched Melvin write the number down. He already had Tina's number, from monitoring her calls, but really didn't want to share anything with the private detective. He and Melvin had swapped howdies on past cases, and like most law enforcement officers, Kamu made it a point not to work with free-lancers. They always pushed the rules to get what they wanted, and Melvin more so than most. Still, the PI was astute and thorough, and he admired his tenacity.

As they left, Melvin asked Detective Kamu, "You know he's lying, right?"

"Sure. I just want to make him nervous, and see what he does." Kamu sighed. "Do you want to help me keep an eye on him?"

Melvin said he needed to get to Oahu, and

wouldn't have time.

"Humph." Kamu shoved his pen into his shirt pocket.

Oblivious to the detective's angst, Melvin said, "I think the girl only has a couple of choices, if she left the island—Maui or Oahu. There isn't anywhere here on Molokai she can hide. I've got friends on Big Island watching for her, and you have Maui covered like a blanket, so I'll head to Oahu and see what I can find. Besides, I have more freedom to get information than the police."

"Uh huh." Kamu put on his sunglasses and strode to his car.

Melvin stopped by the office and dropped off his report on Danny Ipo. He informed me of his plan to catch one of the late afternoon flights over to Oahu. Before he left, I got more specifics from him about Silva and Barton, so Patty could type it up. She would also do background checks on their financial history and any criminal record they may have.

GARY CARR

CHAPTER 12

The late afternoon sun dipped towards the ocean, when I finally tossed all my notes and files in my briefcase. I told Patty to lock up. I was headed home so I could think where it was quiet.

She laughed and said, "You just want to go home and sit around in your board shorts and drink wine."

"You're obviously a mind reader." That was exactly what I *wanted* to do, but, as usual, I'd sip my evening wine in my usual dress slacks and polo shirt. Patty was always giving me a hard time about over dressing. She calls it my "haole hangup." I am what I am.

As I went out the door, she called, "I would love to see those cute legs in a pair of walking shorts. You should wear real island clothes to work tomorrow."

"Yeah, yeah," I said as I opened my car door. On the drive home, I thought of Jimmy's drug dealings. What if he was killed by drug runners? Maybe he was on their boat, and they stabbed him. They might have thrown him overboard thinking the sharks would get him. Instead, he washed ashore. I shook my head and wondered if it was a plausible scenario. There hadn't been any boats out on the East End that night. The water was extremely choppy from high winds. Besides, how could they have gotten ahold of the butcher knife? That was the million dollar question. Whoever killed him had to have access to the knife—a knife that was on the prep table at the family reunion, and used by a number of people to prepare Huli Huli Chicken.

The thought of Huli Huli Chicken pushed my thoughts in another direction and made my mouth water. It would be nice to have some for dinner. Damn, I was too close to home, and I really didn't want to turn around to shop for ingredients. Even though town was only five minutes away, a blip in mainland time, island time was different. Five minutes was like fifty.

I pulled into my driveway, and after taking my shoes off, headed to the kitchen to see what I could rustle up. I managed to find some frozen fried chicken and thawed it out in the microwave. I covered it with a mixture of soy sauce, ketchup, hot sauce, and brown sugar. Sniffing the finished product, I realized I'd fixed my own version of Huli Huli. After my great barbecue feast, I poured a glass of Prosecco and headed to my favorite chair on the lanai to contemplate the day's activities.

As the sky grew dark, I was entertained by what I call my fighter squadron–a group of twenty or so little birds–the islanders call "white eyes." They are a small, light beige bird about the size of a golf ball, with a large white patch around each of their eyes. They weigh next to nothing, and fly almost everywhere as a group. As they dart from to tree to tree, they remind me of a group of fighter planes flying in formation. One major difference, however, is that they usually spend a lot of time being blown backwards by even the slightest winds. For them, it is one tree forward, two trees back! Seems like an apt metaphor for this case.

With my second glass of wine, I started getting philosophical and telling myself how lucky I am to be able to live both on Molokai and in San Diego. Both places are so different from each other, and yet if you take the people out, they are similar in that no matter how many times you look out of the window, you can usually see something beautiful.

My ex-wife used to say that. Of course, my ex-wife used to say a lot of things. The fact that she very seldom shut up is why she is my ex-wife. We get along much better now, because she usually spends time here on Molokai when I'm in San Diego.

After my third glass of Prosecco, the old Latin saying, "In Vino Veritas" took on more meaning. I came to the conclusion that I was over-thinking this whole case. Nothing is complicated on Molokai. I just need to relax, and surely everything will work itself out.

CHAPTER 13

I hit the office again, about seven the next morning, and had pretty well outlined my day by the time Patty came in. We shared a cup of freshly brewed Molokai coffee while we went over the day's schedule. For me, it would be a lot of phone calls to forensic experts, the DA's Office, and checking in with the San Diego office to make sure things were all right there. For Patty, a lot of paperwork, typing, and making sure all the files were in order. I knew sometime during the day I would get a call from Melvin. I asked Patty to call Kamu, when she had the chance, and chat him up for new information. She said she would, but didn't want to work him too much, because he might get the wrong idea. She batted her eyelashes at me, in case I didn't understand the undercurrent of her remark.

I reread the information on blood typing and DNA that I'd found on the Internet. I knew most of it by heart now. There are four basic blood groups, and depending on genetics, children can have different blood types than their parents. It depended on RH distribution. The RH factor accounts for there being eight different blood types. Since everyone who was at the beach the day Jimmy was killed is related, they may or may not fall into the same type. I concluded that other than thinning out the crowd, the blood typing wouldn't have much of an impact.

DNA evidence is an entirely different story. I reminded myself to have my expert in California connect me with Hawaiian experts. If necessary, I can have a local on hand to present technical facts for Tala. The most obvious defense to DNA cases is to claim cross-contamination of evidence. I'd be checking the details of all the DNA tests to make sure meticulously strict handling procedures were used. If Dr. Wong is as lax with the DNA sampling as he was about taking blood type tests, this may never get to court.

I called Dr. Bartholomew Symington's office in San Diego and left a message with his receptionist to have him call me as soon as possible. She assured me she would have him call just as soon as he got out of court, where he was testifying.

Symington and I have been close personal friends ever since our college days together, and even though I only need one pathologist, it would be great to have Bart around to bounce ideas back and forth.

Just the Right Amount of Wrong

He is one of the few people I *really* trust. Besides that, he is probably the best forensic pathologist on the planet.

Symington called me back before noon. I asked how it went in court, and he said, "Just fine. It was another hour of explaining how DNA testing works and how it differs from what most folks see on television crime shows." I told him about the case I was working on, and asked if he had time to come over and find a local pathologist to sign on as an expert witness.

"I'm always up for a vacation in Hawaii, especially if you're paying for it!" He added, "I know a doctor who works at Queen's Hospital in Honolulu who also contracts with the military as a forensic pathologist. I'll contact him and see if he is interested. I'll also check to make sure he isn't working for the State of Hawaii. I also know a couple more pathologists at the University of Hawaii who are doing research on genetic mapping and DNA profiling."

I told him, "Catch the very next plane you can. I need you here as soon as possible. We will be back before the judge in a few days."

"I just need a few hours to get to the office to put my schedule in order, throw a few clothes in a suitcase, and I'll be there."

"Be sure to text me with your arrival time, so either Patty or I can pick you up. Don't worry about lodging; you can stay with me here on Molokai."

"I would rather stay with Patty."

I laughed and said, "That's up to her!"

CHAPTER 14

Melvin flew back to Oahu on the first flight of the day. He was tracking Tina. He'd started by seeking out several of the tent camps at Wainae and Waipio Point. No young girls had joined the community in the past few days, so Melvin decided to head around the island, closer to the North Shore. He'd see if any of the surfers or the shrimp wagons had seen her. When he got there, one of the shrimp truck operators claimed he saw someone who looked like her riding around with some young people just about sunset yesterday. He described the vehicle as an older, white Toyota van. When the van stopped, one of the men came over and bought four plate lunches to go. They drove off, heading south. The van was local, and three of the guys were regular customers. He noticed the girl because they usually only bought three meals.

Melvin thanked him and drove slowly down the

road. Maybe he'd spot the van parked by the myriad of houses that skirt this stretch of highway and face the sandy beaches. As he approached "Pipeline," Melvin's cell phone rang. It was Detective Kamu. He'd been working the phones again, and had picked up a GPS signal from Tina's phone. He asked if Melvin would check it out. Melvin keyed the coordinates Kamu gave him into the GPS on his rental car.

"I'm driving near there right now," he said. According to the sweet voice on the GPS, he was only three-fourths of a mile from the address. As he arrived at the location, he noticed a white Toyota van parked in a carport next to a small, stilted house. A large, gated home flanked the small house on one side, and a small parking lot, crammed with pickups, surfboards and surfers, was on the other. Melvin pulled directly into the driveway.

He let Kamu know he'd call as soon as he was finished checking the place out. Just as he got out of the car, a young Hawaiian stepped out on the porch, and informed him he couldn't park there.

"Private property, braddah," he drawled.

"Oh, sorry," replied Melvin, pointing to the full parking lot. "It's full, and I'm having trouble with my rental." He kept walking towards the young man. "Do you think I could borrow your phone?"

Melvin could tell the man was struggling with helping a stranger and protecting his home, and its precious cargo. "You know how *haoles* treat Asians?" He had reached the steps.

"Ah, come on up!" The man motioned Melvin up the steps. "The phone's in the house."

Works for me, Melvin thought. He climbed the five wooden steps up to the front door and waited while the young man searched for his phone in the dim interior. Melvin glanced through the door, and hit pay dirt. Sitting on an old sofa watching television, was Tina. She turned and looked curiously at Melvin. He gave a nonchalant salute, and she turned back to her TV show. Nobody to worry about, her look said.

When the young man had retrieved his phone, Melvin thanked him and proceeded to call Detective Kamu. Kamu listened to Melvin's cockeyed message of a troubled transmission and being afraid to drive. He caught on quickly to the real message.

"Can you send somebody, please? I'm in someone's driveway."

Kamu said he understood and told his dispatcher to alert Oahu police immediately, and to send officers quietly to Melvin's location.

Melvin asked, "About how long do you think it will take?" After Kamu gave his best estimate, Melvin asked, "Could you hold a minute?"

He put his hand over the receiver and said to the man, "They estimate it will take thirty to forty-five minutes before they can get a tow truck here. The closest one is at the Polynesian Cultural Center. Would it be okay to leave my car in the driveway until the truck shows up?"

The man nodded, "yes," and Melvin relayed the message to Detective Kamu. He hung up and handed the phone back, thanking the young man.

"I'll just wait in the car." As he headed down the stairs, the young man stopped him.

"Come on inside. It's more comfortable."

"Well, if you insist. Thanks."

As he entered the house, the young man announced that "Braddah, here, got a busted rental. Da kine say they sendin' a tow, so he gonna hang here for a while."

The young man indicated Melvin should have a seat on the sofa, and asked if he would like a beer. Melvin declined and sat down next to Tina. He chuckled inwardly. If only Kamu could see him now. Together, he and Tina watched a re-run of "The Deadliest Catch." When the police arrived, he certainly hoped that title didn't fit this situation.

Less than twenty minutes later, Melvin saw, through the open door, an unmarked police car pull up. Two plain-clothes detectives got out and strode to the foot of the stairs. One climbed the step carefully and knocked on the door. Tina glanced over and then looked back at the television, bored.

"Someone's at the door!" She said under her breath that there were just too many visitors today. A moment later, Melvin's genial host came through, drying his hands on a dish towel. Melvin got up and walked behind the man.

When the cop asked for Melvin, Melvin put his host in a stranglehold. He said to the cop, "I'm Melvin, and this is the young lady you are looking for."

By this time, Tina was on her feet, and running toward the kitchen door. Melvin handed the man to the officer, and had her in three strides. "You need to come with me, Tina."

The cop at the bottom of the stairs ran up the steps and into the room. He shackled Tina, read her rights to her, and told her what she was being arrested for.

"What do you mean, a material witness in a murder case?"

"It will all be explained soon."

She went meekly down the steps, and was placed in the back of the police car. Melvin thanked the owner of the house for his hospitality and assured him everything would be all right with Tina. "She's just being taken in for questioning."

The young man gave him a one-fingered salute and told him to get out of his house.

Melvin pulled out his cell. "Got her, Boss."

"Not surprised. Call me once you've interviewed her." I said.

On the drive back to Honolulu, Melvin called

Detective Kamu and filled him in on Tina's arrest. Arrangements were made for Melvin and a policeman to transport Tina back to Molokai where she could be swabbed for a DNA test.

CHAPTER 15

Symington called, letting me know he could catch a four-thirty afternoon flight out of San Diego. That would put him into Honolulu at about eleven tonight, which would mean an overnight stay on Oahu before he could catch an early flight to Molokai. He could do a lot of what I needed on the phone, unless I had something that just had to be done tomorrow morning. Otherwise, he would take the six forty-five flight tomorrow morning and arrive on Molokai early afternoon. We agreed on the morning flight, and I told him I would pick him up at the airport. I told him Tina's samples were taken to the state lab.

Symington called back mid-afternoon to tell me his friend, Dr. James Revis, from Queen's Hospital, had agreed to join us as an expert witness. He instructed Dr. Revis to get copies of the results as soon as they were completed. He told me they would be searching for any anomalies in the results, and consider how things like time in the water and a lack of fingerprints on the knife might affect the case.

Melvin and the officer arrived at the airport with Tina about four o'clock. He called Detective Kamu, and Kamu said he would be right there to pick her up. When Kamu arrived, he thanked Melvin for his work in finding Tina and getting her back to Molokai. The two exchanged a hearty handshake, and the detective transported Tina to the Molokai Police Department where she was put in a holding cell until they could take DNA samples, and the DA could question her.

When Kamu questioned Tina about her disappearing act, she said the reason she ran was because she was afraid of needles. When he looked at her like she was crazy, she conceded she was also afraid whoever killed Jimmy might come after her.

"Now, why in the world would you think that, Tina?"

"One of my friends told me they were looking for me because of Uncle Jimmy's murder." She began chewing on a fingernail. "Is Danny going to be in a lot of trouble?"

"The least Danny can expect is to lose his job." He told her that he suspected a lot more wrongdoing by Danny, and it all depended on what else they learned.

That upset her, and she went silent.

Just the Right Amount of Wrong

Before calling it a day, I phoned Taniko and gave her a status report. I tried to sound as positive as possible. On my way home, I pulled over at one of the beach parks near the wildlife refuge, and sat at one of the concrete picnic tables listening to the surf splash on the shore. Watching a couple of sand crabs fight for territory got me to thinking that Jimmy's murder might have been the result of fighting over territory. We needed a deeper look at Jimmy's background. I called Melvin on my cell. Melvin said he had a list of everyone at the reunion and would use that as a start for getting more information.

I left the beach park, when my stomach sent me a message that it was empty. Rice, a green salad, and fresh fish sounded great, so I headed back into town. I noticed some local fishermen beaching their boat by a small launch, and pulled over to see if they had anything to share. Proudly, they showed me their superb catch.

They had a few larger bottom fish and a plastic bucket about half full of manini (Black striped trigger fish). I picked out about a dozen of the manini. Not bad for ten dollars. I'll clean the manini tonight, and wrap them in ti leaves before throwing them on the grill. Three or four tonight should be good, and then the rest for tomorrow, when Symington arrives.

After dinner, I avoided the Prosecco and lanai. Instead, I pored over several Hawaiian law books I kept on hand. I studied deep into the night, renewing my memory on Hawaiian evidentiary procedure. So far, the delays by the DA and medical examiner were in Tala's favor, but I didn't want to miss anything.

CHAPTER 16

I woke up a little after midnight in my recliner. My glasses were askew on my nose. The law book I had been reading was lying on my lap. I gave some thought to getting up and going to bed, but then decided I was very comfortable right where I was. I put my glasses and book on the lamp table, pushed the recliner back a little more, shut the light off and went back to sleep.

The problem with my recliner is that it is too comfortable, and every time I sleep in it, I wake up groggy and full of kinks. The next morning, I stretched painfully before getting up. Never again, I vowed.

It was Saturday, and so I was surprised when I got to the office at a little past seven to find a standing-room-only crowd congregated. Why was the crew there early? I knew why Patty was there. Instead of finishing file work yesterday, she'd opted

103

to do homework. This morning, she was catching up on office work. She hadn't forgotten to make coffee, for which I was thankful–as were Melvin and Kamu. The conversation between the two men centered on what they knew about Tina and Danny Ipo. They seemed eager to give me their reports and get back out in the field.

At nine, Emily Sanders, an attractive clerk from the DA's Office (surely not the grouch?) stopped by with some forms I needed to sign. These verified me as Tala's legal representative, qualified to practice law in Hawaii.

I asked Miss Sanders to have the DA forward any new information he would care to share by fax, and she said she would pass along the request when she returned to Maui that afternoon. She said she'd be around Molokai until then, taking care of a number of court matters.

"Your boss makes you work weekends, Miss Sanders?"

Looking not at all like a grouch, Miss Sanders smiled prettily. "We do what we have to for the cause."

She sounded like his campaign manager. Still, the DA must be a tireless fighter. I admired that for a moment, but then thought if his motive to arrest Tala wasn't publicity, I could be in trouble.

Upon Tina's arrest, Danny Ipo had also been brought in for questioning. What he said was very interesting. In Kamu's report to me, he said Danny confessed to being a smuggler. He is tied to a ring of wanna-be hoods who use barges to transport people and contraband, from one island to another.

It had started out harmless enough, getting relatives a free ride so they could work off Molokai. Then, somebody thought they should make money at it, and began charging. Relatives looking for a break stopped coming, but it heralded the illegal goods trade. Transported from island to island, untaxed cigarettes gave way to marijuana, and then the hard stuff. It also gave undesirables a way to travel from island to island without using public transportation.

When Kamu clued Danny into all the felonies he could be charged with, he gave up all he knew about his side business. Kamu contacted detectives on the other islands, who arrested Danny's contacts there.

I picked Symington up at the airport, along with our newly hired local expert witness, Dr. Revis. He and Symington had been on the phone, and decided to meet at the airport where they could start work immediately. My friend's tall, angular frame next to Dr. Revis's stoutness reminded me of Abbott and Costello.

105

Revis had wanted to meet me before he flew over to Maui, where he would check out a lab near the courthouse to use for his headquarters. I liked the man, and felt Symington had done a good job finding him. We left Dr. Revis at the airport, and drove into town.

When I got back to the office, it was empty. Kamu and Melvin were out *sniffing scent* in different directions. Patty had left a note saying she was going to the library to use the internet for personal business, and then she'd go to the post office for our mail. Patty has always been afraid to do personal e-mail in the office because she thinks I can recover anything that was ever done on our computers. Since it was to my advantage, I never told her any differently.

Symington found a little space where he could write and use the phone. I busied myself with the information Patty had been able to get on Moses Silva, Isaac Roland, and Lono Barton.

The DA himself called me in the late afternoon to tell me the test results were complete, and copies would be faxed in the next few minutes. This gesture of sharing went south halfway through the first fax. Their machine must have developed a problem because it quit sending, mid-page. When we called to report the snafu, the clerk who answered the phone said they were aware of the problem and had sent for a repairman. However, she informed me, the repairman was in Lahaina and by the time he could get to Wailuku, it would be well after six o'clock. I told her to send the results to me as soon as she could. I also asked her to call Patty beforehand, so Patty could make sure everything was all right. She said she would and hung up.

When Patty returned to the office, I told her the clerk would call and asked her to please get the results to Symington and me, whenever they came in. Since I knew Patty would be at the office well past six, I told her, "You're more than welcome to study while you wait, and I'll, of course, pay you double-time."

"If you don't mind, I'll just call her and give her my cell number. Then when they call, I can come back to the office and get the fax."

"Okay with me!"

"Does that mean I still get double-time?"

"Sure. Why not?"

Symington and I headed for the house and a feast of manini. Symington was a sushi sort, and quite pleased at the opportunity to eat fresh fish. For dessert, I'd picked up some ripe mangoes and papayas from the sidewalk vendor across the street. I let Symington into the house, and he took his shoes off and placed them on the mat just inside the door. Absentmindedly, I followed suit. As I placed my shoes on the mat, it hit me. "Way to go," I chided myself. "You did it again! It's your house; you can wear shoes if you want to."

After Symington got settled into the guest bedroom, he joined me out on the lanai, dressed in walking shorts, tee shirt, and "slippahs." In my matching island haute couture (board shorts, tee shirt, and this time, tennis shoes), I offered him a chilled glass of my Italian sparkly before I fixed dinner, and he accepted.

"Still on the Prosecco, I see."

I knew he preferred heavily oaked Chardonnay, but it was chilling in the refrigerator for dinner. The evening passed pleasantly as we discussed the case and enjoyed the manini. Just before nine o'clock, Patty called. She was heading my way with the faxes from the DA's office.

"Don't expect me in early on Monday, Boss!"

"Sorry, Patty. I know it's late. I'll make it up to you, somehow."

"You bet you will. See you soon."

Symington and I began poring over the documents, as soon as Patty dropped them off. For the next couple of hours, we took a lot of notes and discovered we might have several points in our favor. We wanted to get an early start in the morning, so we headed to bed before midnight.

CHAPTER 17

The next morning, Symington and I called Dr. Wong to review his test results.

Symington asked Dr. Wong if he'd completed all eight DNA tests. When Dr. Wong said, "Yes," Symington began questioning him as if he was an attorney, and Dr. Wong was on the witness stand.

Q: "From these eight tests, are there any that match the blood type on the knife?"

A: "Yes! There are five. This is primarily due to the fact they are all family members. The other three, although not the exact type match, are within the same group. Again, only indicating they are related."

Q: "What were the results of the DNA tests?"

A: "Of the eight DNA tests, only four show possible matches to the DNA found on the knife."

Q: "Who are the possible matches?"

109

A: "They are those of Ms. Tagahashi, Tala Pualani, Isaac Roland and Tina Roland."

Q: "You said *possible* matches. Not *exact* matches?"

A: "That is correct. The deterioration of the sample from exposure to the sea water and time, prevent an exact allele match. However, two of the matches fall within a 90% reliability level and one at a 60% level."

Q: "Who falls within the 90% level?"

A: "Tala and Tina. The other 60% sample was from Ms. Tagahashi."

Q: "So what are you saying? That Tala and Tina have the same DNA?"

A: "No sir. What I am saying is that since they are so closely related, and because we could not do a complete profile due to the condition of the sample, these two individuals fall within a 90% match."

Q: So, again paraphrasing, this means that Tina has as much chance of matching the blood on the knife as Tala does?"

A: "Yes sir."

Q: "So how does Tala's mother come into all of this?"

A: "We were able to get a 60% match of the alleles from the sample taken from Ms. Tagahashi."

Q: "What significance does this have?"

A: "Well, since she is Tala's mother, she would naturally carry a lot of the same alleles, but to a lesser extent."

Symington thanked Dr. Wong for sharing the information, and then asked him to send his report to us in an e-mail, rather than using the fax machine. Not only would this give him more time to study the results, it also meant not having to send Patty back to the office.

GARY CARR

CHAPTER 18

I knew the DA wouldn't let us off the hook, so I needed to incorporate what we'd just learned into the information we'd already gathered. Add meat to it, so to speak. But, what did I have right now? Tala is sitting in jail. Her father is dead. Her mother is doing what she can to help. Her cousin, Tina, and her Uncle Isaac have both been found, but nothing of substance was uncovered. The DA's original charges are based on circumstantial evidence. I felt there was enough reasonable doubt to defend Tala, but I still didn't have a clue who really killed Jimmy and why. That was of utmost importance, not only for Tala's sake, but also for her mother's. I decided to look at this from the DA's point of view.

MOTIVE FOR MURDER: Tala and her mother running from Jimmy's abuse over the years. Abuse, fear, and feeling threatened are powerful arguments for murder. Aunty Kiolani's testimony of seeing Tala

113

have "words" with Jimmy certainly added weight to that.

OPPORTUNITY: Tala was at the reunion, in close proximity to the victim, and was seen handling a knife similar to the one found in Jimmy's back. She also had a cut on her hand. Tala had taken a walk at dusk on the day of the murder with no eyewitness to corroborate she'd only gone down to the shore and not out to kill Jimmy.

INTENT: Really, the DA had nothing here. He was going to have a tough time building on this without getting into a lot of supposition. The only intent was a rash statement by Tala, made with the typical passion of a teenager. It will be easy to dismiss it as an emotional response anyone could make, especially if said under duress by a detective pushing the limits of interrogation.

My work would be to emphasize that mother and daughter had made a plan on how to respond to Jimmy, if he showed up in their lives again—and it *wasn't* to kill the man. I also needed to find out who Aunty Kiolani had actually seen having an argument with Jimmy, as I believed Tala's adamancy that it wasn't her. Usually it was easy to deconstruct eye witness testimony. Because this was a relative, it might be a bit more challenging.

Then there was the knife. Casting doubt on the weapon would be a little more difficult, as the DNA reports were pretty strong. Of course, finding

114

Jimmy's real killer would take care of all of this. Good thing Kamu and Melvin were working on that.

Later that day, I got a call from DA Akumu. He'd heard from the coroner's office that there may have been a mix up with the DNA tests which meant a delay. A lab technician had called, saying he was uncomfortable with some of the results, and rechecked his findings. What he discovered was an anomaly with Tala and Tina's results.

The original profiles of the two DNA samples were nearly identical. The tech worried he'd tested the same sample twice, and possibly failed to test Tina's. There was a question on Isaac's results, too. It appeared that his DNA was a close match to the two girls–much closer than the tech had originally determined. To be absolutely certain of his findings, the tech was going to retest all three. Once that was completed, he would get the results to the DA as soon as possible.

I continued to press the DA for information. His office finally called and assured me I would get the results as soon as they were available. I hung up, elated. This is the kind of thing you hope for as an attorney. They were handing me an acquittal on a silver platter, if this thing goes to court. Sloppy police work, inaccurate forensic testing, thin circumstantial evidence, and a hurry to arrest someone to look good in the press! The only thing that would be better is for someone to step up and confess.

I thought about how close I was to getting Tala back home with her mother. Would that be the end of it for me? Taniko's painful eyes came back to me. She needed answers, and she deserved them. Call me old fashioned, but I needed to see truth and justice prevail, even if I have to wrangle it to the ground and tie its legs, all by myself. Well, I guess I wasn't on my own. I was grateful Symington was now on the team, and Melvin's skill at thorough and unswerving investigation was priceless. Even Kamu was growing on me.

CHAPTER 19

Symington and I were a bit dazed by what we'd just learned. The doctor let me ramble on about meeting the speed test for the arraignment, that my client was not being afforded proper due process, and how all this could get Tala's case thrown out.

Symington let me wind down, and then asked. "Did you get the significance of the girls' DNA?"

"What?" I said.

"Tala and Tina have the same DNA."

"No, they were *nearly* identical," I reminded him.

"They are about 90% the same."

"Doesn't that 10% make a huge difference?"

Symington looked at me like I was from Mars and sighed. "The chance of two individuals with that high of an allele match without being sisters is highly unlikely. They could actually be identical twins, or at least fraternal twins."

117

GARY CARR

My mouth formed a wordless "O," as the significance dawned on me.

"I'm going to call Dr. Revis and see what he thinks."

I listened, as Symington talked to Revis. "Can you please check our sample results to see if they are the same as Dr. Wong's? If they are, please run a match test to see if the girls are sisters. I'll be there as soon as I can."

When Symington hung up, I asked him if Wong's lab just screwed up the samples.

"Yes, it's more than likely. They've screwed up all the forensics, so far. But, what if he didn't this time?"

"Good question. I'll take you out to the airport, and we'll arrange a charter if you can't get a seat on the next flight to Maui."

On the way to the airport, I called Melvin and told him about our latest news. He said that answered a question he had regarding scuttlebutt he picked up from a couple of Tala's relatives.

"I was talking with a cousin, who said he'd watched both Tala and Tina off and on at the reunion, because they both were wearing nice halter tops. When I asked him if he saw Tala near her father at any time, he said no. As a matter of fact, when she tried to run to her mother, he put her behind him, and wouldn't let her pass. She never got near Jimmy.

"When I asked him why Aunty Kiolani thought

118

Tala had an argument with Jimmy, he said it wasn't Tala doing that. It was Tina."

I said, "Great! That's cleared up."

Melvin said, "Apparently, Tina didn't know anything was going down. She was just safeguarding the Huli Huli Chicken, until it was done. Jimmy had gotten out of his car and passed Tina, cutting up chicken. Jimmy reached for a leg already sizzling on the grill, and Tina brandished her knife at him, telling him to wait for everyone else. Jimmy just laughed and then started talking to Isaac."

"Do we have any witnesses to this?"

"The kid said lots of teens were hanging around, sneaking a beer. They'd testify, but no one asked them."

"This just keeps getting better and better."

Melvin whistled low. "Hey Boss, if the girls are sisters…"

"That would explain the mix up with Aunty Kiolani. But, that may mean Tina is the one who killed Jimmy!"

"Holy crap!"

"'Holy crap' is right! This case is getting complicated. Let's see if we can discover anything more from the relatives. Cater some food out to the Church Community Center on East End, if you have to, but get them all together and talking."

"Will do, Boss."

Symington listened to what I'd just learned, and

said, "Congratulations, Harry. I think you've won."

We lucked out on the flights, too. Symington caught an Island Air flight to Oahu that was just starting to board. I bought his ticket, and the clerk printed out a boarding pass. Symington grabbed his briefcase and laptop and dashed to security. He boarded with three or four minutes to spare. On my way out of the airport, I stopped at a snack vending machine and selected a Spam and cheese sandwich. For dessert, I opted for a Cornetto ice cream cone. Pure Hawaiian comfort food—delicious! The only thing better would have been some slow-roasted pork on sweet bread.

CHAPTER 20

Devouring my Spam sandwich, I figured I'd better give Taniko a call. She could put to rest any misunderstanding regarding Tala and Tina being twins, as she was the mother. She'd know if she'd given birth to two girls or one.

And what about Isaac being a closer match to the girls than Dr. Wong originally thought? I forgot to ask Symington about that, but would tonight. I jotted down a reminder to call the DA with the new discovery of Tina being the one with the knife. He wouldn't be happy that one of his star witnesses had been wrong about what she'd seen.

Ha! I thought, as I bit into my ice cream cone, savoring the cool sweetness on my tongue. I may be able to get him to drop the charges in a couple of days! After my hasty meal, I found a seat on one of the benches outside the terminal, and called Patty at home.

She was as excited as I was to hear the news. "By the way, Lono Barton stopped by, wanting to see you. I told him you'd be in tomorrow. He said he'd see you first thing, on his way to work."

"Thanks. I want to talk to him, too."

I gathered my stuff and put it all in the briefcase. As I put my cell into my pocket, I looked over at the rather large man who'd sat down on the bench. He was staring at me.

"Ain't you that lawyer fella from Kaunakakai that's helping Tala Pualani?"

I really didn't have time to talk, but I nodded as I snapped the briefcase shut and stood up.

"I hope you are a good lawyer, 'cause there ain't no way that little girl killed that big pig, Jimmy."

Seeing he wasn't a friend of Jimmy's, I sat back down and asked him what he knew about Jimmy and his murder. He spent the next twenty minutes telling me all about Jimmy and the Pualani family. It was very interesting, but the only new information I got was that Jimmy had recently put together a group of three or four cohorts, and was trying to shut down all the drug trade on the island, except theirs.

The man said they were getting muscle and financial help from Maui. I asked for names, but he claimed only to know rumors. All he gave me was his name.

"I don't want to get involved, but maybe you could check things out, and help Tala."

I thanked him, gave him my card, and asked him to call me if he heard any more rumors, especially if the rumors had names with them. He chuckled and said, "The only thing I remember is it started with "K.""

We parted ways, and I called Melvin. "I have another name for you to work on."

"Keeping me busy, Boss!"

I had surreptitiously snapped a picture of my new "friend" with my phone as he walked away. I forwarded the photo to Melvin's cell and explained this guy knew a lot about Jimmy who was trying to muscle his way into being the only drug trade on the island.

Melvin assured me he'd get right on it after he finished up with Tala's relatives. He was almost done.

"Have you found out anything about Isaac being related to the girls?"

"As far as I understand, he's in no way a part of the family by blood. He married Taniko's sister, making his family connection to Jimmy as being his brother-in-law."

Melvin added, "Taniko's sister, Pearl, married Isaac a couple of decades back. They had a son who died in a surfing accident on Oahu. Tina is now their only child. Isaac and Jimmy got along fine in the early years, and even ran some pot together for a while. They grew apart when Jimmy started getting deeper in drugs.

"Regarding Taniko's family, an older sister moved to California many years ago. This is the one Taniko and Tala lived with in San Diego, and who left her a million bucks, when she died of cancer. Pearl is her only other sibling.

"All of Jimmy's relatives are on the mainland, and haven't had any contact with him in years."

"Superb, Melvin. I'll be in touch."

Finding Harry's airport contact was easy. Melvin recognized him from the photo and knew he would probably be hanging out at one of the snack shops or in the shade by the bank.

The rotund man, who called himself the "Mayor of Molokai," was something of a local celebrity who spent a lot of time at the Saturday market in Kaunakakai. He played slack key guitar and talked story with anyone who stopped by. Melvin knew some of his family on Oahu, and that gave him the in to start a conversation. Melvin got a good lesson in how drugs were being trafficked on and off the island.

When pressed, the "Mayor" went into deeper detail on Jimmy's latest activity. He still didn't want to name names, because some of his family was involved.

"There was a meeting on the East End the night

Jimmy was stabbed. The meeting was called to talk over how things would be done on Molokai, and who would be in charge. Everyone thought Jimmy would fill that spot, but he never showed up.

"Everything's slowed down quite a bit since the murder, and the shipping yard bust. Several people have gone into hiding, and no one on Maui is taking credit for Jimmy's death. Usually that kind of message is loud and clear. I know that sweet girl, Tala, didn't do it, but there are quite a few people who are interested in knowing who killed Jimmy. The answer will determine who's in charge, now."

Melvin thanked him and assured him everything was being done to help Tala.

Drs. Symington and Revis worked together to recheck and verify Dr. Wong's results. Symington called me just before noon, the next day, to confirm that not only were Tala and Tina sisters, but identical twins. The thing that floored me was that Isaac—not Jimmy—was their father.

I called Taniko immediately. She broke down in tears, and I didn't have the heart to scold her for not telling me. It was a secret, she said, that she's had for seventeen years, and had hoped it would never be discovered.

"Jimmy was getting more and more abusive.

125

Isaac showed compassion, and one thing led to another." I could hear shame in her tone. "I wound up pregnant with twin girls. The thought of either one of them having to put up with the abuse Jimmy was dishing out was more than I could endure.

"I finally told Isaac I was carrying his girls. It was impossible for me to ask him to leave my own sister and young nephew, but I didn't want my girls to suffer at Jimmy's hands. Isaac said he would convince Pearl to take one of the girls as her own, and he did.

"When Jimmy found out I was pregnant, all he could talk about was taking his son to do this and do that. He said if it was a girl, he'd use her for fish bait! I almost ran away then, but couldn't find the courage. I stayed." Her shoulders drooped in a gesture of defeat, and she stared down at her hands.

"Pearl faked being pregnant," she continued, "and when the girls were born, she was their midwife. Jimmy was gone when they came, so he never saw the two together. Pearl carried Tina out to the car, and she and Isaac went home. I held my Tala, and mourned the loss of Tina.

"Pearl had 'her' baby a few days later, in their car on the way to the hospital. No one was the wiser, and we moved forward—one to more abuse (for Jimmy was furious with me for having a girl), and the other to her real father. Harry, Tala doesn't know, and neither does Tina."

"I'm afraid, Taniko, that everyone is going to know, soon."

She began to weep.

GARY CARR

CHAPTER 21

Lono Barton came into the office next morning to tell me about the drug network being in a tizzy over Jimmy's murder and the shipping yard bust. I told him I already knew that. He countered that there were new rumors about the Maui boys being behind Jimmy's death. He said he could get more info if I was willing to pay. I gave him $20 and told him not to bother unless he really had something useful. I also told him to talk to Melvin in the future. I didn't want to place myself in a position of becoming a witness.

Detective Kamu made several arrests on Molokai from the information Danny had given him. One of them was a big player on Maui who swore he had no knowledge of Jimmy's death. He had read it in the newspaper just like everyone else, he claimed.

Another guy Kamu arrested gave the same story, but he told the detective that most of the guys were more afraid of Isaac than they were of Jimmy. He said Isaac was the real brains behind the operation, and Jimmy was just a big-mouthed enforcer. Well, this indeed was news!

Kamu called Harry and asked to borrow Melvin, again. Could he go over to Maui and shake some contacts down to verify that Isaac was really the boss? Harry agreed, but muttered something about sending him a bill. Kamu smiled. Like that was going to happen.

Melvin went to Maui and uncovered several leads in Kahalui and Lahaina. Most of the network was involved in selling "Maui Wowee" to the tourists. Things had started to ramp up the last few months, however. A new supplier on Molokai wanted to start pushing meth. None of the contacts knew who the supplier was. That was need-to-know, and only Jimmy and Isaac knew. They had worked directly with the supplier. Most agreed that Isaac was the smarter of the two. Melvin informed Harry of his findings before he called Kamu.

CHAPTER 22

Playing a hunch, I called District Attorney Akumu to see if the DNA evidence had changed his mind about Tala's guilt.

"So are you ready to drop the charges against my client?"

"Funny you should ask. I was just coming to that conclusion, myself. Dr. Wong has confirmed Tala and Tina are identical twins. Also, Detective Kamu thinks that Aunty Kiolani probably confused the two girls." I heard Akumu sigh. "Drug dealing is a much stronger motive than a family feud."

"So, what are you saying?"

"There's a lot more to this than I originally was led to believe by my ADA. Dropping the charges now allows me more time to build the case, and I can re-arrest her if I feel we have enough for a conviction."

"Yeah, and if you *lose*, it is bad politically, not to mention the potential for double jeopardy."

"You're right. There is always that chance. I'll call a press conference for this afternoon, and send the paperwork to the courthouse. Tala will be released right away. Oh, and Isaac Roland bonded out this afternoon."

I called Taniko with the good news. She was delighted. I told her I'd arrange a charter flight to pick Tala up on Maui, and invited her along. She said she'd be at the airport within the hour. I felt very good after the phone call.

When we arrived at the jail, Billy had already received the papers and the matron was collecting Tala. There were tears and squeals of happiness from mother and daughter, as Tala's handcuffs were removed. Tala hugged her mother, grabbed her bag of personal belongings, and we swiftly left the building and headed home.

About that time, the DA started his press conference on the courthouse steps. The media had gathered and formed a tight knot around him like vultures at a fresh kill. They pushed and jostled as they jockeyed for position, snapping photos and thrusting microphones in his direction. The DA hesitated for a moment, then cleared his throat and thanked everyone for coming. He said he had officially concluded there was insufficient evidence at this time to bring Tala to trial for the murder of Jimmy Pualani. He blamed Dr. Wong and his assistants for erring in the collection of evidence.

He cleared his throat again and cast a furtive glance over his shoulder. He spotted Dr. Wong at the back of the crowd, and noted him slipping away flushed and obviously angry. He regretted using the medical examiner as a scapegoat, but so goes politics.

"I still feel Tala Pualani is the prime suspect in this case, but due to the DNA results which show that Tala Pualani and Tina Roland are identical twins, we are adding Tina to the suspect list as the investigation continues."

The press erupted in a din of overlapping conversation and they pelted the DA with questions. He held up his hands until the tumult had subsided, and he spoke a little louder.

"Along with the twins, we have arrested a number of people involved with drug production and trafficking. You can be assured I will do anything necessary to bring justice to Jimmy Pualani.

"That is all." He turned away from the barrage of questions that trailed after him as he climbed the steps and disappeared into the courthouse.

GARY CARR

CHAPTER 23

That evening, I was invited to the Rolands' house to share a meal and celebrate Tala's release. Tonight, I wasn't treated like a *haole*, and was welcomed with warm smiles and big hugs. The Roland home was near the ocean and provided a scenic backdrop to the large grassy area that served as their yard. Numerous tables were set up, covered with a large spread of food.

I'd never seen Tala out of her orange jail uniform. Tonight she glowed in a purple sun dress. Her makeup was flawless, and a yellow hibiscus graced her ear. She hugged me, and thanked me for helping her. She saw a friend, and hurried after her. I saw the precocious teenager I guessed she'd been before her arrest.

Taniko approached and asked if she could talk privately. We moved to a quiet corner of the yard and sat down. "If the girls are re-arrested, will you

135

represent them both in court?" There was a shadow of fear in her eyes.

I explained that an attorney is not allowed to represent more than one client on the same charge, but I assured her, if they did get arrested, I had a good lawyer in mind for Tina.

"Taniko, I am almost positive this is the last time you have to worry about the girls."

"I want to be a hundred percent sure, Uncle!"

I was pleased she addressed me with that title of respect.

"Will you continue working for me, to find the real killer, please? I have the funds to pay you until the killer is caught and the girls are forever free from suspicion."

"I'm at your service, ma'am, for as long as you need me."

Later, I gathered with Taniko, the girls, and Pearl. Isaac, the father of the girls, was not in sight. Taniko told me, "After the DNA results were exposed Pearl and I talked over the ramifications and decided, for the girls' sake, it would be best to worry about their future and not dwell on the past."

A sheen of tears filled Pearl's eyes as she added, "I'd always thought Isaac was a little too close to Taniko, but when my husband came to me with the truth and the idea of the ruse, because I love them both, I forgave them and agreed to the plan.

"This afternoon, we sat down with the girls and

told them the whole story."

I turned to the young ladies and asked what they thought about being twins.

They hugged each other, and squealed. Tina spoke up and explained they'd been curious at first, but then they were joyful. It explained why they'd felt a special bond the moment they'd met.

Isaac being their father had elicited different reactions. Tina had never questioned Isaac being her father as that is all she had ever known. For her, that would never change. The knowledge that Pearl wasn't her biological mother had thrown her a little. In her heart, Pearl would always be her mother, and Taniko her aunt. That is the way she wanted it to be. She'd asked the two women if that was all right with them, and they'd agreed.

Tala told me, "Well, I am happy to know that monster isn't really my father! But, I need time to adjust to knowing that Uncle Isaac is." She looked at her mother, shyly. "I'm taking a few days to get used to the idea."

Taniko hugged Tala. She reached over and took Tina's hand. "I'm so sorry you girls have had to deal with this. I'm forever grateful to my sister for her forgiveness and taking Tina as her own."

Pearl wiped tears away. "Taniko, when I lost my son, I was devastated. If it weren't for Tina, I'd be childless, now. I had no idea that such blessings could come out of such sorrow."

I felt like an intruder in this intimate conversation, and excused myself. Besides, the delicious aroma of food called to me. I filled a platter with broiled parrot fish, sticky rice and a bowl of green papaya chicken and joined several of the men gathered around a small table. I relaxed and enjoyed Hawaiian culture at its best.

It was a wonderful experience to be accepted into a Hawaiian family and gave me great sense of belonging, unlike anything I'd felt since my wedding day. When our marriage went sour, I was set adrift. As I opened that part of myself that had been closed so long ago, I'd forgotten how comfortable being part of a family was.

I realized I felt the same kind of kinship with Patty, Melvin, Symington, and even Kamu. Strange bedfellows, but in a way, we were family, too.

Taniko was at the food table, delicately picking out a little of this and that. She laughed, and I realized I'd never heard her laugh before. Despite her reserve, I detected an unmistakable sweetness underneath. I understood why Tala would defend her mother, even if it meant murder.

As I was finishing my chicken, Isaac approached the table and asked if he could sit. Surprised by the request, I made room for him. "It's your house, Isaac.

You can sit anywhere you like."

He sat down and said he was pleased I would continue to represent Tala, and would help Tina, if she needed it.

"It's my pleasure."

"I know I'm in trouble because of my, uh," his gaze swiveled to the men next to me and he lowered his voice, "business. But that doesn't concern me nearly as much as the DA wanting to pin the murder on one of the girls."

"I agree."

"Can I come by your office tomorrow morning and tell you my involvement with Jimmy?" He looked around. "I don't want to ruin the evening's festivities by talking about that worthless piece of crap."

"Any information you can give me may help me clear the girls' names. I'll look forward to seeing you, then."

Isaac held out his hand, and then left. He headed to the beer cooler, and grabbed a couple before answering his cell phone. He disappeared into the shadows.

It was time for me to go, too. It had been an eventful day, and I had a full schedule tomorrow. I found Taniko to say goodbye.

Just as I was getting into my car, Officers Draper and Davis pulled into the drive.

"Mr. Walters," acknowledged Draper.

I nodded at the men. "What brings you here, officers?"

"We wondered why all the cars are parked along the road." Davis kept looking towards the entrance of the house.

"Just celebrating."

"Do you think they have any food left?"

I raised my eyebrows. "You'd have to ask them."

They took me up on my challenge, and walked around back, where the party was going on.

CHAPTER 24

I checked my cell on the way home, and discovered I'd missed calls from Melvin and Symington. I pulled over to the side of the road, and returned them. I invited both to come out to the house when they got back on Molokai. We could go over all that had transpired over a bottle of Prosecco.

I wasn't too far from home, when I saw flashing lights approaching fast from the rear. I pulled over, cursing under my breath. I was only going three miles over the speed limit, for crying out loud!

When the police car whizzed past me, instead of pulling behind me, I let out a sigh of relief. I recognized Draper at the wheel, and wondered where his partner was. It's probably another wreck on the other end of the island, otherwise surely Davis would have been with him.

Symington's rental car was in the drive when I got home. He met me at the door with a cold glass of

Prosecco, and proudly proclaimed he had bought a case from Misaki's. I clinked his glass, took a big gulp, and then set the glass on the counter.

"I need to change, Symington. Don't touch that glass."

After getting into shorts and a tee shirt, I joined the doctor on the lanai. I heard Melvin drive up, and met him at the front door. He'd parked his rental car facing the highway.

I indicated his parking job and said, "In case you need a quick getaway?"

"I park like that because it's easier to hook up jumper cables. I'm always having a hard time with these rentals."

"Got it." I handed him a glass of wine. "Need to freshen up?"

Melvin took a small duffel he'd brought in to the bathroom. He emerged a few minutes later wearing a multicolored aloha shirt and shorts.

"The rumor mill is going full force, now that Tala's been released."

"Oh?" Symington said.

"Everyone wants to know who killed Jimmy, at least at the lower levels. The higher up you go, the less they care. That's funny, since he was supposed to be working with them to expand the drug trade here. They seemed to think this was a family deal, or someone outside of the drug ring."

I filled them in on the party, and that Isaac was

coming in tomorrow morning to discuss Jimmy. He may be able to offer a clue on who killed the man.

"Taniko is keeping me on retainer because she wants us to solve Jimmy's murder once and for all, for the girls' sakes."

"I was hoping she'd want that," said Melvin. "I hate loose ends, and wouldn't be able to move on until this is solved, one way or the other."

The knife was the key, we all agreed. For an hour, we discussed how someone could get ahold of that knife.

Symington offered, "The blood had to come from somewhere. The fact that there were no fingerprints on the knife means the killer either wore gloves or wiped the handle. That left only trace blood on the blade, which could have come from the cuts the ladies sustained while preparing the chicken."

"Damn Wong for his ineptitude!" I slammed my glass down on the table a little too hard. Wiping up drops of wine, I said, "I'll give him credit for one thing, though. He was able to discern the trace blood from Jimmy's blood. That tells me the blood had dried on the knife long before Jimmy was stabbed."

When we tired of the subject, Melvin gave us the rundown on the people he had interviewed that day. His impression from the Maui people was they had little interest on what was happening on Molokai. They implied Jimmy and Isaac were just errand boys.

143

They thought Isaac was smarter than Jimmy, but insisted neither one ran anything.

"They seemed to think it was funny that these two guys fought about who was in charge, when neither one was. When I asked them who, in the drug world, would be interested in offing Jimmy, they said there just wasn't enough business on Molokai for the big boys to get involved, much less go to the trouble of killing Jimmy over territory. Murder always brings too much publicity."

I filled empty glasses with the remaining Prosecco and said, "For a place where nothing happens, this has been one hell of a week!"

CHAPTER 25

Just then, the phone rang. As I picked it up, I noticed the name on the caller ID. "Detective Kamu," I mouthed to the two men.

"Aloha, Kamu, what can I do for you?"

He was looking for Melvin and asked if he was there. I said he was, but before I could pass the phone, Kamu said, "Just a minute. You need to know that Danny Ipo was killed earlier tonight, after he ran his truck off the road on the West End. The local cop, Draper, called me because he knew Danny was connected to my case. He said he didn't want any evidence messed up, like it had been in Jimmy's death.

"I hurried to the scene and sealed everything off, then called Dr. Wong. He's there now, collecting evidence. Preliminary report is Danny was killed in the crash. There are no other related injuries.

"I think he must have been drinking, and maybe

145

smoking, too. I found a small amount of pot in his glove compartment."

By this time, I'd put the phone on speaker. "You're on speaker, detective."

"Good. This all seems too coincidental for me. Can I borrow Melvin and his fancy cameras, to get some additional photos? I'd appreciate his insight, too, and will even pay for his time, even if I have to take it out of my own paycheck."

I said I wouldn't mind, but I'd let Melvin decide if he wanted to be a paid police consultant.

Melvin spoke up. "Where is it exactly, Kamu?"

The detective gave directions.

"I'm leaving right now, but Kamu, don't let anyone know I'm working for you, okay?"

I closed the cell, and Melvin grabbed his keys. Symington went outside to his car and came back with a plastic case the size of a tissue box. He handed it to Melvin.

"Have you ever taken samples before?"

Melvin opened the box and perused its contents. "I have."

Symington was pleased. "Get me as many as you can. Let's not rely on Dr. Wong, this time."

"Okay." He waved. "I'll be back when I'm back."

I looked at Symington and said, "I hope his cover isn't blown."

"I'm sure the detective will maintain it, using

some ruse for Melvin being there."

"It may be too late. If someone deliberately ran Danny off the road, then they might know that Melvin was with Kamu when they questioned him. But, that may be a lucky break. Not many people would know that. Limits the suspect pool, I should think. Thank goodness it's not our problem."

"Harry, you're not thinking. Of course, it's our problem."

"Why would we be getting into Danny's death? I was eating with all the suspects at their house when this happened."

Symington said, "Well, that gives *them* a nice alibi, but what if someone else is arrested? You're the only criminal attorney on the island, and my guess is we have a better handle on this than the DA does."

"Hmm. I'm not sure I'm ready to take on a new client. I really need to head back to San Diego, soon." For some reason, that depressed me.

"It's a good reason to stay and work on Jimmy's murder, don't you think?"

My attitude brightened, and I grinned at him. "Are you sure you're not just trying to get a longer Hawaiian vacation?"

Symington saluted me with his glass.

Melvin called about an hour and a half later, and said from everything he could see, someone ran the kid off the road. There were few people at the scene, other than Officer Draper and Kamu. He had successfully taken photos and gotten samples for Symington. His secret identity remained intact.

"Dr. Wong actually helped me get samples. He apologized for messing up on Tala's tests. The body was taken to Molokai General."

"I'll need to copy everything and send them to Kamu, in the morning."

"Can't wait to see what you have, but," I yawned, "it can wait until the morning, too."

"Right, Boss. I'll head back to my condo, and my computer. See you tomorrow.

The next morning, Symington, Melvin, and I assembled at my office. Patty kept our coffee mugs filled, for which we all were grateful. Melvin had his laptop open and was flipping through pictures of the scene that he'd downloaded before going to bed last night. We all put our heads together and watched.

Patty looked at the contorted and bloody body of Danny, and exclaimed, "What a waste of a life! Of course, he was already wasting his life in the drug trade, but still...Now, there is no chance to turn back and make something of himself."

"What's that?" Symington said, pointing to the truck's driver side door. It had a dent in it, and a swath of white paint through it.

"Kamu noticed that, too, and said it could have

been left by whoever hit him, or it could have happened at another time. Only testing it would answer that question."

We all agreed it looked like Danny was deliberately run off the road. It happened at the steepest part of the hill, going out to Mauanloa. Skid marks made by Danny's truck indicated a sideways slide.

Melvin replayed the evening to us. He said Dr. Wong had inspected the body thoroughly, and found no bullet or knife wounds. Wong thought the cause of death was most likely from heavy internal injuries and blunt force trauma. Danny's head had gone partially through the windshield. Kamu had already called and told Melvin we'd have a copy of Wong's report when he did.

Kamu and Melvin had stayed at the scene, until the tow truck had pulled Danny's crumpled pickup out of the deep ravine and loaded it onto a flatbed. The pickup was taken to the fenced lot at the police station, where it would undergo closer examination.

Officer Draper had been handling traffic, what little there was, and after the tow truck left, he offered his help to Kamu. The detective had dismissed Draper, saying he had everything under control. To Melvin, it had looked like the officer wasn't very happy with that.

I said, "When Kamu called this morning, while I was eating breakfast, he said you had been 'the epitome of excellence.' He said you were exacting and precise, noting every bit of possible evidence with your camera. I think you have a fan, Melvin. He wondered why you worked as a private investigator and not in law enforcement."

"None of his business." Melvin's face said it wasn't ours, either.

"Anyone need more coffee?" Patty chirped.

CHAPTER 26

Molokai is the last place, you'd think, where people killed each other. And yet, here was possibly a second murder in just a short while. It had been three years since the last one, and the one before that was five years ago. Both of those were domestic violence cases. The first was a husband killed by his wife who shot him after he'd beaten her. The other was a woman, strangled by her drug-crazed boyfriend, who thought she was a three-headed dragon.

Detective Kamu had investigated both of them and wasn't anxious to ever handle another murder. But, at least with domestic violence you knew the reason right away. Jimmy's murder, and now Danny's suspicious death, left a lot of questions.

If Danny Ipo had been run off the road, Kamu surmised, it probably was to keep him quiet, as he had unsavory ties in the shipping and drug scam he helped operate. Kamu made a mental note to check

151

with Oahu authorities on whether they'd tracked down Danny's pick-up men. Three arrests had been made on Maui, but they weren't talking.

Kamu climbed into his car. Worse than finding a young man's head stuck in a windshield, Kamu hated his next task more. He braced himself for notifying Danny's family of his death.

Dr. Wong had prepped Danny's body for autopsy last night and then went home to sleep for a while. He arrived at the hospital early, carrying a steaming cup of coffee that he sipped as he stood in front of the elevator. The doors slid open and he stepped inside. He sighed as they closed again.

When he reached the basement level that housed the morgue, the assistant, who was temporarily assigned to help him, was already there setting up. Danny's body had been pulled from refrigeration, but was still on the gurney. Wong crumpled his cup and tossed it into the trash, then helped the assistant place the body on the autopsy table. He pulled the stainless steel cart, covered with a neatly arranged assortment of surgical tools, closer to the autopsy table and snapped on Latex gloves. They were ready to begin.

As he recorded each step of the process, Wong gave precise details of his observations. He took his time and proceeded with the utmost caution and diligence. He couldn't stand another humiliating press conference from the district attorney. Right now, he was out to prove he was a good medical examiner.

He told the digital recorder in his pocket that the body was Danny Ipo, a male, nineteen years old, found at the scene of a single vehicle crash. The body was identified, by a driver's license found in his wallet. The decedent resided in Kaunakakai.

The body was clothed in an optic green tee shirt, denim jeans, boxers, white cotton socks, and tennis shoes. Dr. Wong noted no unusual matter on the socks or shoes and removed them. He then gently cut the shirt off, and noted possible oil or grease stains in the fabric. "Non-food related," Wong told his recorder. Along with considerable blood splatter, there were small pieces of safety glass on the shirt. He cut the stains out, and placed the cloth in evidence bags. He did the same with the glass shards. The decedent's jeans had a stain on the right leg, similar to that found on the shirt.

In one jeans pocket, Wong found a wallet containing twenty-three dollars, a Hawaiian driver's license, an ID card for Young Brothers Shipping, an insurance card, and a condom that, from the looks of the worn packaging, was really just a fantasy waiting to happen. The other pocket had a good-luck turtle key chain in it. One key was attached. As he put the key chain into an envelope, he shook his head. It hadn't brought Danny any good luck, the doctor thought.

There was some vegetable matter in the bottom of the pocket, too. Wong carefully turned it inside out and scraped some of the material onto the blade of a scalpel, then tapped the trace into an envelope and sent it to the lab for analysis. He had an idea of what it was, but tests would have to confirm it. Along with the plant matter, Danny's pocket also held a few crystals of methamphetamines. Wong spoke into his recorder and noted that he would run tox screens on Danny's blood. Maybe, he was high on meth when the crash happened.

He was just about to place the jeans in an evidence bag, when he noticed something pink sticking out of a back pocket where the wallet had been. He removed a length of thin satin ribbon. Wong held it up in front of his eyes and looked at it for a moment. It looked just like the pink ribbon collected near Jimmy's body on the beach at Twenty-Mile.

Securing it under the microscope, Wong assiduously examined it. There were two small segments of possible hair attached to it. He slid the hairs onto separate slides and increased the magnification. Yes, the samples contained follicles. Next, he snipped several fibers from the ribbon onto slides. From the evidence locker, he retrieved the ribbon found at Jimmy Pualani's crime scene and prepared samples in order to do a comparison.

Just the Right Amount of Wrong

Wong was elated that he suddenly had a chance to prove his worth as a medical examiner so soon after he'd messed up. He chided himself for growing lazy. A coroner on Molokai had a pretty dull life. Over the past three years, he had dealt mostly with health-related deaths of the elderly, accidental deaths, and the occasional suicide. It was an easy way to supplement his income. That all changed with Jimmy's and possibly Danny's murders. Time to step up to the plate and make sure there were no errors.

Dr. Wong carefully assessed both ribbons. They were an exact match. He logged them into his evidence record. He then returned to Danny's body and re-examined all the clothing. Finding nothing further, he slid the clothes into a bag, set them aside, and resumed his inspection of the body.

There were several large lacerations on Danny's arms, torso, and head. Massive trauma to the head and face was consistent with his hitting the windshield. Wong confirmed that Danny had died from a cerebral hemorrhage and extensive internal injuries as a result of the accident.

He called Detective Kamu to share his findings. He mentioned the ribbon in Danny's pocket, and that he'd tested it against the one discovered near Jimmy's body, and confirmed they were a match. He said he'd found vegetation in Danny's pocket, too, and that he'd sent it for analysis. He stepped out on a limb and told Kamu he thought it looked like marijuana. Regarding the meth crystals he'd found, he informed the detective he would be transporting Danny's blood samples to Oahu for a full toxicology analysis. It could take several weeks for complete results.

After he hung up with the ME, Detective Kamu mulled over what Wong had told him. He had sensed Danny was in a lot deeper than he had let on. It surprised him a little that meth had been found on him, though. He hadn't seemed the type to use. He'd been clear-eyed and rational when Kamu interviewed him. He wondered what Melvin's take on this would be. Usually an "outsider's" two cents wasn't wanted, but Kamu liked Melvin's style, even though he was somewhat of an enigma.

CHAPTER 27

First thing the next morning, Kamu interviewed Danny's guys, the ones who'd been harboring Tina. He told them to be careful with their answers. Depending on the depth of their involvement, they could be arrested on charges ranging from smuggling human cargo to any number of drug charges.

"It all depends on what the DA decides."

They told him they'd started helping Danny to pick up a few extra bucks. The one who'd allowed Melvin to use the phone was named Kimo. He'd worked for Danny first. He was a delivery truck driver, and his first job was to sneak a cousin of Danny's to the Big Island. Danny had told him his cousin had made some local thugs mad and needed to disappear. It was an easy gig, and Kimo agreed to more deliveries. Pilipo and Bane joined Kimo a year later. They agreed that all they did was drive a truck and deliver their cargo where they were told. They

157

claimed they didn't know anything about drugs.

Tina's case was personal for Danny. He'd asked Kimo to transport her, as she needed to hide from the cops. He'd paid the driver an extra two hundred, but Kimo would have been happy to do it for the usual price. He liked Danny.

Kamu asked if there was anyone else besides the three of them who worked for Danny and was told no. "If there was," Kimo said, "Danny took it to his grave."

Thanking the three men, he said he'd make sure the DA knew of their cooperation.

Kamu returned to police headquarters and called the lab. He'd dropped off the paint samples from Danny's accident scene and hoped they would have something for him soon. A call from them later that morning relayed the information that the white paint was from a late model Ford. It was used by Ford the last three model years as their standard white paint and was used on both sedans and pickups. The lab tech also found wax and detergent residue on the paint, indicating the vehicle had been recently washed. He'd also checked motor vehicle records and found seventy-three vehicles registered on Molokai which could have that paint finish. There were another dozen or so that could have used the paint for repairs or repainting. The tech was sure he could shorten the list by twenty-one, because that's how many county and state vehicles were on the island with that paint color.

Kamu decided to delegate the list to the two local cops.

Patty had gone home to her classes, and Symington, Melvin, and I were eating our plate lunches in silence. We all were a little tired of talking.

Symington would leave soon to take the samples Melvin had collected last night to Dr. Revis for testing. Dr. Wong had allowed him to collect a blood sample from Danny, and a number of hair samples and what he suspected to be marijuana leaves from the upholstery. Symington was impressed by Melvin's thoroughness. Once Dr. Revis and he did their tests, they'd share their results with Dr. Wong. Perhaps, he would appreciate confirmation of his findings, before the DA got excited and arrested someone.

I was just about finished with lunch, when my phone rang. Caller ID said it was my San Diego office, and for once I wished I could put them off.

Lifting a "just a minute" finger to my office mates, I answered it. My secretary updated me on my caseload, and then asked when I was returning. The prosecutor in the San Diego District Attorney's Office had called to see if I would be willing to move up the trial date for one of my clients. If not, he would schedule someone else.

My client had been arrested on embezzlement charges, and we were trying to work out a deal with the company to drop or reduce the charges, if the money was returned. Negotiations were going well, but were delayed when the company's attorney had been sidetracked by contractual work. Since my client was out on bail, and there were no objections from the prosecutor, we had postponed the trial for forty-five days. That's when I had decided to take some time off and go to Molokai.

I told my secretary that we were nearly through with Tala's case, but I expected more work here in the near future. I told her I would personally call the Assistant District Attorney and tell him no. She then went through a litany of other matters, which were piling up, and asked how much work she should send me.

After a few clarification questions, I said, "It would be easier to just fly back to San Diego for a few days. I also want to talk with my client, and see how she is holding up under the strain. You can expect me in the office around ten o'clock tomorrow. I will have to catch one of the late red-eye flights from Honolulu."

Symington and Melvin stared, open mouthed, at me.

"What?" I said, staring back.

Just the Right Amount of Wrong

Symington spoke first. "You're going back to San Diego right in the middle of our murder case?" Melvin sat back with folded arms.

I stood up, gathering paperwork. "Just for a few days. I've got a few things to clear up on some other cases. Besides, you all can hold the fort down while I'm gone. If anything big happens, call me, and I'll high-tail it back here."

"But what about this stuff with Danny?" asked Symington.

Melvin chuckled and said, "Looks like you're hooked, Doc. Tell you what, while the boss is away, let's see if we can't solve this for him."

This pleased Symington. "Great! That's the main reason I'm staying, Harry. Until now, it's just been technical stuff, but now that I'm in the thick of things, I'm enjoying the chase immensely."

"Fine. You two do just that." I slammed the door a little too hard.

It's not that I was really mad, I thought, as I packed my suitcase at home. But, I am the "Boss" and should therefore be present when the case is solved. I clicked my briefcase shut and locked the door behind me.

161

GARY CARR

CHAPTER 28

The Hoolehua Airport on Molokai has a personality all its own. Like the rest of the island, it has a laid-back attitude and a quiet sense of purpose. A few tourists have confused that with being lazy or uncaring, but quickly found out the hard way how seriously they take their jobs. Good paying, steady jobs, like those at the airport are hard to find on Molokai, and workers aren't going to do anything to jeopardize them.

After getting my boarding pass, I emptied my pockets, removed my shoes and belt, made the usual dumb comment about my pants falling off, and placed my briefcase and suitcase on the conveyor belt. I was motioned through the metal detector by a large jovial young man who had just recently joined the Transportation Security Administration team.

I had gotten to know him over the past few months because of the number of flights back and

163

forth to San Diego. His smile faded, when the alarm went off, and he asked me to step back. I checked my pockets, again, and sure enough, I pulled out a key ring. I handed it to the young lady by the conveyor belt who then placed it in one of the plastic bowls. The smiling agent motioned me through.

I set off the alarm, again, and then all hints of happiness disappeared. He asked me to stand on the two painted footprints on the floor and raise my arms. I did so, and he scanned me with the hand wand. He checked my trousers, then my torso, and as he neared my wrists, the wand went off. A big smile returned to his face, and he tapped the wand on my wrist watch.

Well, son of a gun! I removed my watch, and this time it was smooth sailing.

He waved me into the secure waiting area and said, "Gee, Mr. Walters, it's not like you to be this forgetful. This murder case got you all stressed?"

Feeling sheepish, I said, "I guess so."

The other three passengers in the waiting area were fixated on my movements, and when I sat down, they eyed me curiously. One was an older, skinny guy, a local I recognized. The couple next to him quickly found me boring and returned to their hugging and kissing. They must be on their honeymoon, I guessed.

Over the years, I'd learned not to start conversations with people in airports. It almost always results in lengthy personal histories, or opinions I wasn't interested in on subjects I could care less about. I sat down on the bench and took out my files. Soon, I was lost in my work, but briefly emerged from the world of legalese, when I heard the local guy ask the couple where they were from.

They informed him they were from Canada,

"Canada. Bet it's cold there, huh?"

"Not now," the young man said. "It's summer."

"Well, if it's warm there, what are you doing on Molokai?" he asked.

In unison, the couple said, "It's our honeymoon."

The bride gushed, "We got married on Maui and came over here for a few days to be alone."

I sighed. Here comes the airport oration!

The old guy reminisced about when he was their age, and how he had married a gal from Big Island. They were together for twenty years, had a couple of kids, and then she got tired of him and left.

Maybe she was just tired of hearing you *talk* all the time, I thought, shaking my papers, noisily.

The old man continued despite my mental chiding. He drank heavily for several years because of the divorce, but quit a few years ago. It was affecting his health. At one time, he had been a very large man, but had lost over one hundred pounds trying to avoid diabetes. Then, he had to get testosterone patches, because he had grown tired and was losing his interest in women. He clicked his teeth and added, "If you know what I mean." Now he was back to his old self, he assured them, and had two girlfriends.

Just as I felt my blood pressure rise, they began the boarding process. Grateful, I joined the queue to embark.

When I arrived in Honolulu, I took a taxi to Ala Moana Shopping Center. Since my flight to San Diego didn't leave until eleven o'clock, I had at least four hours to kill. I would much rather spend the time shopping some of the exotic shops than sitting in the airport.

One Asian-themed store there has three floors with goods ranging from hardware to food. I headed straight for the food. After selecting more than I should eat, I found a seat and waded into things like pickled ginger, octopus tempura, and a variety of sashimi, with soy and wasabi sauce. This was one-hundred-eighty degrees from my usual fare of Mexican food in Old Town San Diego, or the sausage, peppers, and onion sandwiches at Filippi's, in Little Italy. Tossing my sparse leftovers into a bin, I was reminded of why I enjoyed both San Diego and Hawaii. Both offer amazing opportunities to enjoy diverse cuisine.

At Honolulu Airport, all of the hominess of Molokai disappeared. At best, a feigned politeness was what you got from staff. The TSA people treated their duty like they were guarding the President of the United States. I was pretty sure if you had a sense of humor, you weren't going to work there. Fortunately, I removed all the necessary metal this time and got through security with no problem. Sitting amidst a couple hundred other weary souls was very different from Molokai's airport. No one wanted to talk, and from what I could see, the only thing people cared about was their plane being on time.

Since I had booked at the last minute, I was stuck in coach class. I wound up in the middle of a three-seat row, toward the rear of the plane. Now I get to play fat-butt-bingo, again, I thought, bitterly. The situation looked better when a young Hawaiian girl, about Tala's age, sat down in the window seat. Before the plane took off, she informed me she was going back to school on the mainland. Soon, the lull of the plane's engines worked its magic, and she closed her eyes and dozed. The aisle seat was taken by a late-model piece of fluff that, in my younger days, I would have taken a run at, but not now. I didn't need that kind of complication in my life, anyway.

Any chance of changing my mind burst when her husband, a buff naval commander, sat down across the aisle from her. They complained loudly to each other that they couldn't get seats together. I cordially offered to trade my seat, and they accepted. I happily moved over to the aisle seat, and they snuggled together.

Looking at them reminded me of what I'd lost in

my divorce. I was hit by a wave of nostalgia and loneliness, remembering how my wife used to curl up to me on long flights. I quickly shook the thought out of my head and pulled a book from my briefcase. I decided to engross myself in the latest Carroll Multz mystery, "Chameleon," a story about an undercover cop who winds up marrying a mob boss's daughter. That would make for some interesting Sunday night dinners, I thought as I began Chapter One.

I awakened a couple of hours later, just as the stewardess was picking up the last batch of trash. After we landed in San Diego, I took a taxi to my elegantly appointed luxury condo located on the tenth floor of an exclusive high-rise that overlooks the waterfront. The view alone is worth the several million dollars I had paid for the place.

I bought it before construction was even completed and dropped another couple mil customizing the interior with the finest stone, exotic woods like African Bubinga cabinetry, imported tile, and custom fixtures. My balcony projects beyond the glass wall facing the sea and runs the full width of the condo. It is shielded by a series of engineered glass panels. I enjoy a complete outdoor kitchen and dining area. Not a bad place to come home to.

I sighed and glanced around as I walked in, then tossed my keys onto the table in the entryway. I headed straight for the bathroom and took a soothing shower under four jet sprays and enjoyed a one-hour power nap on my king-size bed. Then, I jumped into my black Lexus and drove to my office.

Life in San Diego is more for show, but the noise is cacophonous. The crowing roosters of Molokai are replaced by blaring sirens, airplanes and endless streams of traffic noise and honking horns. I passed more cars on my way to the office than I see in a month on the island. I was already homesick.

At the office, I waded through my secretary's gauntlet of questions and messages, answered them mechanically, and then got down to work. The sooner I got back to Molokai, the better.

I called my embezzlement client, and she agreed to come in at two-thirty p.m. I called the company attorney and asked if he had time to meet with us. He agreed, as long as we kept it short. No problem, I assured him. It would only take ten or fifteen minutes if they were agreeable to our offer.

He was agreeable, but really slammed for time. Could we come to his office with the papers all ready to sign? Of course. Next, I contacted the prosecutor and informed him of our agreement. I promised to have the signed papers to him before quitting time. He said he would contact the court clerk. Maybe he could get on the next morning's docket to present the agreement to the judge and close this case.

That went well. I wondered why it went so smoothly on the phone from San Diego, rather than on the phone from Molokai. It occurred to me that here in San Diego I took on a completely different persona. My ex used to tease me about getting up in the morning, putting on my shark suit and going off to work. I guess she was right about that.

The meeting with the company went better than expected. They agreed to drop the charges if all the funds were returned along with additional interest payments to be made over the next two years. They also agreed my client's personnel records would reflect that she resigned.

After convincing them to drop the request for interest payments because of the new evidence on sexual harassment, the agreement was signed, sealed, and delivered to the prosecutor, who said our court time was in the morning at eight fifteen. Then, I called the office and told my secretary I was headed to my client's house for signatures and would go home from there. I would be in tomorrow after I finished at the courthouse.

Next, I dialed Melvin to see what was happening on Molokai. His cheerfulness made me even more homesick.

"Heya, Boss, where you stay?"

I told him I was just checking to see if he'd solved the case, yet.

He laughed out loud. I pulled the cell away from my ear until the noise died down.

"That's funny, Boss. No, there's nothing much new here. Dr. Symington is doing his microscope magic, and Detective Kamu has those local cops running around the island checking out all the white Fords. I talked to a few more of the local boys about the drug network on the island. They said it hadn't changed much over past five or six years until about a month ago. They said Jimmy and Isaac had been at each other's throats, and both seemed secretive. There was a rumor that their disagreement was about running meth. Same old stuff we've been hearing." He added, "I'm nearly convinced this was done by locals rather than outsiders. No one I've talked with can recall any new faces on the island around the time Jimmy was killed or when Danny had his so-called accident."

I told him to keep digging.

"I'll be back in three or four days, especially if it all goes as well as today."

"Aloha, Boss."

When papers were signed, I told my ecstatic client I'd see her the next morning. On the way to my car, I stopped by a small fish taco place on 'B' Street where they had great mahi mahi tacos. I took my dinner home, and after putting my briefcase on the counter, my coat and tie over a chair, I grabbed a beer and sat down at the table. Then it dawned on me, I still had my shoes on. It always amazes me how habits change depending on where we are.

My delicious tacos did nothing for the loneliness that crept in as the evening progressed. I turned on

171

the television, hoping a John Wayne western would keep me company. No such luck. My thoughts traveled over the Pacific Ocean to Molokai. Damn it, I really hadn't wanted to leave without answers to who killed Jimmy and Danny. And if I was going to be honest with myself—and why wouldn't I be?—I really hated to leave Hawaii.

Turning off the television, I concentrated on what I had left to do here, and what would be required for me to spend an extended period of time on Molokai. I slept well that night.

The ADA tagged to prosecute my embezzlement client met me at the courthouse the next morning. He presented our agreement to the judge who readily signed off on it. When we left the courtroom, I said goodbye to my client and told her to stay out of trouble. Then I turned to the ADA. Ray Williams had a good reputation as an assistant district attorney. I felt he was going places, possibly to judgeship. I asked him if he had time for coffee. I wanted to pick his brain.

We grabbed our coffee at a little café around the corner from the courthouse. It was full of people from the legal world. Ray listened to me describe Jimmy's case and how different the legal system worked on the islands. I could tell he was a bit surprised by what I told him, but anyone in the legal arena knows that every area, even within a district, has its "quirks." His eyebrows arched as he polished off his coffee and pushed his mug off to the side.

"It's gotta be tough working in such a different legal environment. It all sounds a little "backwater" to me. If the case you described was here in San Diego, I would be tempted to think there was something a little fishy going on in the DA's Office."

"That possibility has definitely crossed my mind," I admitted. "It *is* an election year."

I worked diligently over the next two days, and had the San Diego office situated where they could live without me for two or three weeks. I called Patty to tell her when I would be returning to Molokai.

"Any news?"

"Nothing but a few procedural matters, and some new gossip about Danny's death."

"Can't wait to hear it all."

"Something for you to wonder about on your long trip home…Melvin and Symington have discovered a more direct connection with Danny and Jimmy. Jimmy had helped Danny set up his smuggling operation at the shipping company, and had set up the contacts on the other islands."

"Good to know. Hey, where are my sidekicks, anyway?"

"Melvin's on Maui talking to his contacts. He's trying to verify what we've learned about Jimmy and

Danny's connection. Symington is still on Oahu, working with Dr. Revis on the evidence they found at Danny's wreck. Oh, and Kamu would like to talk to you as soon possible."

This time, I made sure I could get a first class seat on my flight back to Molokai. I instructed the flight attendant to let me sleep, and she brought me some sound-deadening earphones and a sleep mask. Blissfully unaware of noise, I woke up just as the plane descended for its landing. The attendant touched my shoulder and told me it was time to sit upright.

It was a struggle to come back to the real world. I'd had a strange, disjointed dream that Taniko had killed the DA, and wanted me to ship his body in a shipping crate to San Diego. I told her attorneys weren't allowed to ship bodies by boat. We could only transport them by airplane. If my maiden aunt was still alive, I could have asked her what the dream meant. My own interpretation was that I should call Taniko.

CHAPTER 29

I met Symington at the Island Air terminal on Oahu, and we flew back to Molokai together. He was an excited bundle of information. He and Dr. Revis had their test results, and he couldn't wait to tell me all he knew.

"Danny had both alcohol and cannabis in his system, but not high enough levels to impair his driving. The vegetation found in the vehicle was also cannabis. The paint samples were from a Ford, as Wong had thought, but the most interesting fact was that the hair samples from the ribbons matched Tala's and Tina's DNA."

Symington talked nonstop all the way to Molokai. He was delighted to have another mystery to solve, and spent the rest of the flight trying to engage me in speculation on how Danny had one of the girls' ribbons. That question moved to the top of the list I would pose to Melvin and Detective Kamu.

It ranked right next to how the matching ribbon was found on Twenty-Mile Beach next to Jimmy's body. Who knows? I may be representing Tina, after all. My thoughts screeched to a halt. Oh, God! What if they were Tala's ribbons and hair, after all?

Symington blithely carried on. He thought "we" may have another suspect to represent. I cogitated on that, and wondered about the strange direction things were heading. First one twin is arrested, and then the other could be guilty. Who knows, maybe they did it together, like "bad seeds," and they are excellent actresses. No one but the killer or killers knows the truth. I shook my head. I was getting too dramatic. Still, I'd put in a call to the girls as soon as possible.

As soon as we landed, I called Patty and asked her to set up a meeting with Taniko and her girls– tonight, if possible. I also asked her to set up a meeting in the morning with Detective Kamu. Of course, Melvin and the good doctor would meet with me tonight, and we'd update each other.

I made a quick stop at Misaki's for Prosecco, but had to settle for a California Chardonnay. Next stop was Friendly's for groceries. Symington offered to buy the food, as he and Melvin had pretty well eaten everything in the house. When we arrived home, Patty called and said Taniko and the girls would meet with me at the Rolands' home whenever I wanted. I left our meal of frozen fried chicken with Symington, and headed to the East End.

Pearl had joined Taniko, Tala, and Tina. They stood on the front step waiting for me. Each looked a little curious, but there was a tinge of fear, too.

"Harry! Has something happened?" asked Taniko. She felt for Tala's hand. "Have they found who killed Jimmy?"

I wanted more than anything to put to rest her fear. I decided a roundabout approach to the ribbon issue was needed.

"No, my dear. Nothing yet. I wanted to show you the photos of Danny's Ipo's wreck and see if anything stood out."

They ushered me inside, and when we were seated at the kitchen table, I laid down the photos, one by one. Tina stifled a cry, and tears welled up in her eyes. I started to turn over the photos of Danny's body, to ease the situation, but Tina stopped my hand.

"It's okay. I want to see them."

As we continued looking at the photos, she picked one up and looked at it closely.

"Why do you have a picture of my hair ribbon? What has that got to do with Danny's wreck?"

The question of the day had been asked, and now I wanted an answer. "Tina, how *did* your hair ribbon get in Danny's pocket?"

"You know, Danny was my boyfriend."

I nodded.

"We were, er, kissing a couple of nights before Jimmy was murdered, and one of my ribbons came out." She looked quickly at Pearl. "Rather than lose them, Danny put them in his pocket. I forgot all about them. Danny must have kept them with him, thinking he'd return them when he saw me next." She buried her face in her hands and wept.

"Did you know Danny was in the drug trade?" I tried to be gentle with my words.

"I guess I didn't think much of it, since my dad grows pot. I figured Danny was working with him."

Pearl encircled Tina in an embrace. "I'm so sorry." She looked at me. "We know Isaac has been involved in drugs, but we never talked about it."

"No more secrets, okay?" I looked at each of the ladies. "There's no telling where this whole thing will wind up, and I don't want to be the last to know if any of you are in danger."

There was a round of adamant yeses, and then I looked at Tina. "I'm sorry to ask this, but I need to. Did you have anything to do with Jimmy's murder?"

Tina's eyes widened, and she shook her head vigorously. "No, no, no, Mr. Walters!"

"I think it's been a hard enough evening for Tina." Taniko glanced down at the pictures and gathered them into a pile. "May I walk you to the door?"

I picked up the pictures and tucked them into the manila envelope they'd come in. "I'm very sorry to have put you ladies through this. Especially you, Tina. I'll see myself out."

Just the Right Amount of Wrong

Getting back into my car, I felt relief. I believed Tina. Whether anyone else agreed, I was going to move on to other avenues, and I hoped my team would agree. Little did I know how wrong I was.

Tina went into hysterics as soon as the door closed. "I need to get off the island right now!" she shouted. The older ladies looked mystified and tried to calm her. "Whoever killed Danny may be after me!" She covered her face and moaned.

Pearl put a comforting hand on her shoulder. "Why would you think such a thing?"

"I told Mr. Walters a lie. The night Uncle Jimmy was murdered, I heard Papa leave. I quickly called Danny because I wanted to spend some time with him. We planned to drive out to the old dump at Twenty-Two Mile. But when we got close to Twenty-Mile Beach, we saw Papa's car. We were afraid he would see us so we turned the lights off and stopped. That's when I saw two men fighting on the beach. Danny and I got out of the car and hid in the naupaka. Danny recognized them first. It was Papa and Uncle Jimmy!

"We watched as Papa knocked Jimmy down and then stabbed him in the back. It was horrible! He dragged Jimmy over and threw him into the mangroves, then ran to his car and drove off, his tires

179

screeching."

Pearl and Taniko looked at each other, and then back at Tina.

"When Papa was gone, we hurried down to Jimmy. Danny checked his pulse, but he was dead. We didn't know what to do next. I was so afraid for Papa! I started to panic, but Danny said he'd take care of things. He took a tissue out of his pocket and wiped off the handle of the knife. That must be how my ribbon dropped on the beach. I helped him brush our footprints out, and then we got out of there."

Taniko exclaimed, "Why didn't you tell us, Tina? Tala would never have been arrested if they knew Isaac killed Jimmy."

"I was too afraid. That's why I had Danny help me run away to Oahu."

"Tina, we've got to tell the police."

"I know. But, what if whoever killed Danny is looking for me? What if Papa killed Danny too?"

"Your father would *never* harm you," said Taniko, as she looked over at Pearl, tears welling in her eyes. She touched Tina's chin and moved it so she could look into her eyes. She smiled, sadly. "Tomorrow we must tell that detective the truth. He will be able to help us. Okay?"

Tina sniffed, and then nodded. Taniko reached for Pearl's hand. "It will be all right."

Just the Right Amount of Wrong

On my drive home, I started thinking about how the other ribbon had wound up on the beach at Twenty-Mile. If Danny had them both in his pocket, how did one wind up at the beach? Had Danny been the one to kill Jimmy? What if he'd been hired, and then was killed to keep him quiet? Boy, Symington will have a field day with this theory!

When I walked through my door, the house smelled savory and wonderful. The clanking of utensils and small talk going on in the kitchen were welcome sounds after Tina's weeping. Melvin and Symington had followed the cooking directions on the package of frozen fried chicken and had put a salad together for our dinner. Some fresh Hawaiian Sweet Bread from Kanemitsu's Bakery topped off the meal. After eating, we sipped Chardonnay and reviewed all of our information.

I threw out my new theory, and just as I thought, the doctor ran with it. His main question was who would have hired Danny?

Melvin had a little too much wine and asked me if he could use my couch for the night. "Of course," I replied. When he and Symington turned on the television and immersed themselves in a PBS special, I wandered out on the lanai. I sat in the waning daylight, enjoying the mystery of Molokai at dusk. I sipped my wine until the sky went dark, then said goodnight to my two friends and slogged off to bed. A small sense of foreboding followed me.

CHAPTER 30

Kamu was waiting for me outside my office. "Morning, Mr. Walters."

"Likewise, detective. I understand you have something for me."

"I was hoping to have a copy of the report on the Ford and the paint chips, but those idiots, Draper and Davis, have been dragging their feet looking for it."

The detective's cell rang, and his demeanor became serious. He said, "I'll be right there. Call the ME."

We all were frozen in various poses, waiting for Kamu to let us in on the conversation.

"Somebody killed Isaac. His body is out by Sandy Beach in the cave. Some surfers had stopped to dump trash in the barrel and found his body. They called nine-one-one, and the local officers are at the scene. With Isaac potentially related to the other crimes, I better cover this alone. I'll share what I can

183

later. I'll also make sure Dr. Wong has his ducks in a row."

When he left, it was quiet in the office for a few moments. Then we were talking all at once.

"Well, hell's bells!" Symington blurted.

"I better call Taniko," I said.

"Let's all stay calm," said Melvin.

"I'll make coffee," said Patty.

For the next few hours, we sat around drinking coffee, and running this new murder around and around, trying to make some sense of it. Just as we finished our sixth round of coffee, Detective Kamu called me.

"Dr. Wong estimates Isaac was killed late last night. He said he'd been stabbed with a butcher knife, just like Jimmy. There is a lot more material at the scene. Officers are there interviewing and Wong is collecting evidence. Most of it appears to be trash, and that just prolongs the investigation. As soon as the body is transported, I'll release the two cops, and you can send Melvin out here. I welcome another set of experienced eyes."

When Kamu finally called, Melvin rushed out, promising to call us later when he had more information. The detective stayed on the line and gave me a meticulous account of what had happened up until now.

"I interviewed the surfers who found the body," he began. They hadn't seen anyone else in the area, and they had no clue who "the dead guy was." The way they found him propped up against the cave wall, they originally thought he was asleep, or maybe passed out. They emptied their trash, and since he hadn't moved, they went a little closer. That's when they saw he was dead.

The detective didn't move the body until Wong showed up, and that's when they saw the knife. Kamu directed Draper and Davis to take down the surfers' names and personal information, while Wong collected evidence. Then Isaac's body was loaded into the ambulance and chauffeured to Molokai General. Kamu had relieved the officers, and then he called Melvin. He was going to the DA's Office next, but wanted Melvin to hurry to the scene to get his take on the situation. He said he'd call, once his interview with the DA was done.

When Kamu called again, he said the DA was incredulous at the newest turn of events. "Three murders on Molokai," he'd exclaimed, "and two are exactly alike!"

Kamu had been surprised when the DA asked him if he was still on good terms with Tala's lawyer and his investigator.

"As far as I know," he'd replied.

The DA then asked if he would call them to see

if they could help. He didn't want any mistakes this time. He wanted to be absolutely positive of the evidence, before he arrested somebody or worse, gave incorrect information when the press inevitably caught wind of it. Kamu had assured the DA he'd call, and get back to him after he got an answer.

Kamu sounded tired after relaying their conversation. "So, here I am asking. You interested?"

I said I would make Melvin and Dr. Symington available, but I didn't want any direct involvement, since I might be hired to defend anyone the DA arrests. I rang off, and swiveled my chair around to face the window.

This about-face by the DA gave me pause. If what I felt about him was right, then he would jump at the chance to arrest someone, if only to get publicity. I could be wrong, though. What if the last circus made him realize he'd better watch his step or he'd lose all credibility, and that would mean a loss at the polls.

Upon rethinking the DA's offer, I called Kamu and said I would decline the DA's offer, just to avoid any conflict.

Kamu understood, and said he'd pass that along. While I had him on the line, I asked if Pearl had been notified yet.

"No. I'm on my way there, now," he said, weariness heavy in his voice.

"I don't envy you. I'll wait an hour, and then

call them to see if they need me."

"I'm sure that is a good idea." He signed off.

I didn't wait. I called Taniko immediately, and told her the police were heading their way. She wanted to know why, and I said, "Just call me as soon as they leave, and tell everyone not to say a word."

I called Symington and told him I wanted to know anything Dr. Wong knew, and to do what he needed to make that happen. Surely, Dr. Wong would share this information with Symington and Revis, even if for simple professional courtesy. Symington said he'd call the ME and offer his help.

"We'll see what happens."

Melvin drove out to the rocky shores of East Molokai, and located the cave where Isaac's body had been found. Melvin took a moment to appreciate the raw beauty of the rock-strewn shore and crashing surf. He hoped he'd have some time, when all this was over, to do a little fishing before going back to the noise and big city confusion of Honolulu. He carefully took photos of the roadway, the dirt pull-off by the front of the cave, and the cave itself. The cave was used for various reasons. It had been tagged as a sacred place by some of the locals. The youngsters use it as a place to make out. Local fishermen often build fires and take shelter there from sudden storms.

187

It was also a place to drink beer and relieve one's self.

Numerous footprints dotted the soft dirt, and Melvin meticulously photographed them all. It would have been nice to have done it before the medical examiner, Kamu, the cops, and all the witnesses had tromped all over the place. He also took photos of the blood pools and spatter.

Drag marks led Melvin to believe Isaac was dragged from the entrance of the cave to the back wall. At the entrance, there were several small blood pools and a larger one a few feet away. At the back of the cave, the largest blood pool had settled under the body. A trash can had been moved forward so that the body was mostly hidden from passersby on the road.

Melvin picked up the can, and discovered a clear footprint. Why hadn't it been cast? He shook his head. Dr. Wong! He looked around for Kamu. He was talking to someone, so Melvin went to his car and got his plaster casting material out. Returning to the footprint, he framed it, mixed the plaster, and then poured it carefully over the print. When the plaster dried, he lifted the shoeprint, and took several photos to verify his findings. He compared the print to his own size ten shoe, and guessed it was from a size twelve or thirteen. Probably a leather oxford or "slipper," judging by the smooth sole impression.

That could match about half of the male, and maybe a third of the female population on the island, he thought, ruefully. He waited for the plaster to dry completely, then gathered his paraphernalia and headed back to his vehicle.

He watched where he stepped as he approached his car. That's when he noticed some white patches at the edge of the road. Sunshine reflected off of them, or Melvin would have missed them altogether. He stooped, and took out some tweezers, placing the jagged chips of white paint carefully in a plastic bag. Maybe they are from the same car that ran Danny's vehicle off the road, he thought.

Tina was comforting Pearl when I entered the Roland house. I offered my condolences on Isaac's death. Pearl managed a tremulous "Aloha," and then she burst into tears.

I waited a few minutes. "I hope I'm not being inappropriate, but I need to ask what Detective Kamu told you."

Taniko said, "He was very polite and sympathetic. He said Isaac's body had been found at the cave, and would be autopsied. Pearl asked him how he died, and he said he was stabbed, just like Jimmy. He thought the two deaths were related.

"I asked him when he would know, for sure, and he said it would depend on the autopsy results. He said we would probably have to account for our whereabouts over the past twenty-four hours. Harry," she laid a hand on my arm in distress, "does he think one of us could have killed him?"

"It's his duty to check everyone out, Taniko." I looked at Pearl. "Depending on the time of death, you probably don't have anything to worry about. Let's just get through this, and not worry about tomorrow, okay?

"Do you remember where Isaac was last night?"

"I remember something!" Pearl blew her nose delicately into a tissue. "Around eleven p.m., Isaac made a phone call and then told me he had a meeting to go to. It was business, and he'd be gone for a few hours. I was mad he had to leave, but it's not unusual for him to do this.

"When I woke up this morning, he was still gone, but I didn't get worried. That's not unusual for him, either."

"Did you tell Kamu this?"

"No. You said not to talk."

"Okay. Ladies, again, I'm so sorry. I will get back with you as soon as I hear anything." Taniko walked me to the door.

"The nightmare just keeps going on, Harry."

All I could do was hug her.

Symington called to say he was helping Wong with the autopsy. "I haven't been able to get in touch with Dr. Revis, but I left him a message."

"Hold off on talking to him, Symington. Let's just keep him in reserve. I may need a purely independent expert to raise the question of reasonable doubt."

"Right. I'll call you when the autopsy is done."

Dr. Wong began the autopsy with the standard process of notating clothing and foreign matter. Nothing of consequence was found. He started on the body next. He took tissue samples of hair, saliva, and blood. He then swabbed the knife handle and blade, and removed it from the body.

Dr. Symington noted it was expensive stainless steel, and identical to the one used to kill Jimmy. It had been dusted for fingerprints, but they were either smudged or unusable.

Wong validated the cause of death as exsanguination from the stabbing. Symington concurred. Next, they tested for alcohol and toxins present. Both were negative, but it could take weeks for the complete tox results.

Symington suggested Isaac was stabbed from behind. There were no physical signs of struggle, so it looked like he was taken by surprise. "Either the killer was able to ambush him, or two or more people were involved—one to distract him, and another to stab."

"Sounds plausible to me," Wong said.

When the DNA testing was finished, both Wong

and Symington double checked the complete process, to make sure there weren't any mistakes. The only DNA on the knife was from Isaac. Symington began a second test just to be sure. While Symington was getting the second set of tests ready, Wong found the files from Jimmy's death to compare photos and information on the knife. They were exact, most likely from the same set found in the Roland's kitchen. Both had minor traces of chemicals from Huli Huli Chicken.

"I need to inform Detective Kamu of this."

Symington said, "I better call Harry, and give him a heads up."

When I got Symington's call, I decided to bring Dr. Revis on board. Though the DNA tests were rechecked and redone, I wanted Revis to check, too. I got Revis on the first ring, and asked if he could join me at my home for the next week. He called his office and then called me back to say he could.

I phoned Taniko, and told her the news. She panicked, but I told her it's highly unlikely the girls would be arrested. "Since they were released from Jimmy's murder, they have been in your company. This knife didn't have their blood or DNA on it, so I doubt the DA wants to look like a fool again."

I asked her to make a list of everyone at the

house the last few days. I wish I could get ahold of Isaac's cell to see his caller list. I bet Kamu already bagged it. "Melvin will stop by sometime and pick up the list," I told her, "most likely tomorrow. Call me if the police show up. Taniko, don't worry. It will be all right."

I called Melvin, and gave him instructions. He told me he'd been talking with a number of people, focusing mainly on anyone seeing a white vehicle on the Kam V Highway.

"One older fellow had seen Isaac near Our Lady of Seven Sorrows Church. He was on his way home from work, around eleven-fifteen last night. Isaac drove passed him and waved a Shaka out the window."

That coincided with Dr. Wong's estimated time of death.

To complicate matters even more, Officer Draper called Kamu to tell him they had found Isaac's car at the old dump site just a few miles down the road. It had been ransacked and the windows were smashed. Kamu instructed them to cordon off the car with police tape, and block the gate so no one could enter the area. The detective called Melvin and asked him to meet him at the dump.

They thoroughly went over every square inch of the car together, but found nothing useful. The car had been wiped clean of fingerprints.

GARY CARR

CHAPTER 31

Patty perked up when I walked into the office. "Give me all the details!"

I leaned against the file cabinet and told her everything.

"The whole island is in an uproar, Harry," she exclaimed. "People are beginning to worry about a serial killer being on the loose."

"Understandable. Why don't you get the word out that we are looking for a white vehicle with a sizeable ding on the front fender? That would help immensely. Do it quietly, though, because if Detective Kamu finds out he will probably get upset. He would consider it interference, I'm sure."

Kamu met with Draper and Davis to see how

195

they were coming with finding a dented white vehicle. Draper said he was reviewing traffic reports, and Davis was still checking out the automotive shops and gas stations.

"Do you think you could step things up a bit?" Sometimes, he thought the island laissez faire was more a hindrance than a help, at least where a crime investigation was concerned.

Next, he dropped by Molokai General to get the autopsy and test results from Dr. Wong.

Wong pointed out the knife was identical to the one that killed Jimmy, but reiterated the only DNA found on it belonged to Isaac.

The detective shook his head. This is nuts! The girls were home and had no reason to kill their father, as far as he knew. So how in the hell did someone get the matching knife? The only motives he could come up with were possible connections to drug dealing. With Isaac dead, it may mean a new player is trying to take over, or else this is a revenge killing. Kamu looked at the ME's report. "Did you find anything else that might give us a clue?"

Wong shook his head. "Wish I could offer more."

Kamu left the building and found his car. He called Melvin and was told about the footprint and paint flecks.

"Could you hold off informing your guys until I have a chance to tell Harry?" asked Melvin.

"No problem. I need time to digest all this and put together a complete report for the DA and Chief of Police."

Melvin briskly walked into my office and immediately transferred all his photos to my computer, while making a CD copy for Kamu. Together, we made a scaled photo mock-up of the footprint. We kept one of the paint chips in a separate bag, but Melvin put everything else in a box for Kamu.

We then discussed Isaac's murder. Hashing it over brought us to the same conclusion as Kamu's. Tina and Tala had alibis, so they didn't do it. The question was why did Isaac leave so late at night? Who'd he call? Did he take the knife to his own murder, or did someone else? If it was someone else, how did he get it? Why were there no signs of struggle?

Kamu sat in his car thinking about what Melvin had found at the crime scene. He had missed the paint chips and never saw the footprint, and wasn't very happy with himself. And how could he share this latest evidence without revealing he'd gotten it from a private detective? He might get a good-natured butt chewing, but Melvin's findings could break the case. Kamu hated to admit it, but Melvin was a far better detective than anyone on the force, including him. Having his help was a big advantage, and he was doing it for free, to boot.

As Kamu backed his car out, he glanced at the white police cruiser parked next to him. What the…? He pulled back into the space, and got out. There was a fist-sized dent on the front fender, and some missing paint. He glanced around to see if anyone was watching, and then wrote down the license plate number. He took out his pocket knife and removed a small fleck of paint. Placing it carefully in a tissue, he glanced around again. Then he got in his car, and headed to Harry's office.

Melvin and I were sharing a bowl of poke—raw ahi marinated with soy sauce, sesame oil, kukui nut, and seaweed—when Kamu entered the office. Without asking, the detective took a large pinch of the poke and plopped it into his mouth.

Around mouthfuls and sounds of pleasure, he recounted his surprising find. If the paint found at Danny and Isaac's crime scenes matched the cruiser, we were talking about crooked police!

Given this startling discovery, we all agreed,

including Kamu, to keep the footprint and paint chip amongst ourselves. None of us wanted to think the police were involved, but it wasn't like that never happened. The questions now were who had driven Danny off the road, and was it an accident or a way to keep Danny quiet? Who all is involved in this and how high up does it go? And how was it tied to Isaac's murder?

I suggested I get the footprint mold and paint chip to Dr. Revis, for his eyes only. The other two agreed. Kamu would find out whose cruiser it was, and then go from there. Melvin would continue his own agenda. Kamu gave him some names to check out.

Melvin said, "If I uncover anything I'll let you know. If one of the scumbags over there is the one who supplied my wife with the heroin that killed her, I won't rest until he's dead or behind bars."

Kamu was stunned by Melvin's comment. He thought, "Well, I guess I don't have to wonder about his motivation anymore."

Melvin stepped off the ferry in Lahaina. He was dressed like a local today, a weathered, old Filipino with short-cropped hair and a patchy beard. He adopted a slight limp, and spoke with a heavy accent. He blended in seamlessly.

199

He took his time walking over to the Wharf Center, and waited in back for the public transportation bus to Kahalui. He eavesdropped on several young men who loitered around the waiting area discussing where they could buy some weed. Uncle Sam had the best stuff, one said.

Melvin wondered who Uncle Sam could be. He had never heard of a dealer by that name. He caught the tail end of the men's conversation, hearing the Banyan Tree mentioned.

Melvin knew the Banyan Tree is the main gathering spot in Lahaina. It is over a century old, stands over sixty feet high and has twelve major trunks. Its massive canopy shades two-thirds of an acre, and almost fills Courthouse Square, except for the small museum on the south side. What is now the museum used to be the courthouse, and there are remnants of the old jail nearby.

The young men sauntered off in that direction, and Melvin ambled slowly behind. When they stopped, he waited on the sidewalk by the activity kiosk. Nearly invisible in a thick slice of shade, he kept an eye on them.

As time to board the ferry to Molokai grew close, a small crowd of passengers gathered. Most were hotel and service industry workers heading home, but there were also a few shoppers and tourists. The usual throng of hustlers was present, trying for the easy dollar, but none appeared to be selling drugs. Melvin surreptitiously watched the activity under the guise of a napping old man.

The young men suddenly stiffened and looked ready to run when a police car rounded the corner. Melvin chuckled to himself. People who do things they shouldn't always want to run when they see the police. He choked on his chuckle when instead of running the other way, they approached the car.

The policeman slowed and pulled over to the curb. Melvin watched as they exchanged greetings, the young men forming a cluster by the driver's side door. One placed something in his back pocket, while another took something from a pouch around his neck and handed it to the cop. Pleasantries were exchanged, and the cop pulled away slowly. He disappeared around a corner. The boys went back to the Banyan Tree and examined their spoils. Melvin noted the patrol car number, and managed a cell phone photo of the cop, as he drove by.

Melvin decided it would be a waste of time to follow the young men further. He returned to the back of the Wharf Center to catch the next bus to Kahalui. Melvin was always grateful for any luck he could get, and was amazed when one of the young men entered the bus and sat down next to him.

The forty-five minute trip across Maui gave Melvin a chance to strike up a conversation with his seatmate. He asked where he was from, and if he knew one of the larger families on Maui. The young

GARY CARR

man said he was born on Maui, and knew of the
family, but not personally. Melvin complained about
being old, and his gout getting worse. Adding to his
persona, he cradled his small duffel bag nervously,
and whispered to the young man he'd come to Maui
to see an acupuncturist, and maybe score some "Maui
Wowee."

The young man peered at Melvin more closely.
After a moment, he said he'd just picked some up,
and would share it with Melvin. "If you have any
cash, that is."

"I've just got five dollars."

"I can spare a couple of joints for a fiver." He
discreetly exchanged the pot for Melvin's cash.

Melvin told the young man several times how
grateful he was.

When the bus stopped near Walmart, the two
disembarked. The young man asked, "Where you go
now, old man?"

Melvin nodded his head towards the super store.
"Over to Wally World. I fly a sign, and get a few
bucks for food."

The boy reached into his pocket and pulled out
the five bucks Melvin had just given him. "You need
this more than me. Hope the weed helps the gout. See
you around."

Melvin bowed and thanked him. He clutched the
five dollar bill like a great treasure, as he walked
toward Walmart's entrance. The young man turned

away. Melvin passed a beggar sitting just outside the store, and he placed the five dollars in his outstretched hand. The bedraggled beggar was surprised to see someone who dressed like him give him money, and he called a shaky thanks to Melvin's back.

Melvin found an empty stall in the men's room, and quickly changed clothes and disguises. He had entered a grizzled old man, and left the store a thirty-something professional. He walked down the road to a car rental agency, and got a sedan for the day. Tossing his duffel in the trunk, he headed back to Lahaina to see if he could track down "Uncle Sam."

At McGregor Point, Melvin saw a police car pull into the scenic overlook parking lot. Melvin pulled into the lot and backed into a parking space. Joining a group of tourists, he pretended to take pictures on his cell phone of whales gracefully leaping out of the water. He shot a couple photos of the policeman, as he walked over to one of the parked cars and leaned into the driver's side window. A serious conversation seemed to be going on.

Melvin moved into a better position to see, and took several shots of the cop and the driver of the car. Thinking he'd gotten enough, he got back in his car and called Kamu.

"Ever hear of a dealer named, 'Uncle Sam?'"

"No, but I'll contact vice and see what they know."

"I'm sending you some pictures right now. Tell me if you recognize anyone."

Kamu immediately acknowledged he knew the cop and the driver, an assistant DA named Morris.

Melvin interrupted. "The cop's on the move. He's just leaving the parking lot, headed back to Lahaina. Morris is headed in the opposite direction. I think I'll follow him." He signed off, and jotted down the make, model, and license plate of the ADA's car, then let a couple of cars pass by before pulling out to follow him.

He kept his distance so he wouldn't be noticed. When they reached the Kahalui/Kihei turnoff, Melvin was surprised to see the ADA turn toward Kihei. His office is in Wailuku, near Kahalui. The ADA pulled into Kihei's business district and parked at one of the large beachside hotels. Melvin found a parking space where he could watch. A few minutes later, a different police car pulled up beside the ADA. They, too, had a conversation. Melvin shot more photos with his cell, and sent them to Kamu.

The last leg of this curious journey ended when the ADA drove to the courthouse in Wailuku. He left his car in staff parking, and went into the building. Melvin parked and hurried after him. He wondered if the ADA was here on official business, or was making another contact. Once inside, the ADA took the elevator to the second floor offices of the District Attorney.

Just the Right Amount of Wrong

Melvin waited until the elevator cycled back down, then stopped at the second floor. There was a long bank of windows in the DA's Office, and Melvin could see his quarry sitting at a desk. Just as Melvin spotted him, the ADA pulled a large amount of cash out of his pocket and put it in a manila envelope. He sealed the flap, wrote something on the outside, and tucked it into the center drawer of his desk. He got up and walked toward the office door. Melvin moved back, out of his sight line.

He waited until the ADA entered the elevator, and then walked briskly into the office like he was supposed to be there. Within seconds he was at his desk, and opened the center drawer. The envelope was on top, with the name, "Stan" written in pen.

Melvin heard a noise, and looked up to see a pretty clerk standing in front of him, arms folded. He said, "Well, hello, little lady! Sorry I missed Mr. Morris, but I need to leave him some important information regarding the case we're working on. Looking for a pen. Ah!" He grabbed one out of the drawer and held it up.

The clerk wasn't impressed. "Be snappy about it. You aren't supposed to be back here." She watched Melvin write his note and lay it on the desk. When she turned and headed back to her desk, Melvin snatched up the paper and tucked it into his pocket as he quickly left.

He gave the clerk his most charming smile as he

passed her on his way to the elevator. It seemed forever before the door finally slid open. He could feel the clerk's stare piercing his back while he waited.

He drove the rental car back to the agency, and said he would like a different car as this one was not comfortable for him to drive. Now in a generic white economy sedan, he would dissolve into the island woodwork. He drove to his hotel.

Kamu was the first person on his list of calls to make. When the detective came on the line, Melvin asked him if he knew the man in the second set of pictures he sent. He also relayed the name "Stan" that he had seen written on the envelope.

Kamu said, "Sorry. I've seen him before, but can't put a name on him at the moment. I'll check records and get back to you. As for 'Stan,' that's not ringing any bells either."

I answered my cell on the first ring. Without saying hello, Melvin asked, "Is it in your budget for me to call in a couple of acquaintances to help? I need someone to do some computer trace work. The detective has been providing some of the ID stuff, but we're probably going to have to go much deeper on some of the people we uncover. I'm beginning to sense this is a lot bigger than a couple of cops selling pot. It may also be prudent to get some muscle over here to cover my back side in case things get messy."

I didn't want to know what that meant. "That's fine. We can talk money back at the house. But Melvin, keep it legal, okay?"

"Um, sure, Boss."

He laid out the afternoon's adventure, and I felt the picture was coming into focus. Jimmy and his brother-in-law must have gotten caught up in the shifting drug scene. I thought about Danny's role, and would bet he was just a dumb kid who'd been in over his head. Maybe he'd threatened to snitch, and had to be killed to quiet him.

I shook my head. "So many loose ends," I lamented to no one in particular.

I called Dr. Revis, who confirmed the paint chips from the cave were a match to the police cruiser. "The white paint could be the same on a lot of Fords of the same year, but the primer attached to the paint was one generally used by repair shops."

"Hmmm. And what about the shoe print?"

"I made two latex molds. Closer measurements indicate the print was made by a size thirteen, soft-soled shoe."

"Good job, Dr. Revis. I'll be in touch."

I called Patty in and told her to forget about the white paint. I warned her the cops might not appreciate our looking into their affairs. It could get ugly.

"I'm not afraid of these local cops! Besides, I got this thing going with a big Samoan guy from Oahu. Ain't nobody gonna mess with me, while he's around."

"I would like you to keep mum on this case, from now on. I can sense we may be in some danger. We need to keep your Samoan friend on a need-to-know basis. Got it?"

"I understand." From her solemn expression, I think she did.

Symington called to let me know that Dr. Wong was finishing the autopsy on Isaac. Feeling like a mother hen, I suggested it might be a good idea for him to pack and head home to San Diego. I didn't want any more murders on my watch.

His pause was a little too long, and I heard regret when he replied, "Oh, I see. There must be a good reason for you to ask this, Harry." He sighed deeply. "Okay, you're probably right. I could use the extra time to brush up on several cases I'm a witness for, I'm sure. How about I stop by and get my stuff? I'll head out this evening and give you a call when I get to the airport."

I felt a pang of annoyance at the loss of Symington, but I'd rather he be alive and kicking than present and dead.

While I was on the phone with Symington, Melvin called. He told Patty that an associate of his was flying over in the morning, and to expect him at the office around eight o'clock.

He informed her, "His name is Tyler, and he will be staying with you and the boss, while I am on Maui."

I thanked Patty for relaying the message. It should be interesting to meet one of Melvin's "associates."

GARY CARR

CHAPTER 32

I unlocked the office door just before eight o'clock, and was startled to see a man, the size of my refrigerator, sitting in my office.

He stood and walked towards me. Just as I entertained the thought of running out in the street, he thrust a hand the size of a catcher's mitt in my direction.

"Name's Tyler. Melvin sent me."

I tentatively stuck out my hand. He clasped it very gently, and with a wicked smile, apologized for scaring me.

"I picked the lock and came in so no one would see me. Melvin taught me to stay out of sight."

That would be a great trick. I've never had a bodyguard before, but one the size of Tyler certainly made me feel safe–after I was certain he wasn't going to shove my head down inside my body. Once we got past the "introduction" I went to work and Tyler hung

211

out waiting for Melvin. He was quiet for a big man, and after an hour or so, I almost forgot he was in the office.

When Patty blustered in a little late, she stopped and stared at our silent but impressive guest. The two looked at each other, but neither of them spoke. Not one to be perplexed for very long, she shrugged and plopped down at her desk, ready to work. After an hour had passed without Tyler moving or saying anything, Patty broke the silence.

"Who's the new piece of furniture?"

Tyler laughed and gave a slight wave. "Name's Tyler Wilson. Melvin sent me to babysit you."

Bristling, Patty replied, "I don't need no damned babysitter."

"Take it easy, little lady," I said, adding a John Wayne drawl. "The investigation could get dangerous, and we may need our *babysitter*. I do concede, though, Melvin might be a tiny bit overprotective."

Patty gave Tyler a dour look before getting back to work.

Melvin called at 8:05 a.m. "He there, yet?"

"You mean the quiet giant you sent to my office?"

"Scared you, huh?" He laughed.

"Only a little," I grumbled.

"Think what he can do with someone he *doesn't* like."

"Yeah, I'm glad I'm one of the good guys."

"Let him hang out with you. He's pretty good at blending in, despite his size. With the cops and the DA's Office involved in all this, it's better to be safe than sorry."

I spent the majority of the morning on the phone with San Diego taking care of cases. It felt like I had my feet in alternate realities. Bustling city vs. balmy beach-land. So different and yet, the dregs of society acted like thread to connect the two worlds.

Symington called around noon. He was peevish. "Harry, why the quick exit?"

"Melvin thinks the cops and DA's Office are in cahoots selling drugs. He also thinks Officer Draper ran Danny off the road and may also be involved in Jimmy's and Isaac's deaths."

"Did you just say, 'in cahoots'?" His tone had softened a little.

"I guess my penchant for old John Wayne westerns is showing today. Seriously, I'm not sure you being here is safe at the moment. Melvin must agree about there being some danger, because he sent a mountain from Oahu to be my bodyguard."

He whistled. "I knew something had to be up. Wish I could be there for the final inning. Keep me in the loop, will you? I want to know how this all works out."

I assured him I would. "You're a good man, Symington. Thanks for everything."

213

As the afternoon drew on, my empty stomach roiled loud enough for Tyler to glance at me over his Popular Mechanics magazine. After one particularly boisterous episode, I told Tyler I was going over to the store for something to eat. He seemed relieved.

"Want something?"

"Meat!"

Why was I not surprised?

I asked Patty if she needed anything. She kept typing at her computer and said, "Anything sweet will do, thanks."

When I crossed the street, I noticed officers Draper and Davis sitting in their parked patrol car. They averted their gazes when I looked at them. I got the feeling they'd been watching my office. I wondered if they'd been there all day, and a slight chill ran down my spine. When I emerged from Friendly's with arms full of grocery bags, I noticed that the officers had gotten out of the cruiser and were now sitting on the planter in front of the store. They were talking with one of the old regulars who had homesteaded that spot. As I passed, they rose and flanked me on each side.

"Hello," I said, looking from one to the other. "What's going on?"

Draper quietly growled, "We're just making sure

nothing happens to you. Sometimes when people know too much of things they shouldn't, they have *accidents*. We wouldn't want a fellow member of the law profession to get hurt."

Just as I was working up the courage to bluster, two large hands clasped each cop by the back of the neck, and picked them up off the ground.

"What you want me to do with these pigs, Boss?" My new bodyguard lifted the 200 pound men like they were cereal boxes.

Peering around, I loudly whispered, "Put them down, Tyler. We were just having a friendly chat."

Tyler spoke softly. "I know what I heard. I don't like them threatening you."

Gaining confidence, I smiled at the two dangling cops and said, "Really, Tyler, put the nice men down."

The massive paws released their grip on the officers. Anger and embarrassment boiled up from their collars and turned their faces red. "Certainly you boys wouldn't threaten an upstanding citizen like me, would you?"

They responded in unison, "No, sir!"

"That's what I thought." Nodding to Tyler, I said, "I believe we have an understanding, now."

They backed away and hurried to their car.

I called after them, "You tell your boss he's not screwing around with amateurs. We are going to get to the bottom of these murders, and when we do, you and a lot of others are going to jail."

I looked at Tyler and grinned. "I could get used to this. And where did you come from? I had no idea you were around."

"I told you, Melvin taught me to stay out of sight."

Tyler and I went back to the office, and I put the groceries in the refrigerator in the back room. Then, I called Melvin to tell him what just happened.

"Can you believe those two, threatening me in public?"

"And you told them their boss better watch out?"

"Oh, yeah. I guess I should have kept my mouth shut. I was kind of mad."

Melvin said, "Happens to the best of us. Now you know why I sent Tyler over. I have some more friends I can bring over, if you think we need them."

"No, Tyler should be sufficient. Patty has a new Samoan boyfriend to guard her. Taniko's family isn't a threat, now that Jimmy and Isaac are dead. What about you? Did you get someone to watch your back?"

"Already taken care of."

"Any luck on finding 'Stan'?" I asked.

"Not yet, but I have been on the ADA like a shadow. In fact, I'm tailing him right now. He's headed toward Wailuku with a large briefcase, and I'm betting it contains the manila envelope with all that money."

Melvin and I discussed whether to share with Kamu Dr. Revis's confirmation that the white paint chips found at the crime scenes matched the cruiser. We decided to hold back for the moment. Kamu seemed to be a genuine ally, but at this point we need to be sure of who we can trust Best to be cautious.

"However," I said, "It's a good idea to call the detective and tell him about Draper and Davis."

Melvin agreed. "Depending on his reaction to the cops threatening you, we will get our answer as to which side of the fence he is on."

Kamu answered his phone with, "Hello, Mr. Walters. I was just getting ready to call you."

I filled him in on what had happened with Draper and Davis. "Can you believe they actually threatened me?"

"In a heartbeat," he said. "They have pretty much had the run of the island for some time. I've been trying to tie them into the drug business for several months. I just didn't think they were into murder."

He added, "I saw Symington at the airport. Did he go to Oahu?"

I said, "No. He went back to San Diego. He wrapped up all the tests with Wong, and had to get back to his business."

217

"Good. I was concerned about him, as well. He's a lot better off in California.

"I put some pressure on Jimmy's friends, Lono Barton and Moses Silva. They are afraid of something–maybe the cops. When I told them I was after the cops, they relaxed and said there were two that operated here. They didn't name names, but I think we both know who they are.

"I'm going to need help arresting them. I think I'll call a couple of guys on Maui. Maybe they can fly in today. After we interview those two, perhaps we'll have some answers to the murders."

"Is that a good idea? Couldn't they lead us to other contacts?"

"I doubt it. I think they are just bottom rungs on the ladder. Now that they know we are onto them, I don't think they are going to do anything stupid. Like Draper told you, people who know too much get hurt. They'll gladly go to jail. Maybe I can make a deal with them in exchange for information. And Melvin has some good leads on Maui which these two clowns don't know about, or they would have skipped by now!"

"Melvin's growing on you, huh?"

The detective took a moment before answering. "Yeah. He's good at what he does. You can tell him I said that, too."

When I called Melvin and relayed Kamu's next moves, he thought arresting the two cops was a good idea, and may lessen the danger to me. I told him what Kamu had said about his work, but all Melvin did was grunt.

GARY CARR

CHAPTER 33

The ADA was on the move, again. Melvin had just watched him park his car. Now, with his briefcase in hand, he entered the offices of the Maui County Department of Public Safety and took the elevator to the third floor. Melvin had grabbed his camera, hung it around his neck, and followed him into the building. He trailed behind as the ADA emerged from the elevator and walked about halfway down the hallway, then entered a door on the left. Melvin's eyes quickly scanned his surroundings and he casually approached the directory sign on the wall that listed the offices and their occupants on that floor. There, in bold letters, was the name, "Stanley Johnson, Director of the Hawaiian Drug Control Office." Aha!

Melvin pretended to get a call on his cell phone, and took a picture of the board. He then strolled up to the information desk just beyond, and asked if there

221

was a restroom he could use. He said he had an appointment with Mr. Johnson, but really needed to go to the men's room first. The receptionist pointed down the hall to a sign that read KANE. Melvin smiled and politely thanked the lady behind the desk as he wandered toward the restroom.

Just off the hallway across from the restroom, a small alcove opened to a recessed glass entrance leading to a suite of offices where the Hawaiian Drug Control Office was located. Melvin looked around and stepped into the alcove. As her peered in, he could see across the reception lobby into an executive office located just behind the reception area. There was no one sitting at the front desk at the moment, and the door to the office behind it was partially open–open enough to allow him to see the ADA set his briefcase on the desk and lift the lid. He pulled out a manila envelope and passed it to a man Melvin assumed was Stanley Johnson, the director. Just as the exchange happened, Melvin quickly leveled his camera, zoomed in on the image and snapped a couple of fast pictures. A perfect Kodak moment–or so Melvin thought.

Something must have caught Johnson's eye, for at the exact moment, he swiveled his head and looked directly at Melvin. Melvin knew he had been made!

He dashed into the stairwell, then out of the building and onto the street. Heavy footsteps pounded the sidewalk behind him but he didn't turn around to look. He forced his legs to keep pumping him forward and raked his fingers through his pocket for his keys as he raced across the parking lot toward his car. He clicked the automatic lock. It chirped and he jumped in and rammed the key into the ignition. He sped out of the parking lot, his tires squealing as they hugged the concrete. He didn't slow down or look behind him until he was well out on the main road. When he finally did glance up, he cursed at his rear-view mirror. There was no mistake. The ADA's car was not far behind. Fortunately, Melvin was excellent at evasive maneuvers. He stomped on the accelerator, spun the wheel and took off like a shot. He soon lost his pursuer.

When he was sure he was alone, he pulled into a small parking lot and quickly wiped the car clean. He pulled wires from under the dash to make it look like someone had hot-wired the car before he yanked his duffel bag out of the trunk and slung it over his shoulder. From there he nonchalantly walked to the nearest bus stop.

When he disembarked at the center of Kahalui, he called the police. He told the operator he was afraid someone had stolen his rental car, and wanted to report it. She said an officer would be by shortly to help him. When an officer arrived, Melvin gave him a story of parking the car to do some shopping, and after two hours he returned to find his car gone.

The officer offered to take him to the rental

agency. While Melvin was again recounting his "story," to the young male clerk, ADA Morris and two cops showed up. They pushed Melvin aside, flashed credentials at the startled clerk, and demanded to see the agency records. One of the policemen said they'd just recovered one of their rental cars, and it may have been involved in a crime. The young man behind the counter asked if it was a white Chevy Malibu.

Morris said, "Yes. How'd you know?"

The clerk pointed to me, "That was the car he rented. He just reported it stolen."

Morris looked at Melvin. Melvin held his breath hoping the only thing the director saw was a partial face behind a camera. Melvin relaxed a bit. ADA Morris didn't seem to recognize him. He asked, "What time was the car stolen?"

Melvin answered "At about nine, I think. I was doing some shopping, for about an hour, maybe more, and when I returned, my car was gone." Melvin added just the right amount of indignation to his words.

"We'll need the car to be processed," he told the clerk. "We'll get it back to you, when we are done. Got the spare key?"

The clerk picked up the keys Melvin had just given him, and tossed them to the ADA. Morris grabbed them, and the trio left without a backward look.

Just the Right Amount of Wrong

Melvin casually turned toward the window, and made a mental note of the patrol car number. How many cops are involved in this? he wondered.

The clerk asked Melvin, "Sir, do you want to rent another car?"

"That would be great."

Melvin signed the paperwork and drove out of the lot in a ubiquitous compact Mazda. He drove a couple of blocks and pulled off the road near a public park. He fished his camera out of his duffle bag to see if he got a clear picture of the exchange. Satisfied–and relieved that he had captured the detail, he went in search of a photo shop where he could get his photos printed. As he headed back out on the road, he called two of his associates and asked them to meet him at his hotel. He advised them not to dally because the "game was afoot," the code meaning come prepared for anything.

The first to knock on Melvin's door was Roy. He was just a bit taller than Melvin–close to six feet, and carried his one hundred ninety-five pounds with confidence. His cocoa tan hair with graying temples framed a rugged face. Dressed in jeans, flip flops, and a muted aloha shirt, he looked like every other Hawaiian on the island. If you examined his face closely, however, you'd see the road map of a lifestyle very different from island laissez faire. Small scars etched his face, thanks to a bar fight, his nose was slightly off center, and he suffered from cauliflower ear. Roy's wide, friendly smile was disarming, an unwitting precursor to deadly attack. He'd punched the lights out of many unsuspecting miscreants.

Melvin bid him come in, and gave him a big hug. He was pleased to feel the pistol tucked in his back waistband under the shirt.

The second to arrive was Jess. He could have been Tyler's twin. He towered over Melvin, and outweighed him by a hundred pounds. Melvin knew from experience his size did not impede his agility and speed. And he could break through any door, no matter how heavy or barricaded it was. In his line of work, that came in handy more often than you'd think.

He was of Hawaiian-Chinese heritage, and had been raised in Honolulu's China Town. Like Melvin, he was a master of several languages, including Hawaiian and Pidgin. Melvin welcomed him inside, and asked if he was prepared for the task at hand. The big man revealed the butt of a nine millimeter tucked under his shirt, and then gestured there was more to see. He pulled up his left pant leg to show a large knife strapped to his calf, and then pulled up his right pant leg to display a .38 caliber Saturday Night Special, holstered there.

"Good to see you both," Melvin said, as he led them to the small living area. Laid out on the wicker coffee table was an array of photos. The couch groaned when Jess sat down. He gave the other two men an unapologetic shrug. Melvin showed them the photos of Stanley Johnson, ADA Morris, and the two cops, who had been at the car rental office. He briefed them on everything that had happened, from the murders, to fleeing the ADA earlier that day. When he finished, he instructed Roy to follow Morris. Jess was assigned cop-watching duty. Melvin said he would tail Stanley Johnson. He provided each of them with burn phones, and the phone numbers they needed to be in contact.

"Don't use the cells unless absolutely necessary. I'm checking out of this hotel, and will change my location each day. I'll text you each afternoon at three o'clock with my new location. Of course, if something important happens, contact me immediately."

As he led the two men to the door, he said, "Take care, Roy… Jess."

CHAPTER 34

Tyler jammed himself into the front seat of my car and made a feeble attempt at fastening the seat belt. When he found it to be six inches too short, he cocked an eyebrow at me.

"Drive carefully. I'm not buckled up."

I answered back, wryly. "Not a problem. There are only a couple of spots on this end of the island where you can drive more than thirty-five miles per hour."

Even though I was driving carefully, Tyler gripped the dashboard hard enough to leave dents. I guess he didn't like cars. When I pulled to a stop in my driveway, Tyler quickly opened the door and hauled himself out, mumbling something about how he hated small cars. He said, "I'm claustrophobic."

"I imagine someone your size would be."

He grabbed the groceries before slamming the door shut. I shut off the car and climbed out. He

229

peered around like an attack dog sniffing for danger while I opened the front door.

After dumping the groceries onto the kitchen counter, he did a thorough search of my house. It took only a few minutes for him to get the lay of the land. He pointed out that since we were at the end of the street, we should be able to see any questionable vehicles. Anyone approaching on foot would have to cross the bridge from the garage to the house, or descend a steep gravel hillside. I proudly showed Tyler my "alarm system" and told him how it worked. Straight-faced, Tyler asked if I'd mind if he added his own touches.

At my "sure," he asked if I had any boards in the garage, and some nails or screws. I took him to the garage, and he selected three boards, each about as long as the width of the doorway. He drove nails and screws through the board so that their points protruded above the surface like little spikes. He put one of these tack strips in front of each door and warned me not to forget they were there. Next he took my fish line and strung it across each door about neck high. Tyler insisted we close and lock all doors and windows. With all this fuss, I began to feel maybe I was in danger, even with Tyler around.

Expecting Tyler to relax on the couch after all that hard work, he surprised me when he headed to the kitchen, and started putting groceries away. He held up a hand when I tried to help, and shooed me into the living room.

"Watch some TV. Relax, Boss. I'm fixing you dinner tonight."

Two hours later, I was treated to a massive meal of roast pork, rice, salad, and fresh papaya. Tyler waited while I took my share, then he proceeded to load the rest onto his plate. There were no leftovers that night, nor did I anticipate there would be any.

I slept fitfully, barely escaping time and again, some dark dream stranger trying to break into my home. Each time I awoke, I saw Tyler quietly pacing outside my door. Around five thirty a.m., I dragged myself out of bed. I smelled coffee brewing, and another delicious aroma. When I entered the kitchen, Tyler was fixing a breakfast of rice and fish.

Looking like this was his kitchen, not mine, he greeted me. "Morning, Boss. Care for some coffee?"

I nodded, groggily, and held out my hand. "Hope you made it strong. I didn't get much sleep."

"It should put hair on your chest," he said, placing a steaming mug in my hand. "Did I keep you awake with my pacing?"

I sipped the coffee, gratefully. "No, I think I'm just nervous. I'm not used to being threatened." Tyler handed me a plate of fish and rice. My mouth started watering. "What about you? Did you get any sleep," I asked around savory mouthfuls.

"I don't sleep much when I'm working."

After one of the best breakfasts I've had in a

231

long time, I told Tyler we were staying home today. We could work in my home office, I reasoned, and avoid offering my enemies a public opportunity to make good on their threats. I called Patty and told her to stay home and enjoy her time studying. She said she'd rather enjoy her new boyfriend.

"Too much information, Patty!"

Rather than doing office work, Tyler and I spent the day completing chores around the place, and talking about how he came to know Melvin. I learned they had served in the same army unit, and Melvin was his son's godfather. He hoped we could finish this up so they could all go back to Oahu in time to celebrate his son's first birthday.

Melvin and his men kept busy on Maui. Melvin got more photographs of Stanley Johnson receiving envelopes from two other contacts. The two new guys weren't cops, or at least not uniformed ones. Jess had taken enough photos of the cops dealing drugs to make a family album. Roy had struggled to keep up with the ADA, whose case activity had them both in and out of the courthouse many times. Nothing out of the ordinary happened until just before three o'clock, when Morris entered the parking lot and met with a man in an unmarked police car. Roy snapped a photo just as an envelope exchanged hands.

Roy's and Jess's cell phones alerted them promptly at three p.m. that Melvin had texted them. They noted his new location, and that he would be calling in five minutes on a conference call.

When the call was set up, Melvin asked for summaries of their findings. Delighted with the reports, he said to meet him at his hotel at five, and he would spot them dinner. Melvin met them in the lobby and drove them to Kihei for a fresh seafood meal at one of his favorite beachside restaurants. Over steaming plates, Roy and Jess passed their camera memory cards to Melvin and then went into more detail of their daylong surveillances.

As he listened, Melvin ate his Maui onion encrusted ahi steak, nodding every once in a while.

When their reports were done, he wiped his mouth with a napkin and said, "I think I need to get ahold of the Boss and get him up to speed. He'll give me instructions on where to go from here."

After he placed his credit card in the receipt folder for the waitress, he sat back satisfied. "Boys, you never let me down. We have a little more to do, and then you two can get back to your families and a normal life."

When they left the restaurant, Melvin told Roy and Jess he'd call them tomorrow. He gazed around at the deepening sunset. "I think I'll take a walk on the beach–maybe do some figuring." He didn't tell them he'd come up with a somewhat dangerous plan to capture a murderer. He wanted to make sure he wasn't going to make things worse.

My day with Tyler was relaxing, and I was able to get my thoughts back in order. Maybe it was the stress free day, but as I was folding my freshly washed socks, I suddenly remembered the dinner at Roland's, after Tala was released. It was strange that Draper and Davis had just shown up. And when that call came in, only Draper had left. Davis had stayed. Why it didn't register at the time as off-kilter, I didn't know.

I surmised a possibility. Maybe Draper had left to find Danny and run him off the road. It also presented an opportunity for Davis to pick up a knife from Roland's food table. I decided to call Kamu and see what he thought.

When Kamu answered his cell, he said, "It's your nickel!"

"Good afternoon to you, too, Kamu." I switched ears, and got comfortable on the couch. "Say, do you have any spare time this afternoon? I have an idea I want to share with you."

"Why not tell me right now?"

"I'd rather speak face to face. Can you meet me at my office?

There was a rustle of paper in my ear. "I've got a little more paperwork to finish up, and then I'll be there. Around four p.m.?"

A half an hour. "Works for me! Thanks, Kamu."

When I told Tyler we were going back to the office, he stepped outside and checked all around the car. As I approached, he declared it safe. He repeated his dash-clamping routine all the way to town.

Kamu was talking to the real estate folks next door to my office when we arrived. Eyeing Tyler warily, he asked, "What did you want to talk about?"

"I wanted to talk here so we could look at the files, if need be. I had an idea today, and was hoping to get your thoughts. What if Draper and Davis are not just minions for whoever is trying to control things here on Molokai, but are connected to all three deaths? One or both of them were present at each of them. Why, they could have planted or destroyed evidence. While I was working around the house, I remembered they had been at the Rolands' house the night of the celebration. Draper left Davis there and may have caused Danny's death."

Kamu interjected, "I didn't know they were at Rolands', but what you are saying makes sense to me. Problem is, how do we prove it?"

"I think I have a plan. Have you arrested those two, yet? If not, I have a request."

Kamu shifted on the couch, and shook his head. "They are at the magistrate's giving testimony on a traffic accident. I have the officers from Maui waiting outside to arrest them, when the hearing is over. What do you need, Harry?"

I said, "If you can hold off arresting them until Tyler and I can, well-uh, "interview" them, I would appreciate it."

He looked at me quizzically. "Interview them?"

I gestured toward Tyler. "You may not know it, but my friend here has quite a way with words. Just yesterday, he convinced our two cop friends that it wasn't a good idea for them to threaten me. We just need a little time for a conversation."

Kamu looked at Tyler, who remained by the door, expressionless. "They will be out of court at five. You have until six, and then my guys get them. Still breathing and in one piece, if you don't mind. I will let my guys know. Call me when you are finished with your interview."

When Kamu left, Tyler cracked his knuckles. "Do you want them to confess to the murders, or every crime that has ever been committed on Molokai?"

"The murders will do, braddah. Let's head to the Magistrate's Office."

Tyler gripped the dashboard and closed his eyes, as we drove to the block building that housed the Magistrate's Office. We got there just as Draper and Davis left the building. We exited my car, but when I looked around, I was alone. My hefty sidekick had once again done his disappearing act. Knowing he must be somewhere near, I squared my shoulders and approached the men.

"Hello, officers."

They looked frantically around, and seeing no monsters, their faces reflected relief.

Draper blustered. "What did you do with Superman?"

His next jeer was squelched, as Tyler clamped their necks in his death grip. I mentally gave him the thumbs up sign. Tyler half carried, half dragged them over to the public restrooms and tossed both of them inside. He turned toward me and indicated I should stay where I was. Before he gently closed the door, he told me, "This won't take long."

A few loud clangs and thuds, then a groan, echoed behind the closed door. I stood there chewing my cuticles, feeling glad I was on this side of the door. When it opened, Tyler stepped out carrying the two cops under his arms. They weren't moving.

"Are they alive?" I asked, concerned he had overdone it.

He looked at first one and then the other. "Of course. They'll come around in a little while. Where do you want me to put them?"

"Take them over to their patrol car, and I'll call Kamu. Did they confess to the murders?"

"Oh yeah, they said this all stems back to a Maui assistant district attorney named Morris. He hired

Isaac to kill Jimmy, who'd snooped around until he found out who the real bigwigs of the island's drug trade were. Morris heard Isaac had a beef with the dude, and when approached, he jumped at the chance to off him. Isaac's death, they told me, was a necessity. Tying up loose ends, I'd guess."

"What about Danny's death? Did they have anything to do with it?" I asked.

"They wouldn't cop to that. Maybe his death was purely accidental. These goons promised to officially confess if we get them sentenced to a mainland prison. They're afraid they won't last very long in the Maui prison. I told them there are no guarantees, and then they decided to take a nap."

Finally! This takes the girls off the hook. I immediately called Taniko.

"I have great news. We know who killed Jimmy and Isaac, and you'll be happy to know it wasn't the girls. Forgive me for telling you over the phone rather than in person, but I thought you would like to know as soon as possible."

"Oh, thank God! We thought we were going to have to-- I mean, who was it?"

I was too full of adrenaline to notice then, her words. That would come later, in the middle of the night, as these things often do. Without going into great detail, I told her what I'd just learned.

"It looks like Danny's death really was an accident. I will get with you in person as soon as possible to clear up all the legal matters and give you full details on what happened. Right now, I'm tied up with some other matters related to all this."

"Thank you, Harry!" There was joy in the words.

"My sincere condolences to you and your family, Taniko. Perhaps you can move on, now, and have a happy life."

"All because of you, Harry. I will always remember what you did for us."

I felt a little like John Wayne, at that moment.

GARY CARR

CHAPTER 35

"Uh oh, I've got company," Melvin whispered into the phone. We had been discussing Draper's and Davis's confession and where to go from there. In the background, I heard a loud knock.

"Maui Police, open up."

Melvin replied, "Just a moment." I heard what sounded like a door hitting a wall, and then Melvin spoke with a thick Asian accent.

"Hey, you can't just barge in here, officers! I know my rights!"

Another door slam, and an authoritative voice said, "Cut the act. We've been following you all afternoon. Who the hell are you?"

I heard him give his phony name. He must have offered his driver's license, for he said, "Here, check my ID."

"Knock it off, clown. Are you military or a federal cop?"

Melvin was playing it dumb. "What are you talking about? I'm a businessman from Oahu. I came over to Maui for few days' vacation, and to look for business locations. I'm thinking of expanding."

Dismayed, I heard one officer say to another, "Slap the cuffs on him. We'll take him to Mr. Johnson, and he can find out why this guy has been following him."

Melvin, accent still in place, pleaded, "I don't know what you mean! Here, I am talking with my attorney. You tell him you are arresting me."

A deep voice filled the phone. "This is the Maui Police, who is this?"

"Harold Walters. I'm Mr. Saito's attorney. What's happening?"

The officer said, "We're taking Mr. Saito in for questioning on a drug case. He'll be at the Wailuku Correctional Facility."

I said I wanted to speak to my client first, and he put Melvin on the phone. Melvin kept up the ruse, and said, "Mr. Walters, I have done nothing. Can you help me?"

I told him to repeat out loud: "Right. Don't say anything until you get here."

He parroted what I said and added, "Can you call Tyler and my family, and tell them what's going on?"

I said, "Got it. We'll get there as soon as we can. Does Tyler know how to contact 'the family'?"

"Yes. Thank you." The phone went dead.

Tyler absorbed the details, as I relayed them. He grabbed my cell, and made a call. After he was done, I phoned Kamu, and told him what happened with Melvin, and also what Draper and Davis had confessed to. He offered to take Tyler and me to Maui on the police plane and said we could leave right away.

I informed Tyler of our ride to Maui, and he grabbed my cell again. Before he rang off, he had arranged for Roy and Jess to meet us at Kahalui Airport.

At the airport, Draper and Davis were shackled as they stepped into the plane. We were seated as they passed me. They avoided eye contact with both of us, but gave Tyler, who took up two seats, a wide berth as they shuffled to the back of the plane. Kamu stood guard at the door. The two officers who'd escorted the prisoners aboard told him they would stay on the island until replacements arrived. He nodded and thanked them.

Tyler squinched his eyes shut the entire flight to Maui. When the plane took off, I thought he was going to hyperventilate. Kamu seemed bemused by this show of cowardliness from a seasoned bodyguard.

When we had reached cruising altitude, Kamu undid his seatbelt and headed back towards Draper and Davis. I could hear him shooting questions at them. I sure hoped he could squeeze every last drop of information they had pertaining to the murders. I leaned a little farther out into the aisle to catch the conversation.

"Tell me about your connection to the murders of Jimmy Pualani and Isaac Roland. They reiterated that ADA Morris was their boss, but added this went higher up. To Kamu's question, they replied they didn't know how high up. Their need-to-know level stopped at Morris.

"You say Isaac killed Jimmy, but who killed Isaac?"

I noticed it took a long time before Draper spoke up.

"It was self-defense." He took a deep breath. "Things just got out of control!"

Davis picked up the story. "We'd dropped by the celebration at Isaac's house, but when we got the call about Danny selling dope outside of his own territory, Draper told me to stay and enjoy the grub. After Draper left, Isaac pulled me aside, and said he needed to talk to us, but not then with family around. He arranged for us to meet that night, at the cave. He said he had an envelope to deliver to Maui. But, we were at Danny's accident for hours, and missed our rendezvous.

"Several nights later, he called me and insisted we meet. When we arrived at the cave, he got out of his car and came towards us. I didn't see any envelope and demanded to know what was going on.

Isaac pulled out a big knife and pointed it at us. He said he'd thought it was a good thing to kill Jimmy, but now that he had time to think about it, he could see this had just been a ploy to lessen the competition for the drug trade on the island. He said maybe he was next on Morris' list, and he wasn't going to stand for it. Not without taking a few down with him.

"I'd managed to get close to Isaac and grabbed for his arm and wrist. I was able to pry the knife out of his hand, and it fell to the ground. When I bent over to pick it up, Isaac pushed me and took my revolver. He aimed it at Draper. I reached for the knife and lunged at him. Before I knew it, I'd stabbed him in the back." He looked down at his shackles. "I just wanted to stop Isaac from shooting my partner."

Kamu asked, "What happened next?"

"We dragged Isaac's body to the back of the cave, and cleaned up the scene. Then, we got the hell out of there! Your call brought us back."

Draper interjected, "We'll plead guilty to manslaughter, but no way did we murder anyone."

"Did you kill Danny Ipo?"

Draper piped up, "That was purely an accident! I got a call from one of my informants that Danny was at Paddler's trying to sell pot. I was ordered to stop him, so I left Isaac's and rushed into town to catch him. When he saw my car, he jumped in his truck and took off. I followed him. All I wanted to do was pull him over and warn him to stay in his own territory.

245

He must have panicked. I pulled alongside his truck, and he turned into me. I hit the brakes, but his fender hit my front fender, and it spun his truck. He lost control, and went down the embankment."

"You boys are in a heap of trouble. I sure hope you have good lawyers." He eyed me. "At least as good as Mr. Walters, here." Kamu returned to his seat, as the plane started to descend.

A police van was waiting when we disembarked. It would take the prisoners to jail. Kamu hopped into the passenger seat, and waved a farewell to us.

"Keep me posted, okay?"

"Don't worry. I've got a feeling we're just getting started."

As he drove off, a dark SUV pulled up. I watched as two men extricated themselves from their seatbelts and walked toward us. The sleek, tall one said, "Aloha, Tyler." He held out his hand to me. I shook it, as he said, "I'm Roy and," he pointed to a man who made two of me, "this is Jess."

"Nice to meet you. I'm Harry, Harold Walters."

Roy showed his perfectly aligned teeth in a humorless smile. "How can we help you, Mr. Walters?"

"If you don't mind, I need a ride to the Maui Correctional Facility to get Melvin out of hot water."

The suspension on the SUV groaned when the half-ton of humanity climbed in. Following a brief discussion, it was decided Roy would stay with me.

Jess and Tyler would "take care" of some errands. The term, "plausible deniability" flitted through my mind, and I chose not to ask what errands they were talking about. The vehicle stopped in front of the correctional facility, and Roy and I got out. Then it sped away into the darkness.

We went in, and I presented my credentials to the jailer on duty. I asked to confer with my client. While Roy remained in the waiting room, I was ushered into a small ante room. Melvin was already seated. He explained under his breath why he thought Stanley Johnson headed the drug ring.

He said, "The ADA and at least four cops are involved—the two who arrested me and the two I photographed."

"Right," I said. "Now, let's get you out of here. Do you think they have anything to keep you here?"

"No," he replied, "but who knows what phony evidence they might manufacture."

I patted his shoulder. "Well then, I guess it's time for our little family to beat them at their own game!"

Melvin peered at me. "What have you got in mind?"

I recounted in succinct terms how Tyler got confessions from the two Molokai cops, and that they were now in custody. I then told him that perhaps a similar interview with the ADA would get us some answers.

Melvin nodded. "We also have all the photo

evidence. If we can make sure the DA isn't involved in this, we could give him what we have, and let him run with it. Busting a corrupt government drug ring should be a golden ticket to being re-elected."

The ADA walked in, as I was getting ready to leave. He introduced himself as George Morris, and asked if I was Mr. Saito's attorney.

In seconds I'd sized the man up. His pristine clothing and smooth haircut showed someone who thrived in an orderly world, and yet I knew a part of his life was as messy as it got.

I acknowledged his introduction and told him my name. Oblivious to my insider knowledge, he asked if he could question my client. I said that was all right, and I re-seated myself.

Morris asked, "Mr. Saito, why were you following and photographing me?"

Melvin looked at me, and I nodded for him to answer. He replied, "I wasn't following you. I've never seen you before. I'm here on Maui taking photos and getting information about possible business development sites."

The ADA asked, "Who do you work for?"

"I have my own company."

"May I see the photos you took?"

Melvin huddled with me, and said he'd given the camera with the evidence to Roy, but he had anticipated something like this, and had another camera with property shots on it. It was at the hotel.

Just the Right Amount of Wrong

I told Morris, "Mr. Saito has nothing to hide. He left his camera with the hotel clerk for safekeeping. We will be happy to turn it over to you for inspection in our presence."

Morris took out a cell phone, and gave instructions to have the camera picked up, and brought to the jail right away. He passed the phone to Melvin to give permission to the clerk. Morris excused himself, saying he would return, as soon as the camera was delivered. Melvin and I spent the time going over the Molokai murders, and how we were going to approach the DA.

Morris finally reappeared, camera in hand, and placed it on the table. He asked permission to view the photos on the memory card. I gave my approval, knowing that he probably had already downloaded them to a computer before coming in. There were eighteen photos on the card. All were of buildings, streets, and only a few had people in them. Needless to say, none of the people was the ADA.

Satisfied that "Mr. Saito" was telling the truth, he explained that his office had received several threats because of drug cases he was trying. He had assigned officers to provide protection, and when they noticed Saito's car following him, and he taking pictures, they became suspicious.

Morris said, "I'm sorry for the inconvenience, Mr. Saito. I hope we haven't dampened your desire to start a business here on Maui. You're free to go."

He then turned to me and asked, "Mr. Walters, aren't you the attorney for the girl who was arrested for murder on Molokai?"

I said, "Yes. It seems the DA got a little too eager on that one. My client didn't have anything to do with it."

He replied, "I'll bet that was a break from your usual business on Molokai."

"Yeah," I said, "most of the time I work on real estate and business deals for folks like Mr. Saito." He is either fishing for information or just plain stupid, I thought. He should know all about me by now.

Roy stood up from his chair in the waiting area and joined me and Melvin. As we left the building, I told him Morris let "Mr. Saito" go, after reviewing the bogus photos.

Roy asked, "What shall I do with the photos and prints I stashed?"

Melvin answered, "Give Mr. Walters one set and mail the other to my office on Oahu."

I asked, "Does the photo shop have any copies?"

Melvin said, "No. It's all done on computers and copiers these days and they don't keep anything on file except the amount they charged and your name and address."

I asked, "What name did you use?"

He replied, "The rental agency clerk's. I don't think they're smart enough to look for an account in that name. And, even if they do, all they will get is a description of me and a phony address. That's why they wanted to catch me at the hotel." He laughed. "They had no clue we made copies and switched cameras so quickly."

As we waited for a taxi, I shared my concerns that Morris and Johnson might be on to us.

I asked Melvin, "Do you think we're safe?"

"They may try to dream up a way to have us arrested, but as far as physical harm, we've got that covered, just in case. From what you told me about the deaths on Molokai, the only intentional murder was Jimmy Pualani."

"And his murderer is dead."

GARY CARR

CHAPTER 36

Tyler and Jess joined us a few hours later at the hotel. They had been tailing Johnson, and had new evidence to share.

Tyler recounted their afternoon. "Johnson went to the Bank of Hawaii with the envelope, right after lunch. We followed him in, and stood in line right behind him and watched him fill out a deposit slip. He started to pass the deposit slip and envelope to the teller, and I bumped his shoulder nearly knocking him down. He dropped the envelope and slip on the floor. Jess pretended to catch him, while I picked up the slip and envelope. I handed it back, but not before I got the information on it.

"He was depositing forty-five thousand dollars into a company called 'Island Rainbow Development.' The account number is 0000247013.

"I profusely apologized to the gentleman for being clumsy, and then got out of there."

Jess added, "If you want dinner on Mr. Johnson, I have his wallet." He held up a black leather wallet embossed with the initials, S J. He ruffled through the neat bills. "He can afford it!"

Over a late dinner of Spam and melted cheese sandwiches, we discussed investigating whether the DA was trustworthy. His financials, as well as his political and public profiles, needed to be checked out. For the time being, Jess would track the DA, while Roy scoured the Internet for any information on the Island Rainbow Development Company. Melvin would keep tabs on Johnson. Jess would track the DA, I would find the two crooked cops, and Tyler would keep Morris, the ADA, in his sight.

The next morning, we parted ways. Roy stayed at home base to work his magic on the Internet. Melvin, Tyler, and I joined Jess in returning Johnson's wallet to the bank. The bank's security cameras had a record of him with Johnson, and even if they didn't catch his pickpocketing, they would have Tyler and him on tape.

It turned out Jess didn't even have to go into the bank. Just as he was about to go in, he ran into Johnson, going in, too. Jess exclaimed, "Aloha, Brah! You jus' da kine I been lookin' for!"

Johnson said, "Why is that?"

Jess responded, "You drop your wallet when you left yesterday, and I tried to catch you, but you disappear, man." He held out the wallet.

Johnson meticulously inspected the wallet, and then thanked Jess for being so honest. He withdrew a one hundred dollar bill, and held it out to Jess.

Jess gave him a genial smile and said, "You okay, dude! Aloha." He put his hands in his pocket, and whistled all the way back to the car. Climbing in the back seat, he held up the C-note to us. "Well, we didn't get dinner on him, but this should cover lunch."

We entered a nearby island eatery and opted for the usual plate lunch—two scoops of white rice, a scoop of macaroni salad, and for an entrée, we all chose lau lau pork. Jess and Tyler asked for seconds. For dessert, we ordered haupia, a delicious coconut pudding, and coffee. While we finished eating, we used a napkin to lay out the afternoon's goals.

After lunch, we went to the car rental agency. Melvin, Tyler, and I got our own vehicles, while Jess took the SUV. We separated and headed for our specified targets: Melvin to Johnson's office, Tyler tailed the ADA and Jess the DA. I took on the two cops.

It didn't take long for Roy to access Stanley Johnson's Island Rainbow Development account. He easily ferreted out his "Stan the Man" password. Johnson's ego was his downfall, Roy thought. He copied the account activity for the past three months, and printed it out. He called Melvin.

"I'm in. Most of the activity is bi-weekly deposits of close to one hundred thousand dollars. There are cash withdrawals of twenty-five hundred dollars two days before every deposit. The big money is a two hundred fifty thousand dollar transfer to an offshore bank in the Caymans. I'll try to get details on that account, but the chances are slim.

"I bet the twenty-five hundred withdrawals are for the ADA. The cops and other dealers probably take their cut off the top. If you talk with Tyler, see if he can get me the ADA's checkbook or account numbers, I'm putting all of this on a thumb drive, and sending it to Oahu this morning. I'll have copies for you and Walters also. What do you want me to do when I wrap up here?"

"Stay with Walters. I don't want anything happening to him. It's bad business to let the boss get hurt!"

CHAPTER 37

Jess picked up on District Attorney Akumu at his office. The morning passed with the normal flow of staff and visitors, and nothing caused Jess to take particular notice. At eleven thirty, Akumu left the office and drove to one of the larger hotels. Jess followed him in, and discovered the DA was the guest of honor at a political luncheon set up to raise funds for his campaign.

An attractive young lady approached Jess and handed him a campaign button and name tag. "Enjoy the luau," she said. "Your support will help us get Mr. Akumu another four years to clean up crime here in Maui County." Jess's ears perked up at the mention of a luau. He still had a fifty from Stanley Johnson's reward, and he noticed he was famished again. He could have a mid-afternoon snack and watch the DA, too.

He smiled at the young lady and handed her the

fifty. "We all need to work on the crime problem. I'm just doing what little I can."

Keeping an eye on the DA, he zeroed in on the buffet tables spread with Hawaiian luau cuisine. He proceeded to consume the value of his donation in appetizers alone, and then moved to the entrée table. He sat down at a table where he could still see the DA, but not be obvious. When the crowd had filled their plates and was seated, the DA addressed the audience. He thanked them for coming and for their generous donations. He touched on several cases he had brought to trial as a part of his "war on drugs" in Maui County. He also mentioned Tala Pualani's recent arrest and dismissal, and told the audience he would see the "Killer of Molokai" brought to justice.

Jess said under his breath, "With a lot of help, even if you haven't realized it, yet."

After his speech, the DA shook every hand he could find, thanking each donor with typical political jargon. When he finally reached Jess, he asked, "How was the luau?"

Jess answered, "It'll tide me over for a few hours."

The DA expanded his arms and said, "Please eat as much as you like. You helped pay for it!"

"Why, thank you very much!"

Jess tailed him back to the office and then home. With his binoculars, he could see Akumu enjoyed being with his wife and son. Jess had followed many guilty people, but the DA didn't have the same wizened cast to his eyes, the ever present alertness of someone looking over his shoulder. Still, he continued to watch and take photos. About ten thirty, the lights went out in the Akumu home, and Jess called Melvin with a report on his day. Melvin told him to get some sleep.

After a few hours of watching Stanley Johnson, Melvin concluded the man was a real piece of work. Today, Melvin's disguise was that of a rich businessman, fitting in with the other well-dressed, high-powered executives that peopled the upper floors of the building.

Leaning against a wall, perusing a copy of *The Star Advertiser*, he'd seen Johnson alienate almost everyone he contacted with a caustic wielding of power. His position as boss was loud and clear, demonstrated in his boorish mannerisms and conversation. Johnson's small frame probably housed a huge Napoleon complex, Melvin surmised.

Several undercover officers had visited Johnson at his office, but they seemed to be simply doing their job. Melvin snapped photos, and would have Roy do computer checks on all of them, to make sure.

Late afternoon, ADA Morris showed up. He and Johnson stepped out of the office and went into the bathroom, checking both directions before closing the door. Melvin sidled down the hall to listen. Through the door, he heard the two men having a heated argument.

"I don't care what happened on Molokai. We did what we had to do. You know that! Let the dust settle, and then we can set up our network over there."

Melvin noted Johnson seemed to be the alpha in this tryst.

Morris returned, "But the cops--!"

"Never mind the cops! They know what will happen if they talk. You just keep that damn DA's nose out of things!"

Melvin scooted into a recessed doorway, just as the bathroom door opened. He heard Morris say "Got it," and then the he walked past Melvin, looking straight ahead. Melvin fell in step with him, and followed him out the entrance and into the parking lot.

As he drove off, Melvin noticed some movement to his right, and caught a glimpse of Tyler. On his mark, as usual. They exchanged a nod.

CHAPTER 38

I drove to the old section of Kahalui and cruised by Walmart and Home Depot several times. No cops. From there, I casually drove by the park with the same results. I was about to give up when I saw a police car behind me. My nervous system instantly turned to jelly. I really do wonder if I'm cut out for this. I struggled for breath. It's all fine and dandy on paper, but facing corrupt cops with guns is really scary.

I pulled over and parked under a tree. The police car passed behind me, and I let out a sigh of relief. It wasn't them. Regrouping, I decided to go to the Wailuku and Iao Valley areas. Or, I could go home and forget all about this little adventure. While figuring out where I put my courage, I glanced to my right and nearly had a heart attack! There they were, coming down the street, right towards me. Flustered, I scooted down in my seat until they passed, and then

261

slowly pulled out to follow them.

They proceeded through a busy intersection, and I was a few cars back. I saw them pull over in front of a coffee shop. I looked around frantically for a place to stop. I saw the gas station and zipped in. Keeping my eye on the cop car, I stepped into the little glass enclosed office and asked for directions to Iao Valley. While the attendant named off several streets starting with the letter "K" and ending with "wai," I watched as one cop came out of the coffee shop carrying two Styrofoam cups of coffee. Time to get back on the tail. I thanked the attendant and scurried to my car.

I tried to remember all the tricks for following people that I'd seen on television. I stayed two cars back and didn't do anything to attract attention. This went on for several blocks. I was actually beginning to feel like a hunter. I liked it. I pondered this macho scenario, as hunter and prey moved into a less-populated part of town.

Commercial neighborhoods gave way to industrial buildings, enclosed by sagging chain link fences. Traffic was light, if not non-existent, on some streets. The hunter in me dissolved, as I realized I was lost. Ahead, I saw the patrol car signal, and make a right-hand turn at the intersection. Against my better judgment, I sped up a bit, so I wouldn't lose them. When I turned the corner, they were nowhere in sight.

Just the Right Amount of Wrong

Damn! Now what? I pushed the pedal to the floor, and glanced in parking lots as I flew past them. Still, I didn't see them. Each intersection revealed emptiness. In spite of my fear, an old cliché pushed its way to my mind. You know—the one about "there never being a cop around when you need one." I snickered.

My irreverence didn't last, though. I'd decided to backtrack. When I pulled into an alley between two buildings in order to switch directions, there they were. I hit the brakes, and backed out like my tires were on fire. The patrol's flashers came on, and their siren whooped a warning.

A voice came over the cruiser's PA system, blaring, "Stop the car, Walters! Step out of the vehicle, and keep your hands where we can see them."

I stopped. They knew my name! Both cops got out and pointed their guns at me. They walked carefully toward my car. I instinctively grabbed my cell phone, and punched Melvin's number on my speed dial. I put the phone in my shirt pocket, so Melvin could hear me if he answered.

I truly knew what "terrified" meant. I was so scared I could hardly walk. I was worried I'd do something wrong and they would just shoot me. Or worse, that I'd pee my pants. I didn't know which would be worse.

One of the cops approached me while the other

263

hung back. The one in back had a shotgun. The closest one ordered me to put my hands above my head and lean against the building. He patted me down, finding only my wallet and cell phone. He turned me around and handed them back to me. I noticed he had holstered his pistol. A quick glance at his partner told me he'd lowered his weapon, too.

He said, "Would you like to explain why you have been following us?"

I was shaking so badly I could hardly speak, but squeaked out, "I wasn't following you. W-what are you talking about?"

The officer's expression turned dark, and he shoved me against the wall.

"Start talking or we'll make you wish you had never seen Maui!"

Somewhere deep in my gelatinous fear I found a backbone, and adrenalin charged my anger. I pushed him away from me and said, "You two are the ones who are going to be sorry. When you brought my client in just to see what he had been taking pictures of, I figured you were up to something. I decided to follow you, and see what it was. I just sent your chief a couple of shots of you selling pot, when I stopped at that gas station."

The cop studied my face and then replied, "You dumb *haole*. We haven't sold any pot today. No way you could have taken any pictures. Besides, we've been watching you follow us most of the morning. I think you need to take a little ride with us. We have some beautiful ocean-view property we would like to show you. Get in the car!"

He turned and motioned toward the patrol car. He stopped short when a voice commanded, "Nobody's going anywhere."

I almost wept when I saw Roy standing behind the cop's partner with a pistol held to his right chin, just below the ear. Roy told the cop, "Hand Mr. Walters your gun belt and the spare on your ankle, and then come over here."

The cop hesitated, but then did as he was told. The next moment I was holding two guns. When the cop reached the car, Roy roughly jostled them both into handcuffs. When they were secured, he shoved them into the back seat of their cruiser. He walked over to me and said, "Relax, Boss. It's over." He took the guns from me, and put them in the cruiser's trunk.

"Over?" I said, following him. "You've got to be kidding. What in the hell are we going to do with two handcuffed cops?"

Roy laughed. "Why, take them back to the police station, naturally! Don't you agree, Melvin?"

A voice from my shirt pocket said, "Good idea, Roy. Take a picture of it, why don't you?"

I grabbed the cell and exclaimed, "Melvin? I didn't think I had gotten through to you!"

He laughed. "I've been listening the whole time. That was a pretty ballsy move, threatening them on a

265

bluff! We're going to have to give you some serious in-service if you're going to keep playing this game. That's enough learning for today. Roy will transport the bad guys to the cop shop. Why don't you follow him, and then you can bring Roy back to his car. Tell Roy to leave the envelope of photos I gave him on the front seat, and then turn the siren on. The police will find them soon enough. I'll see you both later."

I hung up, and then relayed the instructions to Roy.

"Got it!"

It suddenly hit me that I was a part of a successful sting operation. And, I was still in one piece. I could get used to this. As soon as my legs stopped wobbling.

Roy slapped me on the shoulder. "Let's go, Tiger!"

I followed the police car across town, and watched Roy park it a block away from the police department, on a quiet side street. I slid under a tree's shade, across the street. I expected him to hightail it out of there immediately, but the cruiser door remained shut. I started to get nervous, and then it occurred to me he was probably wiping the car down. He finally stepped out of the car, and through the open door, I could hear the cops yelling profanities at him and demanding he free them. Ignoring their rant, he locked both front doors and slammed them shut.

Two boys, I guessed to be eleven or twelve years

old, had approached the vehicle and watched the excitement. Roy motioned them to come over, and I saw them converse for a moment. Then Roy handed the boys some money. After a short wave in the cops' direction, he jogged across the street and got into the car.

I asked him, "Weren't you supposed to start the siren?"

"I gave those two boys one hundred bucks apiece to do it. That way we'll have plenty of time to get out of here."

Still worried, I asked, "What if they don't do it?"

"They'll do it! A hundred bucks is like a million dollars to kids that age. Besides, they told me they knew these two were bad cops. They've seen them dealing. I also told them not to describe me, and to say I was just some nice man making a citizen's arrest, and I didn't want to get involved. Those two cops aren't going to ID us. That would mean having to explain how they know us."

We were about two blocks away, in a residential area, when we heard the siren.

Tyler had been able to get a few more photos of Morris talking with Johnson. He had set up an observation post outside the DA's Office, and waited. None of the pictures would be incriminating, but they would help to prove in court the two of them met on a regular basis. When a siren sounded, Tyler's attention was drawn down the street. The next thing he saw was Morris and a number of other people exit the building to see why the siren was blaring. Tyler fell in behind Morris, slowing when the ADA joined several policemen on the sidewalk. Tyler fused with the throng of bystanders congregating by the cop car.

Along with the crowd, Tyler watched one officer work a "slim Jim" metal hook to open the locked car door. The blistering siren didn't bother him, but people around him had covered their ears. After a long, loud seven minutes, the officer finally got the door open. He reached in and shut the siren off. The crowd cheered.

Tyler saw, through the open door, a large envelope on the front seat. He moved closer, as the officer carefully picked it up and looked it over. Tyler used his telephoto lens to get a picture of it. Through the lens, he read the words, "TO THE CHIEF OF POLICE." Then the officer stepped away from the car, so other officers could remove the two cops from the back seat. He'd tucked the envelope under his arm.

About that time, Morris walked up to the officer with the envelope, and identified himself. "You find something interesting, Officer…" Morris peered at his badge. "Officer Ikaika? Morris positioned himself so he could read the envelope. The seasoned cop switched arms and said, "This is evidence, and it's addressed to the Chief. The DA's Office will get this when we're through processing it." Ikaika nearly spit out his reference to the DA's Office.

Morris replied, "No need to get irate, I was just curious. Besides, we're on the same team."

The cop sneered. "You guys have been screwing up a lot of our cases, lately. I've had several drug busts which were thrown out of court, and that murder case on Molokai made the DA's Office look stupid. Maybe a new DA will do a better job."

Morris smirked. "By far, a better job, officer. By far. "

Officer Ikaika looked at the ADA and scowled. "Have your boss contact the Chief," he said, and turned away.

"Hey, man, will do!"

Morris sauntered over to the curb, and took out his cell. Tyler scooted closer, and picked up most of the phone conversation Morris had.

"It's me, Stan. Cruz and Tamashiro were found a block from the police station handcuffed and locked in the back seat of their patrol car. There was a manila envelope addressed to the Chief on the front seat. I tried to take a look at it, but the cop who grabbed it got cocky, and wouldn't let me see it. Apparently, he's pissed at the DA's Office. If I get any more info, I'll call you." He listened for a moment, and then said, "They know enough to keep their yaps shut." He listened again and said, "I'll let you know, as soon as I can find out."

Morris snapped his cell shut and dropped it into his shirt pocket. He watched the officers being removed from their car.

He was surprised when Ikaika, apparently not feeling he should follow his own rules, opened the envelope and glanced at the contents. Holding the envelope up, he said, "Leave those cuffs on. From what I see in this envelope, these two are going to jail." He swiveled his gaze to Morris. "Looks like a couple of dirty cops are going to jail for selling drugs. That is, unless the DA's Office screws this one up, too!" Then he started a parade back to the police station.

Morris pulled out his phone, and walked back to his office. Tyler shadowed him.

"It's me, again. The cop just told me the envelope had photos of our guys selling drugs. Didn't you have someone with a camera picked up this morning?" He listened and then he said, "I'll track him down. We need to find out who's watching us. There is something going on." He listened, then said, "Could be an undercover DEA operation, or maybe the DA's got something going on because of those murders on Molokai. He's had Detective Kamu over there for a couple of weeks." He paused to listen again, and then said, "I'll get what I can, but Kamu and the DA have been close friends for a long time.

Right! I'll use one of the other phones to call you tonight."

Tyler followed Morris back to his office, and resumed his post outside. He called Melvin to give him a report on what had happened, and share the details of Morris' phone conversation. Melvin instructed Tyler to call it a day and head back to the hotel. He'd see him there later.

GARY CARR

CHAPTER 39

The view was good at Melvin's new hotel room. Not that anybody would be getting in much view time. We were meeting for a working dinner. When the gang was all there, we plowed through ten pizzas and several liters of soda in no time. It had been an exhausting day.

As my energy sagged, I wished I was on my quiet lanai, enjoying a mahi mahi sandwich, slathered with caper mayonnaise, and a chilled bottle of Prosecco. On the other hand, a thick slice of meat lover's wasn't so bad.

Melvin snapped his fingers in my face. "Come on back, Boss. We got work to do." He looked around at each of us. "They know someone is watching them. That is going to make what we do next twice as hard."

I gulped. "Twice as hard?"

He smiled at me. "You know, Boss. I think you

273

will be a lot more help on Molokai. If you're over there, it will make it look like you were just called to Maui to represent a client. I'll call one of our associates to stay with you, until further notice."

"Why not Tyler?"

"I think the danger has shifted from you to me. I need Tyler to protect me. Besides, my guy is already on Molokai. Patty's boyfriend," he answered my enquiring eyes. "He's one tough Samoan. Why don't you ask them both to stay with you?"

"Let Patty and her boyfriend stay with me?"

"Don't worry. When he's working he's a shadow, like Tyler.

"Guys, I have to admit today was way too exciting for me. I don't know how you do this for a living! I think I will be much more comfortable back behind my desk, making phone calls and solving problems with a pen. I appreciate Roy's saving my skin today, and I'm really going to miss your cooking, Tyler. As for the case, keep me in the loop, and I'll contact Kamu and the DA and find out what's going on with Draper and Davis. Oh, and the two cops we dropped on their doorstep, today."

Melvin said, "Thanks for everything! Can you stick around for tonight?"

I nodded, and then Melvin laid out the surveillance plans for the next day. "Let's get some rest. We may need it!"

Everyone but Melvin and I left for their

respective hotel rooms. When we were alone, Melvin said, "I want you to take this." He dug in his wallet and extracted five one-hundred dollar bills. He handed them to me. "From this point on, I no longer work for you. You work for me as my attorney."

"What's this all about, Melvin?"

He looked at me. "Are you my attorney?"

"Yes!" I took his money.

"I may be doing some things that are a little outside the law the next few days, and I want the lawyer-client confidentiality on my side if someone questions you.

"You're one of the most honest and decent lawyers I've ever worked with. You are willing to do what you need to see justice is done, and you do it within the law. You also protect your clients the same way. That's why you can represent me and use the confidentiality clause to stay inside your moral and legal boundaries."

I studied his face for a moment and said, "Just don't make too big a mess. I'd like to have you around a little longer."

GARY CARR

CHAPTER 40

I decided to take the ferry back to Molokai. I awoke early, after a fitful night on the couch. After breakfast, I said my goodbyes to Melvin and drove to Lahaina. Before turning in my rental car, I shopped for some gourmet food items, and then went to the drugstore for a case of Prosecco. I waited for the ferry at the Banyan Tree. As I sat there nibbling some Cerignola olives, I watched the human drama unfold before me. There were three different speeds of activity.

The tourists buzzed from kiosk to kiosk along the wharf, looking for the best deals that will succinctly portray their "memorable moments" in paradise. I knew they will leave here with their precious cargo, and then spend a trunk-load of money to see whales leap against the horizon, go fishing and deep-sea diving in spectacular waters, or sunbathe on a pristine, if not crowded, beach. For the rest of their

277

lives, they'll take out the souvenirs and pictures, and recreate those moments, again and again.

The local business owners and workers were a different story. They moved with a steady, purposeful gait around and through the flow of customers. Finally, the local citizens ensured the slow, easy pace of the islands was preserved. They seemed to be at peace with their roles, happy and un-phased by all the hustle and bustle around them.

Occasionally, a babbling eccentric, lop-sided drunk, or wigged-out druggie provided a distraction. Today was a case in point. An elderly Hawaiian, who had "found his Lord and Savior, Jesus Christ," was standing on the corner, proselytizing to the passing cars. Half an hour later, he drew under the shade of The Banyan Tree and found an empty spot on a bench. Pulling out a paper sack scrunched around a bottle, he took a couple swigs from its contents. He unstrapped the guitar on his back and started playing in the slack-key style of the islands. He was surprisingly good at it. His music drew a sizeable crowd, and I joined them in applauding when the man had finished a piece.

For the better part of an hour, he entertained with Hawaiian songs. During his breaks, which were plentiful, he preached. I was disgusted but not shocked when the crowd thinned out during these micro-sermons. Hardly anyone has time for God in their lives, anymore.

Just the Right Amount of Wrong

As they departed, some good souls dropped wadded, folded, and torn bills into his guitar case. It was getting close to the ferry departure, so I walked over to make a donation of my own. I'd really enjoyed the music.

As I approached the guitar case with a ten spot in my hand, the man quietly said, "That's not necessary, Mr. Walters. Melvin pays me quite well. I'll be around until you get on the ferry."

I stopped with my hand midway to the guitar case. I looked into intelligent dark eyes behind grimy glasses, and I realized nothing in my world recently was what it seemed. I smiled at him and dropped the money in. "It's my pleasure. We all need to help each other."

Seldom is the ferry ride pleasant. The Maui channel is usually very choppy, and creates a lot of seasick tourists. Still, the ride is interesting because of the people. A small crowd takes the ferry from Molokai early every morning, returns late at night. The men and women are part of the minimum wage grist which keeps the tourist mill turning. Many family groups use the boat time to sleep, and others share their daily experiences. When I get included in a conversation, which is rare, I'm amazed at how satisfied they are with their lot.

They truly are the people of "Aloha." A kind, loving, and tolerant people, yet they long for the old ways of living. For many of them, modern civilization offers no temptation. They epitomize the saying, "Don't change Molokai; let Molokai change you!"

As we docked, I saw Patty waiting for me. A huge Samoan stood beside her, shading her completely from the morning sun. I waved and stepped off the boat.

"Hello, Patty," I said, as I approached the couple.

Patty gave me a hug. "Harry, this is Honey Boy." Her hand rested on a brown forearm the size of my thigh. "Honey Boy, this is Harry Walters, my boss."

I looked up at him and held out my hand. "Aloha!"

"Aloha, sir," Honey Boy said. "Melvin asked me to pick you up."

"Thank you. Looks like the three of us are going to be spending some time together."

Patty giggled and said, "Won't that be nice?"

I replied, "Yes, it will." I held out the bag of groceries to Honey Boy, who cradled it like an infant, and I tucked the wine under my arm. "Let's head home."

As I walked to the parking lot, I scanned it to see if anyone was watching us. Honey Boy tapped me on the shoulder.

"We're okay, Mr. Walters. I've checked it all out, but it's nice you're staying alert."

CHAPTER 41

Detective Kamu and his hand-picked officers escorted Draper and Davis into booking soon after the two Maui cops were booked. Kamu caught sight of them being escorted away. He asked Billy, the jailer, what was going on.

"These two boys got nabbed by a citizen for dealing pot. Damnedest thing I ever heard of. They found them cuffed in the back seat of their own patrol car. Whoever collared them turned on the siren and locked them in the car."

Kamu immediately thought of Tyler, and the "conversation" he had with Draper and Davis. "Did anyone get a look at who did it?"

"A couple of young boys, but they were too excited to give us anything useful. They each had a different description of the guy. One thought he was a *haole*; the other said he looked like his dad. His dad is a little guy, about five foot nine, and there's no way

281

he or someone his size could have cuffed these two."

Kamu thanked Billy for the information. He finished the paperwork on his two cops, and Billy took them to a cell. Kamu asked the arresting officer about the two Maui cops. He was told about the envelope found on the front seat, with pictures of the cops selling drugs. When the cops were questioned about who brought them to the precinct, they quickly identified Harold Walters. But they didn't know the name of his rescuer.

After getting all the information, Kamu went straight to his desk. First thing on the agenda, he thought, is to do a background check on Harold Walters. He thought there was a lot more to that lawyer than meets the eye.

He stared at his computer screen for a while. He was able to bring up a lot of information on Walters, who was listed as one of the top criminal defense attorneys in California. Kamu was pleased to see Walters had never been arrested, nor reprimanded by the Bar Association. He was licensed to practice law in most of the states close to California, including Hawaii. He had homes in San Diego, Santa Barbara (now owned by his ex-wife, he mentally noted), Molokai, and Acapulco, Mexico. Walters had law offices in San Diego and Kaunakakai, and had operated the office in Hawaii for the past seven years. He hadn't tried any cases in Hawaii, until the recent Tala Pualani hearing. Walters' financial records were squeaky clean, including making regular and on-time alimony payments.

Kamu cleared the screen, and typed in Melvin's name. Hmm. A much more interesting screen, he found. Melvin Momi had retired after twenty years with the U. S. Army, as a Special Forces weapons specialist and lead investigator for the Army Criminal Investigation Division. He had earned a Bronze Star for valor in the Gulf War, along with two Purple Hearts. The first one was for shrapnel injuries suffered while clearing a mine field. The second was awarded after he was shot trying to get behind enemy lines. After the war, he worked for the U. S. Army's Criminal Investigation Command as lead investigator for the Pacific Coast and Hawaii. He had an exemplary financial record, just like Walters'.

Knowing Walters and Melvin were clean made his next task a lot easier. He crossed the street to the DA's Office and asked if Akumu was in. His secretary rang the intercom and told the DA that Detective Kamu wanted to see him.

Akumu opened his door and said, "Come on in, my friend. I want to hear all about the arrests you made on Molokai."

When the door closed, they clasped hands warmly. Kamu sat down when beckoned by the DA, and said, "It wasn't really my arrest. Mr. Walters and his bodyguard had them cuffed and sitting in their patrol car waiting for us."

"What?"

"You heard me. And better yet, they told me all about the three deaths. Here's a copy of my report. Draper and Davis said they'll gladly sign confessions, if you'll make a deal for them to go to a mainland prison."

"I'll consider it. But first, how did Walters get these two to give it all up?"

Kamu cleared his throat. "All he told me was his bodyguard talked to them."

Akumu said, "Who is this bodyguard?"

"I don't know his name, but he's one of the largest men I have ever seen! On top of that, he's smart. My guess is he's tied in with Walters' investigator, a guy named Melvin Momi."

"I've heard of Momi. He's a private investigator from Oahu, isn't he?"

"Yes. He's also former Special Forces and lead investigator for the Army CID."

Akumu tapped his closed lips with his forefinger, thinking. His eyes swiveled to Kamu. "Do you think Walters and his hired help would tell us what they are up to?"

"Why don't you call Walters and ask him? He took the ferry back to Molokai this morning, and should be at his office or home by now. Here's a cell phone number he gave me. Will you let me know if he wants to cooperate?"

"Of course, Kamu."

"Good. In the meantime, I'll see if I can find Momi. He hasn't been answering his cell phone. I hope he hasn't gone dark!"

"Good idea!" The DA looked sheepish. "I guess Walters thinks I'm an idiot after I lost our first sparring match in court. If he talks with me, I'll let him know how this election is affecting me."

Kamu said, "If he says 'yes,' we get some more help, and if he says 'no,' they'll still be out there rattling bushes where we can't!"

"Are you satisfied with the story about the deaths on Molokai?"

"Yes, I think so. The only other scenario that works is the cops doing all three killings. Either way, they're going to jail, and you get a conviction. You should be ready to go on this one!"

"I'm handling it personally. I don't know if I made the mistakes on the last one, or if Morris did. This time, if it goes south, I'll know who to blame."

Kamu nodded. "With all that's going on, I'll keep a close eye on Morris. He has always struck me as overly ambitious. I don't trust him."

Akumu agreed. "But I hired him, so I'm stuck with him, until he does something really wrong. So, let me see if I can get in touch with Walters."

Kamu stood. "A hui hou."

A good informant network was essential for a detective, and Kamu had a large one on the island. At least he knew what Melvin looked like. That is, unless he was wearing one of his crazy disguises. Kamu asked his contacts if they'd spotted an outsider asking questions about the drug trade on the islands. He didn't get much feedback. Momi was good at being invisible. He pulled up to his favorite roach coach for a plate lunch, and to ask the owner if he'd seen Melvin.

He walked up to the window, and saw Leola reading a cookbook on vendor food. He called out, "Aloha, Leola, I'm starving out here!"

Leola laid his book onto a makeshift bookshelf, and stood. "You could go a month without eating and not starve! Do you want to try my new avocado, pico de gallo, and caramelized onion salad? It would be better for you than all that Spam and rice you're always eating!"

"Why not? Is this your creation? Or did you get it off the Food Network?"

Leola said, "Funny story there. This beautiful *wahine* came up and asked if I had any Mexican food. I told her, 'This is Hawaii!' She started to leave, and I called to her, 'Wait a minute! What kind of Mexican food do you like?' She said she stopped because my sign said 'Shrimp,' and she suddenly got a craving for Shrimp Ceviche. I had just found a recipe for ceviche, and told her I'd make her a dish, but would have to charge three extra dollars, as it was a special order."

Kamu heard his stomach rumble, and wondered

how long this tale was going to last.

"That didn't bother her a bit," Leola continued, leisurely. "So, I whipped up a nice shrimp ceviche but it looked too plain, so I rearranged the dish so there was a hole in the center of the plate and put half of an avocado there. Then, I threw a few caramelized onions on top, for color. She loved it! She said it was the best ceviche she'd ever had. Now she and a bunch of her friends come by every afternoon. Hey, if an old Spam eater like you likes it, I'll put it on my menu board!"

"Wait a minute, Leola, ceviche is not really Mexican."

Laughing, Leola retorted, "Yeah, and pasta really isn't Italian, either. I won't tell the Italians, if you don't tell the Mexicans."

A voice behind Kamu said, "I'm an old Spam eater. Can you fix me a couple of those dishes, and make sure there's extra shrimp?"

Kamu turned and found himself staring into a massive chest.

Tyler said, "Aloha, detective. I hear you've been looking for Melvin. Would you like to tell me why?"

"How did you...? Never mind." Kamu turned back to Leola and ordered a ceviche. After Tyler ordered, Kamu motioned him to step away from the coach. He lowered his voice. "The DA asked me to find him, so he could ask him a few questions."

Tyler bristled. "About what? Melvin hasn't done

anything wrong!"

"No, no, my nui friend. Not that kind of questioning. He wants Melvin to help him. He's going to talk to Walters, and if Walters agrees, we want to bring you all on board, so we can break up the drug ring here on Maui."

Tyler squinted his eyes at the detective, calculating his next comment. Matter-of-factly, he said, "I'll call you with an answer, after I talk to Mr. Walters."

Kamu said, "They both have my number. Now, I'm going to try the ceviche before my stomach rumbles out of me!"

Tyler left with his meals, but Kamu sat at one of the outside picnic tables, and enjoyed some of the best food he'd ever tasted. He gave little thought to Melvin until he got in his car and drove back to the police station. He called Akumu to tell him he had made contact, but Akumu was busy, so Kamu left a message with his secretary for him to call.

CHAPTER 42

Roy ran a full background check on Johnson, while Melvin and Jess tailed him. They started at his office, where so far, only one suspicious person had entered the office. He seemed pretty comfortable in the surroundings, and Melvin eventually figured he was probably an undercover man or a regular informant. He was a little too unkempt to be a dealer.

Roy brought Melvin a printout of what he'd dug up on Johnson and then headed back to the new hotel room for more digging. Melvin was surprised to find out Johnson had been a narcotics cop on the Big Island of Hawaii. Newspaper articles made it sound like he'd single-handedly cleaned up the drug problem on Big Island, two years prior. Johnson's larger than life reputation impressed the governor, and he dreamed up a way to use Johnson as a step to get re-elected. The governor created the Hawaiian Drug Control Office and appointed Johnson as

289

director. After that, the number of drug arrests and convictions began to slowly taper off. People in general stopped paying attention, but there was talk about the number of dealers on the street and how few of them seemed to go to jail. After the murder of Jimmy Pualani, all that changed.

Johnson graduated from the Los Angeles Police Academy, and worked in Los Angeles for ten years before moving to Hawaii. There were no commendations in his file, only a couple of reprimands for bucking authority. Melvin concluded that Johnson probably left L.A. because he was about to get fired. When he got to Big Island, he hooked up with whoever he's doing business with now. All his drug arrests made him a real hotshot which led to his promotion. That not only cleared out any potential competition, it connected him to anybody and everybody involved in the drug trade. That scenario fit perfectly with what Melvin had seen here on Maui, and what had led to the deaths on Molokai.

Johnson was a lot harder to track than the two cops. Being a former cop, he knew how to tail, and knew when he was being tailed. In public, Johnson exhibited no suspicious behavior and was never seen in the company of anyone connected to his drug operation. He was slippery and "insulated." Melvin and Jess had been on him almost all day, and came up with nothing new.

They took notice, though, when a bouquet of

fresh island flowers was delivered to his office that afternoon.

"Surely, those aren't for that old cuss," said Jess.

"Maybe an office girl?" replied Melvin. "Go check it out."

The delivery van had "Hale Pua Nui" painted on the side, along with its English name, "House of Many Flowers." The company's phone number and address was stenciled under the name. When the driver got out and opened the rear doors, Jess walked over to it. He watched as the driver sorted through several boxes of prepared flower arrangements and finally withdrew his head, holding a lovely arrangement of anthurium and crab-claw heliconia.

Jess came alongside the driver and joked, "Oh, for me? You shouldn't have!"

The delivery man sighed deeply. "Like I haven't heard that a million times. These are for Director Johnson."

Jess grinned. "His new boyfriend must really like him!"

The delivery man shrugged and said, "Hey, this is Hawaii. What can I say?"

Startled, Jess joined Melvin in their car as the man took the bouquet inside.

Melvin didn't blink at the news. He sat for a moment with his lips pressed together as he thought. "If we can find his partner, we've got some real leverage on Johnson. Since the delivery guy saw you in front of the building, he probably thinks you work there. Let's head over to the flower shop and see if you can get his partner's name. Flash your fake credentials if you have to."

CHAPTER 43

The phone rang, and I heard Patty answer, "Just a moment, Mr. Akumu. Mr. Walters is with someone. I'll see if he has time to speak with you."

I looked puzzled because I had been sitting there most of the morning, chatting with our Samoan bodyguard.

Patty shrugged prettily. "What? It won't hurt him to wait a little. You're more important than he is."

"We both know that's not true, but thanks," I said. "Now would you please ring him through?"

Patty pushed a button and said into the phone, "Mr. Akumu, Mr. Walters said he will be with you in just a moment. If you don't mind holding, I'll ring you in, as soon as he's free."

She put the call on hold, turned and faced me with a big grin. She silently counted all of her fingers and had started in on her toes, when she saw me scowling at her. "Okay, don't get your shorts in a

293

wad. Sheesh." She picked up the phone and said, "Mr. Walters will speak to you, now."

The Samoan winked at me and said, "She's quite the woman, isn't she?"

I said, "I can't argue with that."

"Mr. Akumu," I greeted him. "Forgive the delay. I had someone important in my office." I grinned at Honey Boy. "What can I do for the District Attorney, today? You haven't arrested one of my clients again, have you?"

"Not yet!" Akumu said, drolly. Obviously, he was not impressed at my attempt at humor. "I want to know if you and the people working for you will help me and Detective Kamu get to the bottom of this drug ring." He added, "Kamu trusts you and Melvin, and I trust Kamu. I can fly over to Molokai this afternoon."

"If you're willing to talk, I'm willing to listen," I said, "but first, I have one question I need answered. Why did you arrest Tala?"

The DA didn't answer immediately. "I probably shouldn't tell you this, but what the heck. My opponent has been picking up a lot of support lately because I haven't had many new prosecutions. When my prosecutor, Morris, brought me the information on Tala's blood match, and the fact that she might have a motive to kill her father because he was abusive, I thought I could gain some political ground. Thanks to you, I wound up looking like the fool I was. Kamu reminded me why I ran for office to begin with, and that reason was to clean up crime, especially drugs, here in Maui County. I'm going to focus on my job, and if I get re-elected, so be it. If not, at least I'll know I did my best for the right reasons."

"Good enough. Can you make it this afternoon? I'll be in the office all day."

I turned to Honey Boy after I hung up. "Well, what do you think of that? The DA is coming over here to see us!"

Honey Boy said, "Sounds to me like that detective convinced him you're one of the good guys. Did he say if he is bringing anyone with him?"

I answered, "No. I should have asked though, shouldn't I?"

"That's all right," Honey Boy said. "I'll be ready for them!"

I asked, "What do you mean, 'ready for them'?"

"When Melvin called, he said to go to full alert. That means being prepared for any contingency. Best case scenario, the DA shows up hat-in-hand, to beg for your help. Worst case, he sends a couple of hit men over to make sure you never tell anyone what you know."

"This is crazy," I said, "Do you think he would actually do something like that?"

Honey Boy rose from his chair and looked at me sternly. "Drug dealers are animals. All they care about is the money. They kill millions of people slowly every day and knock off the others one by one whenever the mood strikes them. What makes you think killing you would matter to them?"

Damn! My criminal education was going in dangerous directions. If it wasn't dirty cops, it was a corrupt official, and if not them, there were dangerous drug dealers. What have I gotten myself into?

"Honey Boy, maybe we should get out of this and just let the police take care of it. I never intended for any of us to fear for our lives."

Honey Boy smiled and gently patted me on the head. "We know, Boss. But, we're not going to let you get hurt, and certainly no one is going to get one of Melvin's boys! If you haven't already figured it out, Melvin ain't gonna give up on this until Johnson and his cronies are behind bars or dead!"

"Why is that?" I asked.

"He won't tell you this, and I'll deny it if you tell him I did, but Melvin's wife was a drug addict."

"Was?"

"She got hooked on pain pills she was taking for a back injury. Melvin spent a lot of time away on investigations. Meanwhile, she started taking more and more and finally worked her way up to the hard stuff. By the time Melvin found out she had a problem–and how bad it was–it was too late. She went to rehab and he thought she was doing better.

But while he was out on assignment, she sneaked out of the center, came back home, and overdosed on heroin right in their bedroom. She had been there dead for over a week when he came home and found her. It really messed him up for awhile, and he blamed himself for not being there. He was really devastated by her death and resigned from the Army. A year later, he hung out a PI shingle, and vowed to find the people that supplied the drugs to his wife."

I thanked Honey Boy. I felt bad for Melvin and what he had been through. No way would I bail on him. If we can get through this thing with our heads still attached, Melvin can get his closure and so can Taniko, Pearl and the girls.

Honey Boy excused himself and went out to his car. He brought in a guitar case, holding it with care. He brought it into my office, and after checking to see that Patty was distracted, he shut the door.

By this time I was curious. When he opened the case, I was expecting to see some sort of rare musical instrument, perhaps a Stradivarius, but certainly not an arsenal of arms. "Um…"

"Hold on, now." He removed a machine pistol and a smaller nine millimeter automatic. He put the nine millimeter in his oversized front pants' pocket and strapped the machine pistol into a holster he had under his shirt. He then picked up a .38-special revolver and handed it to me.

"You know how to use this?" he asked.

"Yes, but it's been a while since I fired one." I checked to see if the gun was loaded, and started to put it in the center drawer of my desk.

Honey Boy stopped me. Tuck it in your front waistband under your shirt. You can get to it a lot quicker there." He closed the case and turned toward the door.

I asked, "What about Patty? Should she have a weapon too?"

Honey boy laughed and said, "Dude, you're something else. One minute, you're ready to quit. The next, you're ready to give everybody a gun and go to war. Ain't no way I'm giving that woman a gun! I'm still not sure she's forgiven me about not telling her that I was working for Melvin. We'll send her over to the library, if we don't like the looks of whoever shows up. How's that?"

"That works. In fact, I'll just send her over to do some research before they get here, She can stay until I call her." I busied myself looking for any work I could assign to Patty. I looked up. "Oh, and you are right, though I didn't realize it until just now. Given the right cause, I don't mind going to war. What I do mind is people I care about getting hurt."

"I hear you, Mr. Walters."

"Call me Harry. If you're going to die for me, we better be on a first name basis."

CHAPTER 44

Jess strolled into the Hale Pua Nui Flower Shop, and was greeted by a clerk.

"May I help you, sir?"

"You sure can," Jess said.

"Those flowers you had delivered to Director Johnson this morning, I need to know who sent them."

The clerk bristled and said, "We don't give out customer information. If you want to know who sent those flowers, go ask Mr. Johnson."

Jess reached in his pocket and brought out his fake credentials. He stuck them in the clerk's face saying, "Who bought the flowers? Or do you want me to come back here with a warrant, and check all your sales records?"

The clerk's face turned white as he backed up. "Why didn't you tell me you were a cop? I thought you might be a jealous boyfriend or something. The

299

guy who bought the flowers is George Morris, from the DA's Office."

"Thanks." Jess said, "Now be a good boy, and don't tell anyone I was here, okay?"

The clerk said, "Fine with me. I just sell flowers."

As soon as Jess was out of sight, the clerk picked up the phone and called Johnson. Johnson asked him if he'd gotten the cop's name, and the clerk said, "No." He said his security camera was on though, and he could send him the images from the digital recorder. Johnson was happy about that and told the clerk to clear out all the drugs in the store. Just in case, he instructed the clerk to hold off on any more flower deliveries to his office, no matter who they are from. Johnson then called one of his enforcers.

When the man answered, he said, "I've got a new lead on the snoops from Molokai. One of them was using a cop ID to threaten the kid at the flower shop. I'll send you the photo as soon as I get it along with the description of his car. If he is who I think he is, he can lead us to his boss. If you find them, you know what to do!

"Tomorrow morning, send our Chinese friend over to Morris. He needs to be reminded of what could happen to him and his family if he starts running his mouth. I don't need some dumb love-struck fool screwing up our whole operation."

George Morris began his day, as usual, with a short run in his neighborhood. He returned home and was greeted by his wife and two sons. They were busily getting ready for school and work. After a quick shower, he joined his family at the breakfast table. Morris sipped his coffee, and though he responded to the lively chatter around him, his thoughts drifted toward Johnson. He absently stared into his coffee. The man generated both love and hate from him. Maybe it was the power Johnson had that initially attracted him. The same power had been used, however, to hurt him, too. So why did he keep going back to him?

Johnson wasn't his first gay affair. He had been attracted to both sexes since he came into puberty. He had tried to make sense of it, or at least reconcile with it from the beginning. He had yet to win that struggle. Even though he truly loved his wife and children, he needed more in his life to satisfy his carnal urges. Johnson knew that and had toyed with him in more ways than one. He understood George's love of power, and he felt lucky he'd found someone who relished that as much as he did.

George wiped his mouth with his napkin and

finished his coffee. The boys shrugged into their backpacks while George got up and put his dishes in the sink. He kissed his sons' heads and tousled their hair as they said goodbye and scrambled out the door. He hugged his wife, grabbed his briefcase and left for work.

When he entered his office, he saw three people waiting for him. He stopped mid-stride. One of them was a very attractive Asian woman, somewhere in her late thirties. A Hawaiian male, about the same age, flanked her left, and an older Asian sat on her right. He didn't recognize the men, but his heart leaped into his throat when he saw the woman. She sat perfectly still, impeccably dressed in her red silk blouse and black slacks. Her hair was twisted into a perfect chignon, held in place by an ebony chopstick. She wore little makeup, and Morris could see she had once been quite a beauty. He'd seen her only one other time, those lovely almond eyes, like dark mirrors, reflecting the flames as they consumed a drug lord's home and reduced it to ashes. She'd set it on fire, as a lesson.

"The Chinaman," as she was known, was Johnson's main enforcer. Her reputation as a swift and heartless killer sent even the strongest foes running. Why was she here, of all places? Suddenly the hairs on his neck stood erect.

Morris' secretary looked up from her computer. "Good morning, Mr. Morris. These two gentlemen are from Oahu. They need a few minutes to discuss a case which may come up for trial here on Maui. This is Melvin Momi and Jess Selu." Morris glanced at the two men and uttered a quick, "Aloha, gentlemen."

His gaze quickly turned to the woman. Feigning any knowledge of The Chinaman's identity, he then asked, "And our other guest, Miss Collins?"

"This is Miss Chan from Director Johnson's office," she replied.

Another cold chill ran down Morris' spine and he asked her, "Is there something urgent?"

Miss Chan responded, "No. It can wait until you finish with these gentlemen."

Morris held back a sigh of relief at the momentary reprieve. He ushered Jess and Melvin into his office. As he was closing his office door, he saw Chan approach his secretary and ask where she could find the restroom.

When Chan entered, she checked all the stalls to make sure the restroom was empty. When she was certain of being alone, she pulled out her cell and punched in Johnson's number.

"Guess who I found sitting in Morris's office waiting to talk to him? That investigator, Momi, and one of his men."

Johnson said, "Well, that is very intriguing! I'll get a tail on them immediately. Thanks, Chan. Call me when you've had your little talk with Morris."

Morris shook Melvin's hand and said, "George Morris.....and don't I know you?"

"You may remember me as Mr. Saito, but my real name is Melvin Momi, and this is my associate, Jess Selu."

Morris was immediately alert. "Ah! So, I was right when I thought there was more to you. Well, have a seat, gentlemen. What can I do for you?"

Melvin began by saying, "I'm a private investigator from Oahu. I was recently hired to work for a lawyer on Molokai who was defending a girl accused of murdering her father."

Morris looked wary. "The Jimmy Pualani case. I am familiar with it."

"Yes, that's it. Fortunately for our client, we were able to get enough evidence to have the charges dropped."

As Morris listened to Melvin talk about the murder case, his nerves wound up tight.

Melvin said, "Mr. Morris, I've been watching you for some time now. That's why we are here. We know all about your relationship with Johnson. We know you pass all the drug money to him and help get his people off, when they're arrested. We also know about the flowers you sent him and why!"

Just the Right Amount of Wrong

Morris jumped out of his chair, sending it rolling into the back wall. "Are you here to arrest me?"

"No, please have a seat, Morris. We're here to get more information on Johnson and the people he works for. As a prosecutor you should know the routine. You tell us what we need to know, and we'll tell everyone how cooperative you were, and you might get a lighter sentence. Likewise, if you tell us about Johnson, your wife and kids don't have to find out you swing both ways!"

Morris stared blankly back at Melvin and didn't say anything. He had a vision of his life collapsing like a house of cards. He sunk back into his chair and stared at his lap. Melvin let Morris's nervous system do his work for him.

Finally, Morris broke his silence and exclaimed, "I'm a dead man! Johnson's main enforcer is sitting out there talking with my secretary." He pointed wildly at the door. His anxiety level heightened. He answered the questioning look on Melvin's face and explained, "That woman waiting to see me is called The Chinaman. She does most of Johnson's dirty work! You've got to get me out of here. I'll tell you whatever you want! Just keep her away from me or I'm dead!"

"We can do that, but I need assurance you won't change your mind later. I'm going to record everything you tell me." He yanked out his cell and set the recorder. He turned to Jess. "Call "the family"

305

and get them here right now. We need to get him out of here and somewhere safe. In the meantime Morris, start talking."

While Morris began telling Melvin what he wanted to know, Jess punched in some numbers and relayed the message. Meanwhile, Melvin poked his head out of Morris' office and smiled at his secretary. "We have two more people who are supposed to show up for our meeting. They were delayed, but should be here shortly. When they arrive will you send them right in. He looked over at The Chinaman and cocked his mouth to one side and lifted his hands into the air. "I'm *so* sorry for causing you to wait. I promise we'll be done as quickly as possible." He mustered his most sincere smile and pulled his head back and closed the office door.

Miss Collins smiled and shook her head. I'm sorry, ma'am. Can I get you some coffee or water?"

The woman was unmoved and simply shook her head. "I'm getting paid to sit here. Mr. Johnson said he might be busy, but to wait as long as needed to deliver his message in person." She returned to her People Magazine.

Miss Collins blinked at her for a moment and returned to her work.

Tyler and Roy walked into the office a few minutes later. "We are late for a meeting. Mr. Morris is expecting us."

The secretary stared open mouthed at the

mountains of humanity standing before her. "Uh-certainly. Go right on in." She gestured toward the door and the two men disappeared inside.

For the next few minutes, Melvin explained what would happen next. They would escort Morris out of the office, and take him to a safe house in Kihei. Tyler and Jess would lead, Melvin and Roy would follow, and Morris would be in the middle. It would be extremely difficult to break through the four of them to get to Morris.

Morris said, "What about The Chinaman? She will tell Johnson I left with you or she may even try something in the office!"

"We'll be ready," Melvin said, "and where we are going, Johnson won't be able to follow us without us spottin him."

Everyone's head swiveled toward the door as it flew open. It seems Miss Chan had lost her patience. "What's going on, Morris? You aren't leaving, are you?"

Miss Collins stood behind her, trying to get by. "I'm sorry, Mr. Morris. She wouldn't listen to me."

Morris said, "It's all right. Miss Chan, I've got to go over to the courthouse with these gentlemen. I'll be right back."

"I need to talk with you, *now!*" said Chan, her

voice deepening with growing rage. "Johnson won't like this," she admonished.

Morris shivered. "I have to go." He hurried to Melvin's side. In a single flash of movement, Chan was twirling two nasty looking knives. Morris darted behind Tyler.

"No! You're coming with me!" she said, moving with purpose towards Tyler.

Tyler told the woman, "Put the knives down before you get hurt."

She laughed, slicing the air between them.

Tyler retreated, and joined the others in encircling Morris.

She stabbed at Tyler, but he blocked the move. She feigned a slash at Tyler's face, spun, and landed a heel kick to his midsection. Tyler gave out a short grunt, and ducked another kick aimed at his head.

"Okay, lady, now I'm mad! " He advanced towards her, his fists clenched. "Give me the knives!"

She jumped into the air and came down with both knives aimed at Tyler's head. He knocked the knife out of her left hand and threw his left hand up to block the other knife. Chan was too quick for him. The knife penetrated his left palm all the way to the hilt. He let out an angry bellow that sounded like a grizzly bear. He pulled his hand, knife and all, away and looked at what Chan had done. He glanced up just in time to see Chan coming at him again. He sidestepped her charge and backhanded her over the secretary's desk. He connected squarely and Chan landed, in an unconscious lump, in the secretary's lap.

After screaming and dumping Miss Chan unceremoniously onto the carpet, Miss Collins stared at her and cried, "Is she dead?"

Jess checked her pulse. "She's unconscious. Nice work, Tyler."

"Who are you calling?" Roy was beside the secretary, who'd picked up the phone and was rapidly punching in numbers.

"The police!"

"Lady we *are* the police," he said. "Now let's all get the hell out of here, before anything else happens."

Tyler had removed the knife, and blood was seeping through the wads of tissue he'd applied. "Going to need some first aid," he said matter-of-factly. He asked Morris, "Is there a back way out?"

Morris indicated a side door. Tyler picked Miss Chan up with his good hand, and threw her over his shoulder. He only winced once. Melvin turned to Morris and said, "We are taking you and Miss Collins to a safe house for your protection. If Johnson sent The Chinaman for you, he will probably send someone else. If Miss Collins panics again, she could lead Johnson right to us."

Like a flock of grounded geese, Jess led the group out of the building.

The scene could have been from a *Keystone Cops* movie. Seven people huddled together, led by a stalwart Hawaiian, followed by an unconscious woman tossed over a massive shoulder held by a bloody hand, a middle-aged man trying to calm a near hysterical young woman, while a wiry Asian man and a humongous Hawaiian sandwiched them in from behind. As the motley troupe descended the back stairs, they passed two men, who eyed them warily.

"Need any help?" one asked.

"Nope," replied Melvin. He kept walking.

They continued down the stairs and into a parking garage adjacent to the office building. The group huddled together while Roy retrieved the SUV.

"Did you see those thugs? I bet Johnson sent them." Melvin eyed the door they'd come from. "I expect we'll see them again as soon as they report all this to Johnson."

Roy pulled up in the SUV and screeched to a halt. They all piled in. Tyler secured a seat belt around Miss Chan, and arranged her head so it didn't hang down.

Johnson's men were hurrying out the door when the SUV pulled away. They scurried to their car and screeched after them.

CHAPTER 45

District Attorney Akumu landed on Molokai, rented a car, and enjoyed his ride from the airport, into Kaunakakai. He used to come to the island regularly, but not so much anymore. He always appreciated Molokai's beauty. As they crested the hill overlooking the town, he saw the long wharf extending into the opaline water. He marveled at the beauty of the halo shaped barrier reef, and decided that whether he won or lost, he would bring his family here for some fishing and a much-needed break.

Akumu found a parking place near Walters' office. He strolled into the open doorway and was immediately met by a big Samoan.

"Aloha, Mr. District Attorney. Welcome to Molokai. I'm Honey Boy." He held out a ham-sized hand. Akumu shook it. In the space of a five second handshake, Honey Boy patted the DA down, looking

311

for a weapon. When he withdrew his hand, he flashed his bright white teeth at the DA, and allowed him to pass.

Patty smiled and nodded a greeting.

"I'm Keone Akumu, Maui County District Attorney. I'm here to see Mr. Walters."

Patty said, "Certainly, Mr. Akumu. Harry – Mr. Walters is expecting you."

I heard Akumu arrive and came out to greet him. We shook hands. I couldn't help but notice him eyeing Honey Boy. "Wherever I am, he is," I told him.

The DA raised his eyebrows. "Are you in danger?"

"Possibly. What can I do for you?" I gestured toward a chair across from mine and we both sat down.

"First off, let me say how very capable your, um, associates are. I've heard a lot of stories about their skills in the field. Kamu is still talking about some big kahuna, who likes ceviche."

I threw my head back and laughed out loud. "That would be Tyler. He's the best chef around!"

Akumu nodded. "I'm hoping we can work together. You and your men have--"

From the outer office, we heard Patty say, "And woman."

"We know," I called. I looked at the DA and raised my eyebrows for him to continue.

Just the Right Amount of Wrong

"As I was saying, you *all* have managed to unearth details on the murders that for whatever reason, my staff has not. We need help."

I held up a hand. "You can tell Kamu we will be working together. I'll let Melvin know, too. Those two appear to be cut from the same cloth."

"Can we start right now?" the DA asked. "The sooner the better."

"Okay. Let's start with Morris, your ADA. I think there is a lot about him you don't know."

I know he's gone missing. Do you know something about that?" His eyebrows arched as he asked the question. He knew I did.

I took a breath and filled him in; covering everything I could think of from getting photos of Morris passing money-filled envelopes to Director Johnson to the goons at Morris's office.

"We took Morris and Miss Chan, I believe they call her The Chinaman, to a safe house. Johnson and Morris were lovers, but I guess love has grown cold. Now Johnson wants Morris dead."

Akumu tried to keep the shocked look off his face. "I had no idea. But, why is Johnson trying to kill Morris?"

"I think the ADA has been a go-between for the cops selling drugs."

"His convictions were way down this year," the DA explained, "but I thought it was because of a big caseload, and the pressure of my re-election. Now I find out it's because he's crooked!"

"Hey, Boss!" Patty called from her desk. "It's Melvin!"

"Patty, there's an intercom for a reason. Which line?"

"The one that's blinking, of course." She sniffed.

I picked up the phone and pushed the button. "Hello, Melvin? What's happening?"

Melvin told me they were set up at the safe house. "Can you get in touch with the DA and see if Kamu can send a protection detail to Morris's home?"

"Sure can," I said, putting him on speakerphone. "He's sitting right here. We've joined our resources, so we'll keep him in the loop, from now on."

Melvin whistled. "Okay, then. We're at the safe house with Morris and his secretary and Miss Chan. I hope you don't mind, but I won't tell you where we are, and I will be using a disposable phone. I'll call with the number, later, okay?"

I said, "Thanks Melvin, keep in touch."

The DA immediately phoned Kamu and directed him to set up protection for Morris's family. Before he signed off he said he was happy we were all on the same page, now.

CHAPTER 46

Johnson's men were good. They followed the SUV transporting Morris and the others almost all the way to Kihei without being detected. When they neared a one-lane, half-mile stretch of road, they slowed down. They knew the road. It led to an estate barricaded behind a massive stone wall and locked brass gates. They stopped. There was no way they could continue following them, but at least they had cornered them.

They pulled to the side of the road and called Johnson to tell him their location. Johnson ordered them to stay put, and follow anyone who left. He was furious the way things had gotten out of hand. "Call me, if anything changes, "he barked.

Johnson told his secretary he was leaving the office on an investigation, and that he might be gone for a couple of days. He instructed her not to call, unless it was an extreme emergency. "Even then, just leave a phone number."

Johnson drove to a bar in Kahalui, near the airport. On his way there, he called one of his other enforcers, and told him to meet him there. Johnson was on his second Mai Tai, when a non-descript man walked in and sat down next to him. He ordered tonic water and lime.

"You know I hate meeting in bars, Johnson," the man complained.

Johnson gulped his drink down with a satisfied "ah" and smacked his glass down on the bar. He looked at his companion and winked. "Sorry."

"Screw you!"

"Now, now, settle down, Bud. We need a big clean-up tonight. Morris and The Chinaman are holed up on the Anderson Estate. They have four men guarding them."

"The Chinaman got caught?" There was a note of surprise in his voice.

"I'll be replacing her."

"Who are the guards?"

"A guy named Melvin Momi, and three of his enforcers."

"Must have been some trick to get them both out of the building."

"Hmm. Morris has worn out his welcome, and he needs to disappear."

"Isn't Momi ex-Army Intelligence? I heard he quit the service to go after drug dealers. Something about his wife overdosing on smack. What brought him over here to Maui?"

Johnson said, "I did. I had Morris arrest a teenaged girl on Molokai, as a patsy for Jimmy Pualani's murder. He was getting too nosy. The girl's mother hired this fancy-ass lawyer from California, and he hired Momi as an investigator. The next thing I know he's here on Maui, raising hell with our whole operation!"

He ordered another Mai Tai. "Get everyone together, and meet me at the warehouse just after dark tonight. We need to meet and organize a nice little wake-up call for Momi and his friends. Morris is a goner, too. This thing ends now."

"Right." The enforcer downed his tonic water and left. Johnson had one more Mai Tai. He felt better knowing that Momi and Morris would burn to a crisp tonight.

Kamu tucked himself into a corner of the bar's shadowy interior and watched until Johnson's friend left. He got up and ambled out the door, adopting a drunken list as he walked to his car. When he got in his car, he quickly noted the friend's license plate number and called in for identification. On his private cell phone, he contacted Henry Reyes, an officer he trusted, and asked him to tail the guy. Then, he sat back and waited for Johnson to emerge.

When his quarry came out, walking a bit unsteady, Kamu toyed with the idea of arresting him for drunk driving, but decided to let the evening unfold naturally. He followed Johnson into the dusk, using only his parking lights. They ended up in the industrial section of Kahalui. Johnson slowed and turned into the parking lot of an abandoned warehouse. Two other cars were already there, hunkered in the darkness.

Kamu switched off his lights and pulled to the curb about thirty yards back. He switched off the engine and slumped down in his seat to watch. Johnson's bar companion drove past and parked. Reyes would be somewhere behind him.

The two thugs and Johnson's friend got out of their cars and went into a side door of the old warehouse. Kamu used the opportunity to get license numbers and call them in. Two vehicles belonged to known drug dealers. Kamu had arrested one of them himself.

There was a tap on his window, and Kamu started. He automatically reached for his gun, but saw it was Reyes. Irritated, he motioned him to get in the car.

Reyes slid into the passenger seat and grinned. "Good thing I wasn't one of those guys you were following."

Kamu flushed. He was right. A mistake like that

could cause a man to end up as shark food!

"What we got?" Reyes asked.

"Johnson, your man, and at least two, maybe four, more. This could be a dealers' meeting, but most likely it has more to do with them watching the Anderson Estate, in Kihei."

Reyes asked, "Why the Anderson Estate?"

"For your ears only, the Anderson Estate is being used as a safe house for ADA Morris. I set up a protection detail for his family earlier this afternoon then tailed Johnson to the bar. We have some heavy duty crap going down, and that's why I asked for your help."

"Do you think any more will show up?" Reyes asked. "It's been about fifteen minutes since that last SUV pulled in."

Kamu asked, "You thinking about getting closer?"

"Yeah," the officer said. "We ain't getting anywhere just sitting here in the car. Let's go rattle their cages!"

Kamu was about to reply, when his phone rang. It was Melvin. "Detective Kamu, here."

"And just where might 'here' be, detective?"

"At an old warehouse in Kahalui. Where are you?"

"That's why I'm calling. I think we were followed to the safe house. Most likely Johnson's men. He'll send someone after us tonight, and if he does, it could get messy. Can you send in a pizza delivery truck? I'll put Morris and his secretary in the van, and you can take them to another safe house.

"Those goons are still out there just waiting for their chance at us. They are driving a Toyota SUV, Hawaiian plates, license ZTW579. Can you have a patrol car drive by when the van comes out? I'll keep The Chinaman here, as a hostage."

"Fearless. I've heard of her. What's she like?"

"She and Tyler have been getting along real well, since she came to. She even bandaged his hand. She won't talk to anyone else.

"Tyler's no dummy, though. When she started getting friendly, he put a set of shackles on her ankles and handcuffed her to the metal baluster on the stairwell."

Kamu told him about the meeting under the cover of darkness at the warehouse.

"Reyes and I are going to get closer and see what we can see."

Melvin said, "My guess is this is a powwow to order a hit on us. When you get a head count, call me, so at least we have an idea of what we are up against. Perhaps you could stow some fire power in the pizza van?"

"I'm on it, right now. I can get police or even the military to help. You know, you don't have to do this. It's really a police matter."

"I'll do whatever I have to in order to meet

Johnson. I have a bone to pick with him," Melvin said.

"Don't do anything stupid."

"I want to find out who he works for, and I'll get it out of him, even if I have to rip it out."

Kamu said, "I didn't hear that last statement, but I will arrest him when this is all over, if it's all right with you?"

"I'll give you what's left," Melvin replied, and added, "Now I've got work to do," and hung up.

Kamu noticed Reyes was nervous, and said, "If you don't want to be a part of this, you don't have to. Surveillance is one thing, a gun battle's another."

Reyes answered, "I didn't become a cop to shy away from danger." He took out his service revolver and checked it. He touched his pants leg, where his spare was hidden. "Ready."

The two officers didn't have to sneak up to the warehouse, after all. Just then, Johnson and five others emerged from the warehouse and took off in their vehicles. They were dressed in black, like a SWAT team. Each man had body armor and a helmet equipped with night vision goggles. All of them were heavily armed.

Kamu called Melvin and warned him about the army coming his way.

Melvin said, "Thanks. I hope the pizza van gets here soon."

Kamu followed the unit from a safe distance. No

need to keep them in constant view. Even though it was dark, he knew where they were going. Halfway to Kihei, Kamu got another call from Melvin.

"We just sent Morris and his secretary out in the pizza delivery van. The guys across the street didn't follow, but they were on the phone, probably to Johnson. Morris will be transferred to another vehicle at Sugar Beach, in a few minutes. How close is Johnson?"

"They're about ten minutes from Kihei. Add another five to ten minutes to the estate."

"When you get to the resort, see if you can isolate the two who have been watching the road. Or, maybe your patrol officers could hold them until you get here, and then arrest them.

"Good plan! My guys just swung around, and are nearing the resort, right now." Kamu clicked his radio on and reported a suspicious vehicle at the resort. He cautioned the occupants could be armed and dangerous. A patrol car answered back, saying they had the vehicle in sight and were approaching.

Kamu picked up his cell, again. Melvin said, "That was quick! I see the lights. That should keep them from interfering. Kamu, stay outside the estate. Any additional people in our perimeter will only add to the confusion. I'll call you into this, when the time comes. Is that clear?"

Kamu reluctantly agreed.

The SUVs passed through the edge of Kihei and

cautiously approached the estate entrance. Johnson tapped his brakes, slowing at the sight of the police lights. Kamu could see him talking on his cell, and the other cars immediately slowed down, too.

Kamu was right behind them. He saw the officers talking to the occupants in the car. One officer stood watch, with his hand on his still-holstered revolver, while the other was reading what appeared to be identification material from the driver of the car.

Johnson turned to his burly passenger, "Looks like someone called the cops on our spotters. That's going to delay things another half hour. Call those dumb asses, and see if one of them can talk."

The man punched numbers into his cell phone, and the passenger answered.

The enforcer said, "Johnson wants to talk with you."

Johnson grabbed the phone. "What's going on?"

The man replied, "Some lady called, and reported us as stalkers. We told these cops we're doing surveillance in a divorce case, and they said we can go just as soon as they run our IDs."

Johnson said, "As soon as they release you, get out of here! We've got work to do."

"Hold on, sir." Johnson could hear one of the officers ask him who was on the phone. He said it was his boss, checking for updates on their case.

"Okay, sir," the man continued. "We'll be on our

way, soon."

The patrolman radioed Kamu, and said he would let them go and follow them out of Kihei. That would ensure that they returned to Kahalui. Kamu called Melvin with the plans. He said Johnson was just here, so be prepared. "I'll stay close to the entrance."

CHAPTER 47

Johnson and his men waited until the area was clear of any policemen, and then began their assault. They approached the estate from the adjoining golf course. Johnson and the enforcer approached from the front of the house. The other five spread out, spanning the rear and sides. They were methodical, and used their night vision goggles to scan the property for dogs or anyone guarding from the outside.

All of Johnson's men were part of a hand-picked group of his Drug Control Agency. Most were former military and well-versed in assault tactics. They also had access to any type of guns or equipment they might need.

They were unaware that Melvin had locked onto the Drug Control radio frequency they were using, and was listening to a play-by-play of their maneuvers.

Melvin had chosen the estate because he had helped Anderson, the owner, design the security system for the property. Anderson, a billionaire, had spared no expense to make the estate a veritable fortress. There were pressure and motion sensors scattered throughout the grounds. All sections of the property were covered by closed circuit television cameras. Armor-plated panels could cover all windows and doors with the mere flick of a switch, and there was an impenetrable safe room in the basement to be used as a last resort in the event of an emergency.

Melvin had provided his men with silenced pistols, while he carried a tranquilizer rifle equipped with a night vision scope. As two of Johnson's men neared the rear of the house, Melvin took careful aim and shot one with a tranquilizer dart. The man reached for his neck where the dart found its mark. He stopped in his tracks as his knees buckled and he sunk onto the grass. His partner glanced back and saw him lying in a heap. He looked this way and that, not comprehending what had happened. Then, a dart struck him, just as he was reaching for his radio.

Jess and Tyler carried the two into the house and rejoined Melvin. Melvin had his rifle trained on the two approaching from the east. He squeezed the trigger and one of the men slammed backward onto the ground. The other dove for cover and scrambled for his radio to contact Johnson. He was shrieking that everyone around him was dead.

Johnson raged into the radio and gave the order to storm the house. "Kill everyone inside," he screamed.

Melvin pushed some buttons, and the armor plating slid into place. It closed off all access except for the front entrance. Johnson and the enforcer burst through the front door and rushed into the living room. With guns leveled they looked this way and that. It appeared empty, until Johnson saw a bundle by the marble staircase. It was The Chinaman, bound and gagged. He made his way to Miss Chan, while the other three rushed in after him. He cursed her stupidity and put the barrel of the gun to her temple.

Suddenly, a voice came over the room's speaker system and his head shot up. It was Melvin. "Hello, Johnson. Gentlemen. Nice of you to join us for a visit! Slowly put your weapons on the floor, and lock your hands behind your heads."

Johnson raised his gun, but suddenly the room was hit with dazzling light. Johnson and his men were wearing their night vision goggles, and they quickly ripped them off and threw them aside. The bright light blinded them for a brief moment, but it was enough time for Melvin and his men to storm into the room and take them by surprise.

When Johnson's vision cleared he had murder in his eyes. When he saw that he was surrounded, he let loose a string of profanity before he laid down his weapon. His men followed suit and tossed their weapons on the floor. Roy collected the firearms and goggles and placed them away from the prisoners. One by one, Johnson and his men were handcuffed to the balustrade.

When everyone was secure, Melvin walked over to Johnson and pulled him off the floor by his hair.

"You and I are going to have a little talk."

"Kiss my ass."

"Now, Mr. Johnson," said Melvin, "you're only going to make things worse. If you cooperate, and answer a couple of questions for me, you might end up in a nice safe jail cell. If not, the next hour you spend will be the worst you've ever experienced in your life. It's your decision."

Johnson assessed him for a moment, but must have seen the deadly serious look in Melvin's eyes. His bluster suddenly deflated as quickly as a child's balloon "What do you want to know?"

Melvin calmly responded, "The name of the person bringing drugs into the islands, and the name of the dealer who sold my wife drugs."

"Is that all? That's all you want?" Johnson said. "One, I have no idea who sold your wife drugs, but if you let me go, I can find out." He allowed a twinge of hope to edge into his voice, but his instincts told him he was playing a very dangerous game. "Two, you know as well as I do that I wouldn't live twenty minutes if I told you who was running the operation here in Hawaii."

Melvin took a key out and unlocked his handcuffs. He pushed Johnson toward a hallway and said, "I thought you might say that. Looks like we're going to have to do this the hard way.

"Tyler, bring the woman, and follow me to the basement," he called to Roy and Jess over his shoulder. "Get Kamu and have him haul this trash out of here."

Melvin pushed a fake light switch aside to reveal a numbered panel. He tapped in a code, and pressed "Enter." The wall slid open. Johnson's eyes opened wide as a heavy wood panel slid aside and the room opened up.

Inside, a bank of closed-circuit television screens continually displayed different points being monitored in and around the house. The screens and equipment filled one entire wall. Adjacent to that was a bookcase that held a hundred or more books. The remaining wall framed a queen sized bed, neatly wrapped in a hand-made Hawaiian quilt. Attached to the room were a small kitchen, and a bathroom.

Melvin ushered Johnson inside, and pushed him roughly into a straight-backed chair.

Tyler came in behind them, carrying Miss Chan. He dumped her into another chair across the table from Johnson.

Melvin approached a panel, on the inside of the room, and punched more numbers.

The wall rumbled closed. He announced, "Now, no one can hear or bother us until tomorrow. This room has a time lock of twenty-four hours, unless I open it. I hope it won't take you that long to reconsider your answer."

Melvin instructed Tyler to tie Johnson and Miss Chan to their chairs, and to bind their feet. He walked over to the closed-circuit television screens where he could see Johnson's men fumbling with their cuffs. It was fruitless.

He reached into a cabinet and pulled out a square marble cutting board. Even though it was only about twelve inches wide, the heft of the stone made a thud as it was set on the table. Johnson stared at the thing, a puzzled expression stamped on his face. Melvin gave him a humorless smile as he pulled out a claw hammer and set it next to the stone cutting board. Johnson shifted uncomfortably in the chair. Looking at a simple hammer had never in his life filled him with such a sense of foreboding.

Chan's wide, unblinking gaze was locked on him. Melvin narrowed his eyes. "Perhaps we should begin with you." He walked over to Miss Chan and placed her free hand on the slab, held it firmly. His voice was very matter-of-fact. "Tell me what you know about Johnson, or I'll break all the bones in

330

your hand."

Chan's tough façade shattered and she shrieked, frantically tugging to free her hand. Melvin gently tapped her on the forehead with the hammer.

"Perhaps you didn't understand what I said."

She glared at Melvin. "Up yours!"

Before she had time to react, Melvin brought the hammer down full force on her index finger. She screamed and threw her head back as the pain shot through every fiber of her body. Her breath came in gasps like she was hyperventilating. The force of the blow had split the skin on her finger and it was bleeding profusely.

"That was only one finger, Miss Chan. I am prepared to do that to each one of your fingers and then crush both of your hands. Let me ask you again. "Tell me everything you know about Johnson and his operation."

"Kiss my ass!" she yelled defiantly.

Melvin held her hand fast and lifted the hammer above his head.

"Wait! Wait!" she screamed. "What the hell." She glared over at Johnson, anger and hatred reddening her face. She turned back to Melvin. "He'd give me up in a heartbeat. I just work for him on a contract basis. I'm not a part of his drug operation. I heard him talking about a dealer on Oahu called 'The Lizard' or 'The Gecko,' or something like that. If your wife got drugs from around here, that is who hooked her up."

Melvin released her trembling hand. "Thank you, Miss Chan. Tyler, please move her over there." He pointed to a comfortable chair on the far side of the room. "Put something around her hand."

"Right, Boss.

Melvin then turned to Johnson and said, "See how this works? You talk, and no one gets hurt."

Johnson said, "Do what you want; I'm not talking." He folded his lips together in a tight line.

Melvin asked Tyler to step over to the table, and hold Johnson's right hand down on the slab. Melvin looked Johnson directly in the eyes. "How do I find The Lizard?"

When Johnson failed to answer, Melvin grabbed his little finger, and smashed the tip of it with the hammer. Johnson screamed and tried to pull his hand free. Melvin asked him again, "How do I find The Lizard?"

Before Johnson had time to answer, Melvin smashed the hammer down on the first knuckle of the same finger. Johnson screamed, writhing in pain. He yanked Johnson's head back by his hair. "*Where* do I find The Lizard?" he asked again." When the answer was not forthcoming, Melvin moved to the next finger. This time he shattered it like he had Miss Chan's.

Johnson was nearing a state of shock, so Melvin asked for a glass of cold water. Tyler obliged, and

Melvin threw it in Johnson's face. When Johnson's eyes seemed to focus again, Melvin smashed another finger. Both the table and Johnson's hand were covered with blood. Melvin pulled out a small bolt cutter and held it up in front of Johnson's eyes. He told him he was getting tired of playing around. Now he informed the wild-eyed Johnson that he intended to cut off his thumbs then hack off his hands–*after* he crushed them.

By then Johnson was sobbing, and rocking back and forth in the chair. Melvin let him sit for a minute, then picked up the bolt cutter and took hold of Johnson's thumb.

Johnson screamed, "Stop! Please don't. I'll talk! I'll talk!"

Melvin sat down across the table. He folded his hands in front of him, and looked steadily at Johnson. "Who is Lizard, and how do I find him?"

Johnson, through gasping sobs, answered, "He goes by the name 'Gecko,' and deals around Beretania, near Chinatown. He hangs around a soup shop called, Phö Joe's."

While keeping his eyes on Johnson, Melvin told Tyler to call Honey Boy and have him find Gecko. "Tell HB to put him in storage, until I can get there.

"Now, Mr. Johnson, tell me who's in charge of the drug trade you're operating."

Johnson sobbed uncontrollably. Melvin reached across the table and slapped his cheeks. "I'm waiting!"

Johnson said, "It's a group out of Macao. They bring the stuff in on container ships. The only name I know is 'Truong.' I get all my instructions by cell phone, and I don't know how to find him. I tried to track him down myself a couple of times, but only got close enough to know he has connections through the International Marketplace in Waikiki."

Melvin grabbed his finger again, raised the hammer and asked, "You wouldn't lie to me now, would you?"

Johnson cried, "No, No, No! Please, that's all I know! They're going to kill me just for saying what I've said!"

Melvin told Tyler to get Johnson some water and a towel for his hand. He walked over to a television screen and watched Kamu, Roy, Jess, and Officer Reyes take Johnson's men out the door.

Melvin pressed the intercom button and said, "Thanks, Kamu, I'll be out in a minute."

Kamu answered and asked, "Is uh everyone all right in there?"

Melvin replied, "We had a couple of minor mishaps, nothing serious. But other than that, we are all fine. I'll be out, as soon as we can wrap up a few more details to help you make the biggest drug bust of your career."

Kamu said, "I'll be waiting right here!"

Melvin called me at home. "How would you like to become Stanley Johnson's attorney?"

"That's a question I wasn't expecting any time in the near future."

"Stanley, here, was a little uncooperative when we started talking, but decided it was in his best interest to tell me what I wanted. He's worried that the Chinese will kill him, and would like some assurance we can protect him. If you can get the DA to agree to a plea deal that doesn't get him life, and a shot at witness protection, I think he will be a lot more cooperative."

I heard Melvin ask someone on his end, "How does that sound, Stan? We got a deal?"

I could hear an emphatic affirmative.

"What do you say, Boss," Melvin asked. "Can you and the DA cook up another deal?"

I thought it over a moment. "I'll get in touch with the DA. Meanwhile, can you keep Johnson under your protection?"

"Not a problem," Melvin said. "One more thing, Boss, we have this woman called The Chinaman here with us. She's the one who stabbed Tyler in Morris's office. I also want to keep her here, until I can figure out what we should do with her."

I asked Melvin about the assault on the estate,

335

and was delighted to hear no one was killed. Most were just very sore and bad headaches. I closed the call with, "Be back in touch, as soon as I talk to the DA."

Before I could give Honey Boy the details of Melvin's call, his cell rang. He listened and then said, "Copy that." He closed his phone and looked at me. "That was Melvin. Catch you later, Boss man, I'm off. If you get in any trouble, just have Patty kick some ass."

I called the district attorney and gave him what information I had. He had been in touch with Detective Kamu, and was aware that most of the drug ring was in custody. I carefully laid out Melvin's idea on what to do with Johnson. The DA liked the plan, and said it would be easier to present to the court because of Morris's arrest. Having Morris available as a State's witness didn't leave Johnson with a great deal of wiggle room.

I called Melvin and told him the DA would accept his deal. I asked him, "What's your timeline for bringing Johnson in?"

He said, "Not for a couple of days. We need some time to get back over to Honolulu, and see if he's telling us the truth. We also need to keep anyone from finding him. We don't want someone taking him out before we get what information we need from him. Kamu can arrest Morris, and get everyone thinking about him. If he plays it right, the DA should get some good press out of Morris being arrested. Exposing corruption in his own house should be worth a few votes. He can follow that with Johnson's arrest and ride the good news train to a landslide election."

I said, "So when did you become a politician?"

"Since we finally found an honest DA."

I then asked about Miss Chan. Melvin would have Roy do a complete check on her.

"At the very least, she could be charged with assault with a deadly weapon. However, she was cooperative, and even gave me a lead on who may have sold drugs to my wife. "

"Since you're still my client, I want to advise you against doing anything illegal. Now get some rest."

GARY CARR

CHAPTER 48

Kamu hauled all of Johnson's men to jail. He'd called Melvin to give him the news, and asked if he needed any more uniforms to help with Johnson. Melvin requested two more. Kamu complied, and sent Reyes and another trusted officer to the estate.

When they arrived, Melvin assigned one to guard the safe room door, and the other to stay with Johnson. "He may try to commit suicide or something else as dumb." He told the officers he and his other three men would patrol the estate grounds. "I don't think we'll have a problem, but we'll be ready if we do."

Kamu also sent a doctor to take care of Chan and Johnson's hands. "I'll call you in the morning."

Melvin showed the cops to their duty stations. He told Johnson he had a tentative agreement with the DA, and that until it was finished and Johnson signed it, he would be confined in the safe room,

339

under guard.

Kamu was in charge of guarding Miss Chan. He managed to get her story. "How'd you wind up working for Johnson, he had asked?"

"I was smuggled into the islands from China when I was a teenager to work in the massage parlors. When my first "client" tried to rape me, I killed him with a pair of scissors and ran away. I spent several years running from the sex traders and drug dealers. One of the enforcers managed to catch me on Oahu and, before he could deliver me to the boss, I killed him, too. Another dealer heard about me, and sent word that he was looking for an enforcer. He told me if I would go to work for him, I could be an enforcer rather than a prostitute. My new boss liked me and helped build the legend portraying me as a martial arts expert and deadly assassin. I haven't killed another person, but my reputation seems to be enough to strike horror in men's hearts."

Her boss let Johnson use her from time to time, to get a point across. She said she didn't like Johnson, because he was a "two-tailed" pig. He enjoyed sex anyway he could get it, and was always pressuring her to oblige him.

Kamu asked, "Would you like to work with us to find Gecko and Truong? I know Melvin was hard on you." He motioned toward her bandaged hand.

She shrugged slightly. "One does what one has to, I guess. I don't hate Melvin and I understand his pain. Actually I think we might be very much alike. She looked at him for a long moment, searching his face. Why me?" she asked. "Why do you think I could be of any help?"

"Because you're Chinese, and your only other alternative is to go to jail for a very long time. Help us, and you'll probably just do only a month or two in the County Women's Detention Center."

"I've never worked for a Boy Scout before. What do you want me to do?"

Melvin walked in and interrupted the conversation. "You'll find I'm no Boy Scout. Come into the living room."

Tyler, Roy, and Jess were sitting on the couch, when they walked in.

Melvin announced, "The Chinaman, Miss Chan, is working with us, now. Since we don't know if we can trust her yet, if she makes one wrong move, kill her!"

Melvin looked at her and said, "Those are my rules. Any questions?"

"Nope," she said.

Melvin curtly nodded. "Would you prefer Miss Chan, or The Chinaman?"

"My name is Mei Li, and it's been a long time since anyone has called me that!"

Melvin said, "Roy, you and Tyler stay here, and help with guarding Johnson. Jess, I want you to come with Mei Li and me, to Honolulu. We have a gecko to catch. Honey Boy should be in Chinatown by now, and will join us when we get there."

Melvin, Mei Li, and Jess drove to the Kahalui Airport and met a friend of Melvin's, who ran a charter helicopter service.

The friend greeted Melvin, "You're out kind of late, aren't you?"

Melvin responded, "Can't catch geckos in the daylight."

Melvin sat up front with the pilot, with Mei Li and Jess in the back. As they were getting ready to lift off, Jess told Mei Li, "Fasten your safety belt and put your ears on."

She gave him a blank stare and lifted her injured hand, so he reached over and buckled her seat belt, tightening it around her slender body. He took the headset, adjusted it to fit her, and placed it on her head.

"Can you hear me now?" he asked.

"Yes," she replied. "I've never flown before."

As the copter left the ground, she grabbed the handles on the side of the seat and didn't let go until they were out over the ocean.

"Better now?" Jess asked.

"Yes, this is exhilarating, when you get used to it."

She spent the rest of the ride cooing over the bright lights and boats she saw.

Melvin called Honey Boy from the terminal to

let him know they were in Honolulu. Melvin said as soon as they could get a couple of rental cars, they would meet him in Chinatown. Forty five minutes later, they were all seated at a side table in Phö Joe's.

It was nearing midnight, and the restaurant employees were starting to close things down. Melvin and company took advantage of the situation to eat a hot bowl of phö, and were nearly finished when a bus boy nodded discreetly to Honey Boy. The large man lumbered toward the cash register. A young man had just entered the restaurant, and was talking to the cashier. He shut up, as Honey Boy approached.

"Don't mind me, just needed a toothpick."

The man turned away and told the cashier he would make a delivery in the morning. While he was talking, Honey Boy went outside. Melvin sent Mei Li out after him. While they were outside, Jess and Melvin approached the cashier, to pay the tab. Once again, the man immediately stopped talking.

Melvin walked behind him, and applied pressure to a nerve bundle on his elbow. While the pain registered in the man, Melvin quietly said, "Please step outside. I want to talk with you."

The man left without a struggle. When they were outside, Melvin let go of him.

He rubbed his elbow and asked, "Who *are* you?"

"More important, who are *you*?"

"Who wants to know? You don't look like any of the local narcs."

343

Melvin motioned to Jess, and Jess slugged the guy in the stomach. When he stood upright, Melvin asked him if he was Gecko.

"Yeah. I'm Gecko. What of it? What do you want?"

"Come with me," Melvin ordered, and had Jess lead him to the car. Jess pushed him into the back seat where Melvin joined him. Jess got in the driver's side and started the car. Honey Boy leaned into the window and said he and Mei Li would follow in their rental car. Gecko asked Melvin where they were taking him.

Melvin said, "To hell!"

Gecko was quiet for the rest of the ride, which ended at an old airstrip near Pearl Harbor. Melvin told Gecko to get out of car and then half dragged him into the old hangar where they had stopped. Honey Boy and Mei Li pulled up and joined them. Jess found a chair, and plopped Gecko into it none too gently. He tied him up with nylon baling twine he'd found littering the floor.

Melvin faced Gecko and asked, "How do I get in touch with Truong?"

Gecko feebly answered, "Are you crazy? You don't get in touch with Truong. He gets in touch with you."

Melvin continued, "Where does he live?"

Gecko shouted, "Now, you are nuts! Truong finds out you're looking for him, you're a dead man!

Who the hell are you, anyway?"

Melvin paused, and then walked over to a small bag he had brought with him. He unzipped it and removed a syringe and vial of liquid. Holding them in front of Gecko, he said, "You have ten seconds to answer my questions or I use this. Your choice."

Gecko licked his lips. "I don't know anything about Truong, other than he runs things."

Melvin pushed the needle into the vial of liquid, extracted enough to nearly fill the syringe, and removed the needle. He dangled the syringe in front of Gecko's face and squeezed a drop of liquid out. Gecko started to squirm in his chair. He reiterated that he didn't know how to get ahold of Truong. Melvin told Jess to hold Gecko's arm. He injected a small portion of the liquid.

Gecko struggled and demanded, "What is that? You don't need truth serum. If I knew anything, I'd tell you."

"I know," said Melvin. "This stuff is going to make *me* feel much better!"

"What's wrong with you, man?" Gecko yelled, "Why would it make you feel better?"

Melvin pushed the needle in Gecko's arm again, and injected more fluid, and said, "Because this is heroin, and I'm going to keep shooting you up, until you die. Just like my wife did."

Gecko sluggishly responded, "I don't even know you, mister. Who are you?"

345

"Melvin Momi. My wife was Carol Momi."

Gecko eyes were beginning to loll. He managed to say, "I'm sorry, mister, I just sell the stuff." His head lolled to one side, and drool slid from his mouth. He blinked his eyes a few times and mumbled, "Truong has a pretty yacht at Ali'i."

Melvin started to give Gecko more heroin, but Mei Li reached over and laid her hand on his arm. He stared into her dark eyes for several moments. All he could see was Carol's face.

"Why did you stop me?" Melvin asked. "He needs to die just like Carol did."

Mei Li softly said, "Doing the wrong thing for the right reason doesn't make it right. My grandmother used to tell me that, when I was a little girl. It's still the best advice I've ever had."

Melvin dropped the syringe, and walked away.

Mei Li followed. She said, "Don't worry. They'll find this guy with enough drugs and cash on him to put him away for a long time. Let me take care of this, and I'll meet you at the Ali'i Marina."

Jess tugged on Melvin's sleeve and said, "She's right. Let's go see if we can find Truong. He's the one you really want."

CHAPTER 49

Jess and Melvin checked with the slip manager at Ali'i Marina to see how many yachts were registered. The manager said there were only two luxury yachts moored there on a permanent basis. Melvin asked the manager who owned the yachts, and the manager told him he couldn't give out that information. Melvin slipped him a one hundred dollar bill, and he forgot all about privacy laws.

Neither yacht was registered to someone named Truong. One yacht was owned by a movie star, who spent a lot of time on the island. The other belonged to a Chinese corporation, Sunlu. Melvin asked if the Sunlu yacht was used much.

The manager said, "Every month on the third, just like clockwork. They take her out early in the morning and bring her back after dark. I've never seen the owner or crew, and they pay their slip fees electronically."

Melvin thanked the manager, and asked if he would like to make some more easy money. The clerk said, "Sure." So Melvin told him he would give him one hundred bucks for every picture he could get of people on the Sunlu boat. He reminded him to be very careful, though, because rich folks hate paparazzi, and it could be dangerous. Melvin told him he would call him every day to see if he had any photos. He got his cell phone number, and then handed him another hundred, to seal the deal.

As Melvin and Jess were leaving, Mei Li and Honey Boy entered. "There you are, Boss," said Mei Li. "I would have been here sooner, but there was a big traffic jam over on Queen Street. Some naked guy was walking down the street stoned out of his mind, carrying a duffel bag full of money. Everyone stopped to watch him. Look! I even got pictures with my phone!"

Everyone crowded around to see the photos. The manager declared, "Hey, I know that guy. They call him Gecko. He hangs around that Sunlu yacht a lot!"

Melvin pulled Mei Li aside, and thanked her for stopping him at the warehouse. "I've wanted to get even with someone ever since Carol died. Her death left me with an aching sadness and a feeling that there was more that I could have done to help her! When you stopped me, I suddenly realized nothing was going to change what happened. I'm as much to blame as anyone else." He lifted her hand. "I'm so sorry I hurt you."

Mei Li took his hand and said, "Being a good Boy Scout is the best way to honor her memory."

Jess joined them and echoed the sentiment. "She's right, Melvin. Carol loved you because you were her knight in shining armor. Thanks to you, there are a lot of people on the islands who won't be taking drugs tonight."

Melvin took a deep breath. It was the first time in a long time that he'd enjoyed breathing. He nodded at his old friend and his new friend. "Right. Let's get going."

He called the pilot and told him to be ready. They would be flying to Maui as soon as they could get to the airport. Melvin told Honey Boy to stay in Honolulu, and catch an early flight back to Molokai. On the way to the airport, he told Mei Li she could work for him or he could let her out now, and pay her for her time.

Mei Li told him, "You guys are the first people I've had in my life for some time who cared for me, even in the slightest. I'll stay." Then she quipped, "Besides, I miss Tyler."

"By the way," Melvin said, "where did the duffel bag of money come from?"

Mei Li answered, "I got it from his car along with his drug stash." Holding up a sheath of bills, she said, "I've been living off dummies like Gecko for years."

349

Melvin called from Honolulu and told me all that had transpired. Jess would tell me later about the epiphany Melvin had in the hangar. I called Symington and told him it was all over except for the paperwork. He wanted every little detail, so I invited him to fly here. I told him, "Melvin and I will give you a blow-by-blow account."

"I'm on my way!"

Later, that evening, the DA and I talked on the phone, trying to coordinate how to handle the plea bargaining with Morris and Johnson. We set up a meeting for the next afternoon in the DA's Office, and agreed to have Kamu and Melvin join us. I called Melvin and told him I would like everyone to gather at my home after we finished the meeting with the DA.

The next day I picked Symington up at the airport. We got to the house just as the rest of the group was pulling up. Patty was the last to arrive. Looking around at everyone—Symington, Melvin, Jess, Roy, Patty, Honey Boy, Tyler (holding hands with Mei Li), and Kamu—I realized we'd become our own brand of a Hawaiian family. I was struck with a sudden sadness that our adventure together was almost over.

I congratulated them on a job well done, and received an avalanche of accolades back.

"Okay, okay. Enough of the back patting. You'd think I was your boss." A groan went up around the room. We spent the next couple of hours in easy conversation. It was no surprise when thoughts steered towards Jimmy Pualani, the man who'd started it all.

"What a rat!" Patty exclaimed. "And yet, because of him, we are all together." She leaned back against Honey Boy. "I love you all!"

The rest of the room was silent for a moment, and then we all started nodding. It was one of those moments when you know there's a silver lining, even in such a sordid mess.

"Speaking of the underside of society, what about that scumbag, Morris?" This from Symington.

I said, "Morris is just happy to be alive. When we assure him Johnson is not a threat anymore, he will agree to whatever we put together. We have enough charges to put him away for twenty to thirty years. If we charged him with obstruction of justice, in addition to the drug charges, he won't even be eligible for parole for at least seven or eight years. And who knows, with his sexual proclivities, he may even enjoy prison." More groans.

"Getting a judge to sign off on Johnson is going

to be harder. All we have on him is his drug dealing. He could be out in three or four years, with good behavior. Witness protection may be even harder. We have to make it contingent upon his information about Truong being accurate. If the judge gets stiff-necked about procedure, and causes a delay, Johnson may change his mind. If he does, it could blow everything out of the water. The key is Johnson being afraid enough of Truong, and Melvin, to use this as a way out."

It was past midnight when we broke up and headed to our respective beds. I told them I'd call each one the next day, and update them.

The next morning, the DA had Detective Kamu formally arrest Morris and Johnson, and get their signed confessions down on paper. Next, he scheduled time on the court docket for presentation of charges and entry of pleas on the following day. If he could fast-track acceptance of the plea bargains, Morris and Johnson could be sentenced within a week or two.

Our meeting didn't take long. Morris and Johnson had accepted their fate. Morris was pleased that his family wouldn't find out about his "other side," and Johnson knew this was the only way to escape Truong and the Chinese, not to mention Melvin. The DA agreed that keeping Morris and Johnson isolated at their respective safe houses for now would be best. Kamu and his hand-picked cops would guard Morris, while Melvin and his crew would keep Johnson under wraps.

District Attorney Akumu was careful to leak the news of Morris's and Johnson's arrests to a reporter he could trust. He offered the story as the culmination of an ongoing investigation, and added the arrest of Johnson and his drug dealers were a part of his continuing effort to clean up drugs on Maui. This time he stayed in the background and let the reporter pose the story and revel in his "scoop."

GARY CARR

CHAPTER 50

The press, a number of curious onlookers, Kamu, Melvin, the DA, and I, along with Morris and Johnson, were all present, as the judge entered the courtroom. He was the same judge we had for Tala's hearing. As he sat down, the court clerk announced our reason for being there. He read through the written information the DA had presented, and then looked at me.

"Hello, again, Mr. Walters. I see from Mr. Akumu's information that you are representing Mr. Johnson?"

I said, "Yes, Your Honor."

The judge looked at Johnson and asked, "Do you understand the charges against you?"

Johnson stood and said, "I do, Your Honor."

"Do you wish to have Mr. Walters represent you?"

"Yes, sir," Johnson said.

355

Then the judge said, "I understand that these charges against Mr. Johnson are the result of a plea agreement?"

The DA responded, "Yes, your honor, on behalf of the State of Hawaii I accept the terms of our agreement in exchange for a plea of guilty to the charges presented."

The judge turned to me and said, "Does the defendant also understand and agree to these terms?"

"On behalf of my client, I accept the terms."

"And, Mr. Johnson," the judge continued, "do you understand and freely accept these terms?"

"I do."

The judge declared, "I find the confession and plea agreement signed by Mr. Johnson to be in order, and as he has agreed to same, I hereby accept the plea of guilty to the charges before him. He is to remain in custody until such time a sentencing hearing can be scheduled."

The bailiff instructed two court officers to take Johnson out of the courtroom. He was met by one of Kamu's detectives, who waited to return him to the safe house. That took care of Johnson, and gave us the insurance we needed for Morris to stick to our deal.

The court clerk then announced, "The next matter before the court is an arraignment hearing for Mr. George Morris."

The judge was surprised to see me greet Morris,

as he was escorted to the defense table by Officer Reyes. "Mr. Walters, you're not attempting to represent Mr. Morris, are you?" he asked.

I said, "No, Your Honor. That privilege belongs to Mr. David Santos."

David Santos had been District Attorney on Maui, and was instrumental in talking Akumu into running for office when he decided to return to private practice on Oahu. The judge watched as Mr. Santos traded places with me at the defense table.

The judge said, "Mr. Santos, welcome back to Maui. Will you be representing Mr. Morris?"

"Yes, Your Honor."

The judge then looked at Morris and asked, "As an attorney, Mr. Morris, I presume you are familiar with your right to counsel?"

Morris replied, "Yes, Your Honor."

"And have you selected Mr. Santos to represent you?"

Morris again replied in the affirmative.

I left the defense table, and took a seat in the gallery, next to a reporter scribbling notes. The judge then read the plea agreement the District Attorney had submitted. He followed that with the steps of having the State of Hawaii and Morris both agree to the plea bargain.

He then asked the DA, Santos, and me to retire to his chambers. After he shut the door, he paced behind his desk. He said, "Gentlemen, I've got a problem here. There is something about all of this that just isn't right. I'm not exactly sure how you were able to get Johnson and Morris to roll over so easily on a plea bargain. I'm even more baffled as to why Morris would hire Mr. Santos here as his attorney, when Mr. Santos was the one who kept him from becoming District Attorney. It's also pretty obvious from the arrest information, Mr. Walters, that your investigator was instrumental in uncovering this drug operation. Ethically, I think there is a lot wrong with this, but legally, I can't do anything about it, if he agrees to the plea bargain. I just don't want this all to come back and bite us all in the butt!"

Looking at me, he asked, "Do you have any comment?"

I thought for a moment and said, "Someone once told me that doing the wrong thing for the right reason doesn't make it right. But, if you take everything into consideration in this matter, Your Honor, you'll conclude, as we have, that this is just the right amount of wrong!"

EPILOGUE

Sentencing for Morris and Johnson came a few days later, and Akumu had the dealers on a fast track to prison, as well. Draper and Davis were settling into their new home in a mainland prison. Quiet had finally returned to Molokai. Best of all, Truong and his gang were snatched in a DEA and Coast Guard sting, and all were currently cooling their heels in jail while they awaited trial.

I'd invited Symington, newly re-elected DA Akumu, Kamu, and their families along with Melvin and his crew to join me on Molokai for a victory celebration. Invited, along with my crew, was Taniko, Pearl, Tala, and Tina. I hired a local chef to come in and do a full luau for us. Everyone ate and drank freely, and it was nice to see the Aloha spirit return to Molokai, and especially watching it manifest itself in my own backyard.

I sat down by Melvin and asked if he was happy

with the outcome.

He pursed his lips at the question. "I wondered if I'd ever be happy again, after Carol died. Now, I think it's possible." He looked across the yard, where Mei Li was tucked lovingly under the massive arm of Tyler. "I've got Mei Li to thank for that!"

I glanced over at the couple. "I wonder when the next murder will happen on Molokai."

Melvin laughed out loud. "Let's not wait around for that. Surely there's some other crime we can work on together!"

Lifting my glass of Prosecco to him, I said, "Here's to crime."

Just the Right Amount of Wrong

Mounted on the steed of imagination,
I ride to an endless horizon

GC

GARY CARR

Just the Right Amount of Wrong

About the Author

Gary Carr is the son of a contractor. He describes himself as a professional vagabond. He learned construction from his father, but also trained as a chef and used that skill to help pay his way through school. He retained his love of food and cooking, but moved on to work in radio as an announcer and disc jockey, and in television as a newsman. He ultimately retired after 30 years as a school administrator.

GARY CARR

Though he has many interests, traveling has always been a passion that tops the list. It began as a youth roaming the Southwest and traveling across the U.S.A. Eventually his journeys included Europe, the South Pacific, Polynesia, Hawaiian Islands, Caribbean and South America.

Gary lives in Colorado with his wife Shirley to whom he has been married for 45 years. Gary continues to pursue his travel and writing.